Her cheeks aflame, Sophie was temporarily lost for words.

"I had the distinct feeling that, for a moment or two at least, you were actually enjoying the whole experience quite as much as I was," he continued, still concentrating his gaze to the front. Then, with a jerk, he pulled his team to a standstill and swung around to face her, his eyes boring into hers. "In fact, I defy you to tell me that you didn't enjoy it!"

Endless minutes ticked slowly by as the viscount's unremitting gaze seemed to strip away every one of her defenses and lay open her very soul until at last, as a little sob escaped her lips, Sophie was forced to tear her eyes away from his, with the broken whisper, "I...I cannot—you know full well that I cannot!"

* * *

The Rake's Final Conquest
Harlequin® Historical #310—June 2011

DOROTHY ELBURY

lives in England in a quiet Lincolnshire village—an ideal atmosphere for writing her historical novels. She has been married to her husband for fifty years (it was love at first sight, of course!) and they have three children and four grandchildren. Her hobbies include visiting museums and historic houses, and handicrafts of various kinds.

DOROTHY ELBURY
The Rake's Final Conquest

TORONTO NEW YORK LONDON
AMSTERDAM PARIS SYDNEY HAMBURG
STOCKHOLM ATHENS TOKYO MILAN MADRID
PRAGUE WARSAW BUDAPEST AUCKLAND

Recycling programs
for this product may
not exist in your area.

ISBN-13: 978-0-373-30619-0

THE RAKE'S FINAL CONQUEST

Copyright © 2011 by Dorothy Elbury

www.Harlequin.com

Printed in U.S.A.

**Did you know that these novels are also available
as ebooks? Visit www.Harlequin.com**

Chapter One

'I'm so dreadfully cold, Miss Flint! Have we very much further to go?'

'Not far now, Lydia, my dear,' replied Sophie, in as cheerful a tone as she could muster, given that she too was feeling chilled to the bone. Putting aside her own discomfort, she reached across her charge and tucked the travelling rug more snugly around the girl, before peering through the misted glass of the carriage window at the snow-blanketed scene beyond. 'We do seem to be running a little late, but I imagine that this unexpected fall of snow must have *required* our coachman to lessen his normal speed somewhat.'

'Been crawling along like a slug for the past half an hour or so,' grunted the stout, ruddy-faced man opposite. 'Should never have left the Reading stage at all, in my opinion. I warned him that the weather was going to worsen before the day was much older, but would he pay any heed to the worldly wisdom of an old sailor? Not a bit of it—and now see where we are!'

'Hold hard, sir!' exclaimed the elderly gentleman seated at Sophie's right, the clerical collar at his neck clearly indicating his profession. 'One has to remember that these stagecoach drivers are under contract to adhere pretty strictly to the advertised timetables! The poor fellow is seemingly doing his best in what must be the most trying of weather conditions. Surely we should all be applauding his efforts, rather than seeking to find fault with him!'

A low moan emanating from the far corner then directed all eyes towards the couple who occupied the carriage's two remaining seats. As a self-conscious flush covered his cheeks, the young man pulled the woman more closely to him, before saying, 'I am sure that it cannot have escaped your notice that my wife is in a somewhat—er—delicate condition! We had expected to arrive at our destination in Maidenhead with more than enough time to spare but now I feel bound to advise you that it is becoming vital that we reach shelter with all possible speed!'

Since none of the carriage's other occupants could have failed to observe the young woman's advanced state of pregnancy upon boarding the stage at Bath, it was hardly surprising that her husband's words were greeted with a rather ominous silence.

'Fear not, dear lady,' said the reverend gentleman bracingly, leaning forward to give the young woman a reassuring pat on her knee. 'You may be sure that our doughty driver will do whatever is necessary to bring us all safely to the Maidenhead stage well before—'

With a juddering creak the coach slithered slowly to a halt, leaving the rest of the clergyman's intended words of comfort unspoken. The unmistakable sound of the guard clambering down from his perch caused all six passengers to eye one another in varying degrees of alarm. Seconds later, the wrenching open of the nearside door brought about a concerted gasp of dismayed protest as a brisk flurry of snow whirled into the carriage, covering its occupants in a fine layer of ice cold crystals.

'Sorry about that, sirs and madams,' puffed the guard, as he pulled himself up and dragged the door shut behind him. 'Come to inform you that we have hit a bit of a snag. Seems that this snowstorm's a good deal worse than we expected!'

Ignoring the florid ex-captain's grunted, 'Told you so!' he went on, 'Looks to be buildin' up into a fair old blizzard, it do! Driver can't see a blessed thing and the horses is getting fair spooked!'

'You're surely not suggesting that you intend for us just to sit here and weather the thing out?' demanded the young father-to-be. 'My wife is already in a really bad way and I fear that we may well be needful of the services of a midwife before very much longer!'

Cutting through the perturbed silence that followed these disquieting words, the sudden forward lurch of the carriage brought a gleam of satisfaction to the guard's wizened features.

'Peckers up, folks!' he crowed, as he reached again for the door handle. 'Looks like Old Jim's decided to try retracing our steps! Said he'd caught sight of a roadside inn of some sort a while back, so he must be aiming to take shelter there. Just until this infernal wind dies down, at any rate, if we can find the place!'

A second blast of icy weather billowed into the carriage as, once again, the door was thrown open and the guard stepped out to face the harsh elements beyond. Although it was not yet five o'clock in the afternoon, the combination of badly misted windows and thickly swirling snow made it well nigh impossible for any of the passengers to make out exactly what was happening outside the vehicle. Eventually, however, it became apparent that, despite the fact that the turnpike was already inches deep in snow, the driver and his mate had managed to persuade their trepid team of horses into executing a complete turnabout and, now that they no longer found themselves trying to battle against the oncoming blizzard, the edgy foursome seemed to have calmed down at least enough to allow themselves to be led through the snowy wasteland back in the direction from which they had just come.

Throughout the entire manoeuvre the seventeen-year-old Lydia Crayford, her eyes wide with apprehension, had been clutching at Sophie's arm.

'Oh, Miss Flint!' she wailed, as the carriage began to inch its way forward once more. 'Now we will be even later than ever! I cannot begin to imagine what Mama will say when we fail to arrive at the Swan at eight o'clock, as instructed!'

Having borne the brunt of her employer's vituperation on more than one occasion during her six month tenure as governess to the Crayfords' two younger offspring, Sophie had no need to exercise her imagination over the matter. She had little doubt that any blame for returning Lydia late to the bosom of her family would be placed squarely at her door, despite the fact that the assignment upon which she had been dispatched could hardly, in the normal way, have been considered as forming part of her accustomed duties.

Having received urgent notification of a suspected outbreak of chickenpox at the highly regarded Bath seminary at which her stepdaughter boarded, Mrs Crayford, disinclined to allow the event to interfere with her own busy social calendar, had done her utmost to try to persuade her stepson Arthur to take on the task of posting down to Bath to fetch his sister back to the safety of her own home. When that young dandy had flatly refused to be seen 'carting about the countryside with a blessed schoolgirl in tow' Mrs Crayford had simply delegated the undertaking to her own children's governess.

Furnishing Sophie with the cost of one return and one single ticket, plus a shilling or two for any necessary refreshments, she had sent her off to the staging post in Lad Lane, with instructions to board the evening coach to Bath, collect Lydia without delay and bring her back home on the early morning stage.

'That way there will be no need for you to put up overnight,' she had informed Sophie grandly, as she had handed her the five guineas that were intended to cover the full cost of the trip. 'You will have ample time to catch up on any lost sleep on the way. Roberts will be at the Swan at eight o'clock tomorrow evening to meet you. Kindly return here with all speed, for I shall require the barouche to take me on to the Messinghams' rout at nine o'clock.'

Now, wearily reflecting on her mistress's parsimony, Sophie loosened the drawstring of her reticule and, with considerable perturbation, calculated the extent of the small change therein. There was barely enough left for a decent meal between the two of them, let alone an overnight stay! It was to be hoped that Lydia had brought some money with her, otherwise they were going to find themselves deeply embarrassed, always assuming that they eventually succeeded in reaching the shelter the driver sought!

Suddenly conscious that the conveyance had veered sharply to the right, and was now running down a steep incline before eventually coming to a halt, she leaned across her charge and pressed her nose against the windowpane. Through the swirl of the thickly falling snowflakes she could just make out a pair of squat buildings, huddled together in a small hollow just off the side of the post road. Her heart sank, for it was clear that the 'inn' to which the guard had referred was little more than a hedge tavern or local alehouse, and most definitely not the kind of place that would be likely to meet with Mrs Crayford's approval, should it prove necessary to inform her of their unscheduled stop.

Scarcely more than a minute or two had elapsed, however, before the unwelcome sound of raised voices met the ears of the waiting passengers, causing a good many troubled glances to be shared between them. Captain Gibbons frowned and shook his head.

''Tis naught but a den of thieves!' he scoffed, as he peered through the glass. 'Won't be catching me going in there, that's for sure! Strip you of every penny-piece you own and throw you to the wolves as soon as look at you, that sort would!'

'Except that it would seem that we really have very little choice in the matter,' returned Sophie tartly, as she rose from her seat. 'Either we choose to take our chances inside or we stay out here and freeze to death! Come along, Lydia!'

And, holding out her hand, she proceeded to pull the decidedly unenthusiastic Lydia to her feet. Opening the door to the elements, the pair stepped down from the carriage, only to find themselves up to their ankles in several inches of freshly fallen snow. After her initial gasp of shock, Sophie, gritting her teeth, turned back to face the others and advised the young father-to-be that he had better be prepared to carry his wife, since she doubted that the young woman would be able to manage the somewhat treacherous terrain without some sort of assistance.

Determinedly ploughing her way through the rapidly drifting snow towards the building's lighted doorway, Sophie, keeping Lydia's hand firmly in her own, did her best to reassure her shivering companion that she would soon be warm and dry again. Upon reaching the shabby dwelling-place, however, it became clear that the driver was having difficulty in persuading the landlady to provide his passengers with the necessary shelter.

'Oh, miss!' breathed the elderly woman as, with a sigh of relief, she caught sight of the two young women approaching. 'Please tell your driver here that I'd be only too glad to help you all if I could but, as I keep tellin' him, neither the potman nor the young skivvy who usually helps me have shown up—hardly surprisin', I dare say, what with this sudden fall of snow! But even so, miss, I just don't have the facilities for puttin' folks such as you up!'

'You have no rooms at all?'

'Well, it's true that we do have three small bedrooms, miss, but none of them fit for the likes of you and your companions. Plus there's no fires lit, and none of the beds are made up, and without any help I'm just not in a position to assist you, much as I would like to oblige.'

'Three rooms will do very nicely,' said Sophie, eying the woman steadily. 'The young lady who is in the process of alighting from the coach at this very minute is due to give birth at some time in the very near future— unless you wish me to direct her towards your stable in the time honoured fashion?'

'Lord bless us, no, miss!' exclaimed the woman, clapping a hand to her mouth in dismay. 'I'll just go and look

out some sheets and blankets—we don't get that many
paying guests around these parts—it's only the lack of
help that's bothering me, not being as young and fettlesome as I once was!'

A sudden smile lit up Sophie's face. 'Well, then, let
me assure you that I'm perfectly fettlesome and only
too willing to lend you a hand,' she said decidedly. 'If
we could just get Mrs Lucan into bed first, we can take
our time sorting out the rest of the party.' Then, with a
nod at her young companion, she added, 'Come along,
Lydia, I dare say that we will be able to find something
useful for you to do, too!'

'But I have the most fearful headache and I do not
even know how to make beds!' complained the youngster, as she trundled sullenly after the governess. 'I
cannot think what Mama will say when she hears about
this!'

Since she preferred not to dwell too heavily on what
her mistress might or might not have to say about the
matter, Sophie chose not to reply, and applied herself,
instead, to helping the inn's landlady extract a number
of sheets and pillowcases from a large linen press on
the first floor landing.

Quilts and blankets for the bed allocated to the young
couple expecting the baby were found in a shabby otto-
man at the foot of the room's half-tester and, while
Sophie proceeded to instruct her none-too-willing
charge in the niceties of bed-making, both the landlord
and his wife, Webster by name, set themselves to lighting all the bedroom fires.

Consequently, when the somewhat out of breath Jack
Lucan shuffled through the doorway, bearing his whimpering wife in his arms, the first of the three small bedrooms was already beginning to lose its original chill

and, since Mrs Webster had also had the forethought to fetch up a couple of hot bricks from the kitchen range, the young woman was slightly overcome to discover that the bed itself was as warm and as cosy as it was possible to be, given the unusual circumstances.

Discovering that both of the two remaining rooms were even smaller than that which had been assigned to the Lucans, Sophie elected to commandeer the smallest of them for Lydia's use, it being furnished with only a single bed and a marble-topped commode, leaving just enough room at the foot of the bed for the straw pallet that the highly apologetic landlord had managed to locate from somewhere or other. Reassuring Mr Webster that such a makeshift bed would serve her perfectly well for the enforced overnight stay, Sophie then brought a relieved smile to the man's face by adding that she had frequently been obliged to bed down in far less salubrious conditions during her recent travels with her soldier father.

Although neither Captain Gibbons nor the Reverend Palfrey were particularly happy at finding themselves obliged to share the bed in the last of the three rooms, they were both far too relieved to be out of the cold to complain, albeit that the ex-sailor was frequently to be heard muttering somewhat uncomplimentary remarks about the drawbacks of travelling with such a cut-purse coaching company, along with his intention to deliver the owner a pretty sharp set-down the minute they arrived at their destination.

Leaving Mr Lucan to attend to his wife's immediate needs, Sophie, having accompanied their hostess into the inn's kitchen, then enquired as to the extent of provisions available. Luckily, it soon transpired that Mrs Webster was a great believer in the keeping of a well stocked larder, so it seemed that there was very little likelihood of her unexpected guests going hungry—were it not for one unfortunate setback.

'I don't know as how I could rig up a meal for such a large number,' exclaimed their hostess, wringing her hands together in considerable apprehension. 'I've never been obliged to cook for more than two or three at a time—Mr Webster were goin' to kill a chicken for our tonight's dinner, but I don't see as how the one bird can be made to feed the ten of us!'

'It most surely can, if it is made into a hearty stew!' returned Sophie swiftly, as she rolled back her cuffs. 'And, having seen your splendid store of winter vegetables, that should not prove too difficult a task for the pair of us.'

So saying, she sat herself down at the large pine table in the middle of the kitchen and proceeded to attack the heap of mixed vegetables that the landlady was already beginning to pile on to its well scrubbed surface.

'You're a bit of a strange one, miss, if you don't mind me sayin' so,' remarked Mrs Webster, as she took a seat opposite and picked up a potato to peel. 'I'd have said that you must have been in service at one time, if it weren't for the way you speak—sort of genteel-like, if you'll excuse me sayin'.'

'Well, I suppose you could say that I was in service once—in a manner of speaking.' Sophie laughed as she neatly quartered an onion and tossed it into the large stew pot that the landlady had placed on the table between the two of them. 'For the past twenty years or so my mother and I have been following my soldier father wherever his army campaigns chose to take him. We were obliged to spend a good deal of our time arranging sleeping quarters and making the most of whatever provender we were able to get hold of, so I suppose that this kind of thing does seem to come as some sort of second nature to me.'

'A hard life for a young lady, that,' observed the elderly woman. 'Had you no brothers or sisters?'

'Oh, yes!' confirmed Sophie, with a smile. 'I have a fourteen-year-old brother, Roger, but he's away at school now. Mama was determined that his education should not be allowed to suffer as a result of...' Her voice tailed away and her eyes began to mist up, causing her to clench her teeth as she made a determined effort to regain control of her emotions. Even after all these months, just the thought of her father's death the previous year still had the ability to knock her sideways.

'Lost your pa in the war, did you, miss?' Mrs Webster's voice was full of sympathy.

At Sophie's brief nod, the landlady let out a deep sigh. 'Our Jamie was taken, too,' she said quietly. 'Just over four years ago, it were—some place in Spain called Badhow or Bardhoff—never could quite get my tongue around the name.'

'Badajoz,' responded Sophie, much calmer now. 'Yes, I know it well. Such a dreadful battle it was, but our soldiers fought so courageously—you must be very proud of your son.'

'Well, yes. Dare say I am,' returned the other flatly. 'But I'd still far rather he'd stayed at home with us!'

The resultant silence that followed this critical observation might well have continued for quite some time had not the return of the landlord, bearing aloft his freshly slaughtered chicken, served to interrupt the mutual melancholia.

'Biggest one I could get hold of!' he bragged as, sit-

ting himself down next to his wife, he proceeded to
pluck out the bird's feathers.

Some three hours later, fully replete on double help-
ings of the hearty chicken and dumpling stew, chased
down with a glass or two of Mrs Webster's highly intoxicating homebrewed ginger wine, the exhausted travellers
declared themselves ready for their beds.

Having offered to take a tray up to the Lucan couple,
Sophie had found the pair fast asleep, entwined in one
another's arms and, since she did not have the heart to
awaken them, she had crept quietly away, judging that a
peaceful night's sleep was likely to be of far more benefit to the expectant mother than a plateful of stew.

A rather more immediate concern, from her own
point of view, had been her young companion's constant sneezing and shivering fits throughout the evening, both of which seemed to indicate the beginnings
of something ominous. She could only hope and pray
that Lydia had not already succumbed to the dreaded
infection from which she had been despatched to remove
the youngster!

Luckily, Mrs Webster was able to supply Sophie
with a couple of headache powders, but it was not until
she had administered one of these to Lydia, tucked a
wrapped hot brick at her feet and settled her down for
the night, that she was able to turn her mind to her own
needs. Having set out from London with the intention of
being back in Lennox Gardens before nightfall, she had
brought nothing with her apart from the clothes she was
wearing! Had she thought of it before her young charge
had drifted off to sleep, she might well have considered
asking Lydia for the loan of one of her nightdresses,
since they were of an almost similar size. As it was,

having hung her plain but serviceable grey kerseymere gown over the fireguard, in the hopes that the fire's heat might remove the worst of its creases, she was obliged to resign herself to sleeping in her flimsy muslin shift.

Although the straw-filled palliasse was not the most comfortable of mattresses, it was impossible not to smile as she had, as she'd told the landlord, known far worse sleeping quarters, and she quickly reminded herself that, had their doughty driver not found them this little jewel of a lodging, they might yet be sitting in the carriage, probably freezing to death in a snowdrift somewhere!

Snuggling under the heavy quilt with which Mrs Webster had insisted upon providing her, she felt her eyelids droop and sleep was all but ready to claim her when a sudden thought flashed through her mind.

Her reticule! Unable to recall exactly where or when she had last set eyes on the little purse that held the sum total of her wealth, she pulled herself up out of her warm cocoon and, with the help of the flickering firelight, began to peruse the various surfaces of the tiny room. In one of the pockets of her pelisse, perhaps? But, no, she remembered having checked both pockets before handing her damp coat over to Mrs Webster to hang up on the ceiling dryer in the kitchen! As panic threatened to overcome her, she forced herself to take a deep breath and concentrate. And then, as sanity prevailed, it all came back to her. She had placed her reticule down on the parlour windowsill before coming upstairs to help Mrs Webster with the bed-making. She found it hard to believe that any of the other passengers would have helped themselves to it, but then, one could never tell these days! So, judging that it would be better to be safe than sorry, she crept over to Lydia's portmanteau, extracted a large paisley shawl from within and, after thrusting her feet into her half-boots, made her way over to the doorway and peered out into the dimly lit passage beyond.

Chapter Two

Just as she had supposed, the house was completely silent, with every one of its exhausted occupants presumably wrapped in the arms of Morpheus! Tiptoeing swiftly down the single flight of stairs, with only the light from one wall sconce to guide her, she made at once for the parlour. Finding the door shut, she turned the knob gently, unwilling to risk waking either of her hosts who, as she had recently ascertained, slept in the room directly opposite to this one. As she stepped inside, her boot immediately encountered a creaking floorboard, causing her to freeze in her tracks, but then, by the light of the still glowing logs in the fireplace, she spotted her reticule, lying just as she had left it upon the windowsill. Her courage returned and, making a quick dash across the room, she reached out her hand to snatch up the precious object.

'Well, well, well! And what have we here? A cosy little armful come to keep me company, eh? How very accommodating!'

At the unexpected sound of the drawling male voice, Sophie spun round in dismay—only to find herself almost face-to-face with its advancing owner who, as she was soon to discover, seemed bent on relieving her of her shawl. Clutching the totally inadequate covering more tightly about her person, she attempted to back away towards the door.

'Not so fast, my pretty one!' came the stranger's purring undertone, as his hand shot out to catch hold of the shawl's trailing end. Then, with one swift jerk, he yanked it from her shoulders, to leave her cowering before him clad only in her flimsy shift.

'You clearly came with the sole purpose of entertaining me in my hour of need, my sweet, so let's waste no more time on this feeble pretence at maidenly modesty, I implore you!'

And then, before the utterly transfixed Sophie even had time to speculate upon what his intentions might be, the man had stepped forward, pulled her into his arms and, after tipping her head back, set about capturing her lips with his own!

Her initial sense of stunned outrage was almost overwhelmed as an inexplicable trickle of excitement ran up and down her spine, and for countless seconds she found herself seized by the wildest of temptations to simply allow these confusing emotions to run away with her. It was not until one of the stranger's hands slid down her back to cup the softly rounded cheeks of her buttocks that her misplaced wits suddenly leapt into action and, with a swift wrench, she succeeded in tearing herself away from what was becoming an increasingly enthusiastic onslaught on her person.

Breathless with disbelief, she tried to haul herself

out of his reach, but he was too quick for her, his hand shooting out and capturing her wrist.

'Let me go!' she panted. 'Please, let me go, sir. I beg of you!'

A puzzled frown puckered the man's brow, and as the sound of Sophie's voice gradually penetrated his perception a sudden stillness came over him. *No serving wench this, as the girl's cultured tones instantly informed him!* With a strangled oath he dropped his hold and, stepping hurriedly away from her, held up his hands in a gesture of surrender.

'My mistake, ma'am,' he grated, as he lurched back to sink into the fireside chair that he had so eagerly vacated at Sophie's unexpected entrance. 'I fear that I seem to have partaken of—'

But Sophie, seizing her chance, was in no mind to wait to hear whatever explanation her attacker was about to drum up to excuse his extraordinary behaviour. Snatching up the discarded shawl, she dashed towards the door and, dragging it open, fled along the passageway and up the stairs as if all the devils in hell were at her heels!

Raising his head just in time to catch sight of her shapely calves and trim ankles disappearing from his view, Marcus Wolfe, Viscount Helstone, let out a self-deprecating groan. Well aware that it had been sheer madness on his part to have set out from Bradfield on such a night, he could not help but feel that he had been well served for his inanity. Whilst it was true that another hour spent in his father's company might well have driven him into doing or saying something that he was sure to have later regretted, he was not so foxed that he was unable to recognise the possible bumblebath into which he had landed himself, with his attempted seduction of a female who, rather than having been a serving girl eager to earn herself a few shillings in return for services rendered, as he had originally supposed, had turned out to be one of the inn's benighted coach party passengers!

Not that he was especially worried about any consequences that might arise as a result of that rather unproductive foray—past experience had taught him that the passing over of a thick wad of notes was usually more than enough to silence the complaints of even the most devoted of husbands and fathers! He shrugged. In any case, life was too short to allow such petty irrelevances to overset him! Not for nothing had his closest associates designated the Viscount with the soubriquet Hellcat!

Tossing back the final dregs of the bottle of rather inferior brandy with which the landlord had provided him—presumably as some sort of sop for failing to accommodate him with sleeping quarters more appropriate to his position—Marcus sprawled back in his chair with a low growl of discontent. Far from being too short, his life, as far as he was concerned, was well on the way to being too damned long and a sight too dreary for words! Small wonder that his father had termed him a worthless wastrel, much preferring the company of Giles, the younger of the two Wolfe scions. Giles the brave—Giles the hero—good old never-put-a-foot-wrong Giles!

Good grief! What in God's name had got into him that he had actually sunk to reviling his beloved brother, a man whom he loved and respected with every fibre of his being!

As he stared down into the fire's dying embers, Marcus's shoulders slumped in a fit of self-revulsion. It seemed as if the endless round of drinking, gambling and whoring of which his life consisted was finally beginning to affect his reason. It was beyond question that Giles, who for the past six years and more had fought his way across two continents, surviving countless bloody battles to emerge virtually unscathed as a highly decorated war hero, deserved every bit of praise and admiration that could be heaped upon his twenty-seven-year-old shoulders.

It was not that Marcus begrudged his brother even a single one of that young man's well deserved accreditations. His abiding feeling was simply one of envy, laced with a generous helping of resentment—a deep and bitter resentment at having been born the elder of their father's two sons, thus precluding him from opting for the much desired military career that his younger brother had been allowed to pursue. Whilst it was true that a good many members of the nobility had been seen to encourage their eldest sons to join in the campaign to rid the civilised world of Napoleon's tyranny, it had been as a direct result of the loss of so many of those promising young lives that Marcus's father, the Earl of Bradfield, fearing the possibility of losing both his heirs, had flatly refused to countenance his elder son purchasing the commission on which the Viscount had set his heart.

The badly thwarted Marcus, having pointed out that there was more than one way that a fellow might choose to sacrifice his life, had then proceeded to demonstrate several of them, thoroughly outraging his father by occupying his hours with every possible degeneracy known to man.

In direct contravention of the Earl's wishes, Marcus appeared to have gone out of his way to dice with death and had, in the past eight or so years, been obliged to turn up to defend his name in dawn encounters on more than one occasion. Although he had, as yet, never actually killed a man—his aim being so impeccable that a harmless nick in an opponent's upper arm or shoulder had proved more than enough to decide the day.

Whilst he could, if he so chose, drink most of his friends and colleagues under the proverbial table, he had for the most part learned to hold his liquor, preferring to keep a sober head both for his card-playing and for other, more pleasurable activities. For, although he kept two mistresses in comfort in different parts of Town, he did not feel that such arrangements necessarily prohibited him from taking advantage of the many other casual liaisons that offered themselves up to him—a goodly proportion of the females in the upper echelons of the society in which the Viscount moved had proved to be remarkably lax in regard to the marital vows they had taken, hence those somewhat frequent dawn encounters! And, had his skill at cards not been so amazingly superior to that of his opponents, Marcus might well have lost the fortune he had inherited from his maternal grandmother, thereby obliging him to depend upon hand-outs from his father—a situation to be avoided at all costs, as far as Helstone was concerned.

As it was, he could not help but be aware that he was in grave danger of becoming not only an out-and-out rakeshame but also the 'worthless wastrel' his father had termed him earlier that evening—an epithet that did not sit too readily on Helstone's shoulders and one that had caused him to quit the family mansion in a towering fury.

Having finally managed to stumble, half-dead with cold, into this tiny wayside tavern on the Reading post road, only to discover that all its rooms were already occupied, he had been obliged to try and make himself comfortable on one of the most uncomfortable of fireside chairs that he had ever encountered, but with his boots off, a roaring fire at his feet and a half bottle of brandy at his disposal, he had been quite prepared to make the best of it, reasoning that by morning the snow would more than likely have disappeared and he would be back on his way to his Grosvenor Square mansion well before noon.

Although he had been slightly taken aback at the unexpected appearance of the rather comely young woman who had seen fit to invade his privacy, he had merely taken her arrival as yet another token of the landlord's regret at not having been able to furnish him with a suitable bed for the night, as was his due! And, although the girl had turned out not to be the accommodating chambermaid of his fancy, she had certainly been a highly curvaceous little creature, in addition to having been blessed with quite the most kissable lips that he had had the pleasure of tasting in some time.

Throwing on a couple more logs, he stoked up the fire and, thrusting a cushion behind his head, stretched out his legs and placed his feet on the leather-topped log box, having reached the happy conclusion that, provided he got away at first light, he could avoid any inherent complications of coming face-to-face with his late-night visitor—not to mention any irate husband or father that lady might have in tow!

In the event, however, it seemed that the Viscount's good intentions were to be brought to nought. On pulling back the curtain at around six of the clock the following morning, in order to check the state of the weather outside, he was dismayed to find that, rather than having improved overnight, as he had supposed it must, the situation appeared to have worsened to an even more worrying degree.

Despite the fact that the fierce wind of the previous day looked to have finally blown itself out, the continuously falling snow had enveloped the entire landscape in a soft white blanket as far as the eye could see. Whilst this highly picturesque scene was, without doubt, one of awe-inspiring splendor, and more than enough to cause Marcus to draw in his breath in appreciative wonder at Nature's handiwork, it was not long before it came to him that the hasty departure on which he had set his mind was now totally out of the question. It was becoming increasingly obvious that the depth of the snow that filled the little hollow wherein the tavern nestled would make the reaching of the post road well nigh impossible—given that the drifts outside his window were already somewhere in the region of three feet deep! It would take three or four men half a day at least to dig out a passageway up that steep incline to get to the highway, and even then one could not be entirely sure that the post road would even be traversable—there had certainly been no indication of any passing traffic for the past hour or so, as far as he had been aware!

Stifling a yawn, the Viscount ran his fingers over the bristles on his chin and wondered how long it would be before anyone would think to fetch him some hot water in order that he might wash and shave. He had heard various sounds of movement emanating from the passage outside his room, and the welcome smell of freshly brewed coffee had been wafting its way into the little parlour for some time now.

He stood, undecided, for a further moment or two but then, as the smell of the coffee grew ever more

enticing, causing his empty stomach to growl in anticipation, he plonked himself back down on the fireside
chair and began the almost Herculean task of pulling
on his boots—something of a masterly feat, in his case,
considering the lack of both valet and boot-horn!

It was while he was attempting to smooth the creases
of his crumpled cravat into some sort of acceptable order
that, on turning his head, he happened to catch sight of
a small brown leather object that had somehow become
lodged behind one of the legs of the side table that stood
against the rear wall of the parlour. Curious, he reached
down to pick it up. No sooner had he recognised the
object for what it was—a lady's reticule—than his lips
began to curve in amused recall of the previous night's
thwarted encounter.

*So, this was what the young woman had been after
when she had come creeping into his room! It must
hold something of immense value to have caused her to
leave her bed and wander, half-clad, into a gentleman's
sleeping quarters!* Not that she was likely to have known
that it was anyone's sleeping quarters at the time, he was
quick to remind himself, as he unwound the thongs of
the shabby purse and tipped its meagre contents into the
palm of his hand.

A puzzled frown creased his brow as he stared down
at the sum total that he held—a single half-crown, three
sixpenny pieces and a few odd coppers! Less than five
shillings, all told—hardly worth anyone going to so
much bother to retrieve, he thought dispassionately, as
he returned the coins to the reticule and retied its leather
thongs before thrusting it into his jacket pocket.

Finding the passageway deserted, he made for the
door at its far end. Having been ushered through that
same door the previous evening, he had no doubts about

it leading him to the kitchen and to that much needed cup of coffee!

Pushing open the door, he quickly surveyed the scene in front of him. A lace-capped serving wench, clad in a plain grey kerseymere gown, overtopped by a clean white apron, was bent over the range with her back to him, heavily preoccupied in stirring the contents of one of the pots thereon.

'Coffee, if you please, and quick about it!' he ordered authoritatively, as he sauntered across the room and took a seat at the large pine table that dominated the tavern's kitchen. 'And then ham, eggs and mushrooms to follow, I think!'

Straightening up in shock, Sophie swung round to face him, her heart stuttering almost to a stop as she got her first real look at her midnight assailant. Pausing momentarily to take in his remarkably handsome if slightly dishevelled appearance, she found it necessary to take in quite a deep breath of air before she felt able to summon up the necessary self-assurance to respond to his communication. Having spent the better part of the night trying to rationalise the quite bizarre happenings in the parlour—particularly in reference to her own out-of-character behaviour—she had reached the conclusion that, since it had seemed to her that the man must have been in a very advanced state of intoxication to behave in the way he had done, there was every chance he might well have woken with no memory of what had occurred between them.

Not that anything of great moment had actually taken place, as she hastily reminded herself! Merely a fumbled kiss, followed by his slurred attempt at an apology— hardly a matter to get wound up over and, if she were honest, an experience nowhere near as unpleasant as those she had suffered at the hands of Arthur Cray-ford, whose constant attempts to waylay her whenever his stepmother was not in the offing were beginning to cause her considerable disquiet!

'Wake up, girl! I said coffee, if you please!'

She started. It seemed that the man had not recognised her! Which was hardly surprising, really, considering all the effort she had made to bundle her unruly chestnut curls into some sort of chignon, prior to covering her entire head with one of the highly unattractive lace caps she had taken to wearing in her attempts to hold young Crayford at bay.

'There is no more coffee, I'm afraid,' she replied, in as gracious a tone as she could manage in the circumstances. 'Mr Webster has had the last of it—he slipped on the ice while going to collect logs and has been obliged to take to his bed with a badly sprained back. As a result of which, the range fire is now almost out, but should you care to go and fetch some logs yourself, I daresay I might be prevailed upon to provide you with a fresh jug of coffee!'

Thoroughly taken aback, Marcus rose from his seat and in two quick strides he was standing in front of her, an angry expression upon his face.

'I believe you are forgetting yourself, miss!'

'As indeed are you, sir!' Sophie fired back at him, her former apprehension instantly swept aside in her growing indignation at what she felt was an unnecessarily imperious manner on the man's part.

Marcus stared down at her, his eyes narrowing. 'What the devil do you mean by that remark?' he demanded, somewhat belligerently. 'Is it or is it not your duty to wait upon the guests in this establishment?'

'I hardly think so,' she countered, in the most dulcet of tones. 'Since I myself am also one of the guests.'

A puzzled frown shifted across his brow as he continued to peruse her face until all at once realisation began to surface. 'Good God! You're her, dammit, aren't you?'

'She,' corrected Sophie automatically. 'I am she, not "her"—if you are referring to the female who inadvertently invaded your sleeping quarters last evening, that is!'

Marcus's eyebrow quirked in exasperation.

'Never mind the blessed semantics,' he grunted. 'Perhaps you will have the goodness to explain to me what you mean by going around giving folks the impression that you are a serving maid?'

'I believe that was your mistake, sir, not mine!' she answered cheerfully, as she turned back to the porridge pot to give it another quick stir. 'I am merely doing my best to help an old couple who, quite without warning, have found themselves landed with a house full of uninvited guests. Apart from our doughty driver and his guard, who have spent the past two hours clearing a path to the stables and woodshed, it would seem that I am the only one of our party who is capable of being of any practical help to them.'

'Ah! At last I begin to understand,' returned Marcus with an expressive nod. 'I must suppose that this is also the reason you are togged up in that apron and wearing that hideous monstrosity on your head.'

'I beg your pardon!' flashed back Sophie indignantly. 'I'll have you know that my cap is perfectly respectable and generally considered to be quite in keeping with my position.'

'Whatever position that might be I cannot begin to

imagine,' he riposted quickly, having already ascertained that her fingers were unadorned with rings of any sort. 'You are quite clearly not a widow, and unless I am much mistaken a fair few years from being counted an old maid!'

'Really, sir!' retorted Sophie, beginning to feel distinctly nettled at the man's indefensible lack of civility. 'I fail to see that who I am or what my situation is can be any possible concern of yours!'

Whilst it was true that in normal circumstances such pointed questioning of a young woman might be considered rather improper, Marcus suddenly found himself relishing the thought that, given their present situation, no such conventional restrictions need apply.

'Oh, come now!' he cajoled, favouring her with a lopsided grin, the like of which was usually more than enough to leave even the most straitlaced of females quivering in her shoes. 'Since it would seem that we are likely to be cooped up together for who knows how long, it occurs to me that the polite interchange of names might not be considered amiss.'

Then, executing a perfect leg, he added, 'Marcus Wolfe, at your service, ma'am.'

Whilst his roguish smile was certainly enough to bump up her heart rate more than just a notch or two, Sophie's unconventional upbringing had taught her to recognise such guile for what it was worth, and, dipping him what was intended to be a mockingly servile curtsey, she replied, 'Miss Sophie Flint, governess—if it so pleases your honour, sir!'

He laughed, showing a set of even white teeth. 'It pleases me greatly, thank you, Miss Flint and, if you will allow it, I should like to take this opportunity to apologise for that rather unfortunate misunderstanding last evening—I suspect that your impromptu visit was actually intended to retrieve this piece of property. I assume that it *is* yours?'

And, having thrust his hand into his pocket as he spoke, he extracted Sophie's reticule and held it out towards her.

At the sight of her shabby brown leather purse, the blush that had been forming on Sophie's face at the man's mention of the highly discomfiting events of the previous evening quickly disappeared. All at once her summer blue eyes lit up in delight and she favoured the Viscount with a smile of such joyful sweetness that he was momentarily lost for words.

'Oh, thank you, Mr Wolfe!' she exclaimed, as she reached forward to accept the purse. 'I was beginning to fear that I might have seen the last of it!'

Not having seen fit to introduce himself by his correct title, Marcus was unable to bring himself to rectify Sophie's unwitting error. In fact, having experienced a somewhat disconcerting sensation in the pit of his stomach the moment their hands touched, he was very soon of the opinion that, for the short time that they were to be forced into one another's company, to be known as Mr Wolfe might serve him rather well—especially since the yawning, night-capped landlord had been too busy apologising for the lack of a suitable bed to get around to enquiring his name upon his arrival the previous evening.

Forcing his eyes away from her elated expression, he shot a quick look at the dying fire.

'I suppose if I am ever to get that cup of coffee I am so desperately in need of, I had better go and see about these blessed logs,' he groaned, at the same time simulating a world-weary sigh. 'Exactly where is this woodshed of which you spoke?'

Unable to hide her amusement at his feigned expression of virtuous suffering, Sophie raised her hand and indicated the back door. 'Directly opposite,' she replied. 'As I said before, part of the yard has already been cleared of snow and—oh, yes, I'm afraid I forgot to mention—should you happen to require milk in your coffee, you will find Daisy waiting in the adjoining cowshed!'

'Daisy?'

Marcus stopped and turned, a mystified frown on his face.

'The Websters' cow—she is yet to be milked.'

But then, seeing the Viscount's look of utter astonishment, she added hurriedly, 'That was intended merely as a jest, Mr Wolfe. One could scarcely suppose it likely that you also number milking amongst your undoubted talents!'

He gave a low chuckle and a mischievous glint lit up his eyes. 'Such talents as I do happen to possess might surprise even your good self, Miss Flint,' he murmured softly. 'In fact, if you would just do me the service of removing that ghastly monstrosity from your head, who knows what hazardous activities I could be persuaded into!'

The challenging look he cast at her was more than enough to cause Sophie's cheeks to flame in mortification, it having instantly brought to mind her almost wanton behaviour of the previous evening.

'Logs!' she choked, as she gave him a swift push towards the door. 'And quickly—before the fire goes out!'

Kissing the tips of his fingers, he sent her a quick

salute as he exited from the room with the words, 'Your wish is my command, dear lady!'

As she stared at the now closed door, a perplexed frown creased Sophie's brow and she tried her utmost to make some sense out of the somewhat odd sensations that the very vexing Mr Wolfe seemed to have engendered within her. Unable to reach a satisfactory conclusion to her ruminations, however, she gave a brisk shake of her head and forced herself to return her attention to the porridge pot from where, after giving it one final stir, she spooned out a small bowlful to take up to her still ailing charge, along with the very last drop of milk in the jug.

That Marcus Wolfe was the most accomplished rake she had ever come across was without question, and, given his rather autocratic manner and the obvious quality of his perfectly tailored jacket and fine leather riding boots, it would seem that he more than likely belonged to that high-flown set of men about town whom lesser beings such as Arthur Crayford craved vainly to emulate. Clearly the sort of dangerously attractive man that all well brought up young females were taught by their mothers to be on their guard against, and, bearing in mind the rather disconcerting effect that his very presence already seemed to be having on her, Sophie was quick to realise that she would need to keep all her wits about her if she meant to keep her heart safe from Wolfe's compellingly magnetic charisma.

Having spent most of her growing years in the company of men from all walks of life, she could not recall a single one of them having had quite the same effect on her pulse as did this man, who was little more than a stranger to her. Whilst she had never been averse to a light flirtation with the occasional junior officer under her father's command, her heart had always remained entirely her own, and now that she was forced to make her own way in the world she had reached the conclusion that it must continue to remain that way.

With her mother reduced to taking in paying guests in a rented house in Dulwich village, in order that Roger, Sophie's fourteen-year-old brother, might continue his public school education at the nearby college, an advantageous marriage might have been thought to be the ideal solution to the Flint family's financial difficulties. Unfortunately, given that Sophie's current situation as a governess to two young children was something of a drawback insofar as regular contact with unmarried members of the opposite sex was concerned, she had grown accustomed to the idea that the chances of receiving a suitable offer for her hand were distinctly remote. Indeed, it was entirely due to having found herself the unwitting recipient of rather too many highly *unsuitable* offers during her six month tenure with the Crayfords that she had privately determined to consign all gentlemen below the age of sixty-five or so to Hades—or to some other persecution of an equally unpleasant nature!

Her inexplicable reaction to Wolfe's stolen kiss had set her at odds with her normally down-to-earth self, and she could only pray that she had it in her to drum up sufficient tenacity to withstand his flirtatious banter—not to mention the incredibly melting effect he seemed to have on her every time his lips curved in that particular smile of his! In fact she was disconcerted to discover, as she made her way up the stairs towards Lydia's room, it seemed that even the memory of it was enough to make her heart skip more than the odd beat.

Chapter Three

Once she stepped inside the bedroom door, however, one glance at her young charge was more than enough to banish all such heady thoughts from her mind. *Oh, dear Lord*, she thought in dismay, as she stared down at the girl's flushed and perspiring face, *the poor child really looks quite poorly! Now what am I to do?*

'Could you just try and sit up for a moment, Lydia?' she coaxed, and she sat down on the bed where, slipping one arm beneath the girl's shoulders, she eased her gently into a sitting position, before carefully plumping up the pillows behind her back to help support her.

'Oh, Miss Flint!' wailed Lydia, clutching at the governess's hand. 'My head aches so and I feel truly dreadful! Please do not tell me that I have developed the chickenpox, after all—Mama will be so cross with me if I should end up with a host of unsightly scars on my face!'

'Hush, my dear, you must not think such things,' soothed Sophie. 'You have caught a very bad cold, that is all, and if you wish to get better quickly you must try to eat some of this lovely porridge that I have brought you.'

'But I hate porridge!' cried the youngster, eying Sophie's offering with considerable distaste. 'I would much rather have a glass of cold milk!'

Finding herself at something of a stand at the girl's plea, Sophie dipped the spoon into the bowl and lifted it towards her lips.

'As soon as you have eaten all of this,' she encouraged, mentally crossing her fingers as she did so, 'then you shall have as much milk as you want, I promise you, my dear!'

Even if I have to go and milk the blessed animal myself! she averred silently.

Fortunately, since it took every scrap of Lydia's energy to take in and swallow every mouthful of the detested oatmeal, all she wanted to do when she had finished the dreaded ordeal was to slump back against the pillows and drift off to sleep again.

Placing her hand upon the child's fevered brow, Sophie could not help but feel that Mrs Crayford had landed her with an almighty problem. What if Lydia was really sick? Supposing that she *had* caught the chicken-pox? Without a doctor, and only Mrs Webster's headache powders to hand, it seemed that there was very little that she could do to alleviate the youngster's suffering. But then, castigating herself for such negative thinking, she started to ask herself what her own mother, the calmest and most practical of women, would have done in such circumstances—her tender ministrations to the sick and injured having become almost legendary during the family's years in the Peninsular.

Lemon barley water, of course! Mrs Webster is sure

*to have those ingredients, at least! And then I must
bathe Lydia's arms and legs with warm water to bring
down her temperature.*

But after shooting a quick glance at the dying fire,
she could not help but wonder how successful Mr Wolfe
had been in his bid to secure logs—only to experience a slight flutter of dismay when it suddenly came
to her that the future health and safety of the entire
household might well depend on the reliability of that
undeniably handsome but decidedly suspect character
downstairs!

Raised voices from the next room soon had her on her
feet, making for the door. Surely Captain Gibbons and
the Reverend were not at each other's throats again, so
early in the day? She had hoped that, after yesterday's
disturbing goings-on, the ill-matched pair would have
been only too happy to remain in their bed until at least
mid-morning. Apparently not, if the noises emanating
from their room were anything to go by!

Glancing across at the bed, she could see that Lydia
was now asleep, although her restless tossing and turning
did not bode well for a swift recovery. Quickly making
up her mind, she tossed the last of the logs on to the
fire's still glowing embers, left the room, and rapped
sharply on the door of the neighbouring bedchamber.

The wrangling from within ceased instantly, followed
by a moment's silence before the door was flung open
by the Reverend Palfrey, to reveal both of the room's
nightshirt-clad occupants clutching at a tangled heap of
bedclothes.

'I hesitate to bring it to your attention, sirs,' she began,
without preamble. 'But there are sick people on either
side of you, and the walls of this cottage are exceedingly

thin! Kindly lower your voices to a minimum, if you would!'

'But he keeps taking more than his fair share of the blankets!' protested Captain Gibbons, tugging frantically at the quilt that the reverend gentleman, despite his lesser stature, was quite determined not to relinquish.

'The situation is quite the reverse, I assure you, ma'am,' gasped the outraged parson. 'I have awoken time after time throughout the night to find myself totally devoid of bedding. I was merely endeavouring to rectify the matter when this—this—!'

When the epithet he was searching for failed to materialise, his shoulders slumped, and with a resigned sigh he released his hold on the quilt, allowing his adversary to clutch it to his chest in grinning triumph.

'Really, gentlemen!' Sophie admonished the pair. 'One would have thought that you had sufficient wit between you to have reached some sort of reasonable compromise. It seems to me that you have more than enough bedding to accommodate the pair of you. Why not simply divide it in half and each of you roll yourselves up into a separate little cocoon? It's a method that has always served its purpose perfectly well in military circles, I've found, and since it appears that we are to suffer one another's company for a good deal longer than was originally supposed, you might well consider putting it into practice without further delay!'

For a long moment neither of the two men moved nor uttered a word, but then, giving a slow, appreciative nod, the Captain let go of the quilt.

'T'lass is quite right,' he said, with a hoarse chuckle. 'Makes no sense two grown men argifyin' over a set of bedclothes—you take hold of this, sir, and I'll make do with what's left. What say we bed down for another couple of hours before we brave the chill below?'

'Whilst I am perfectly agreeable to that suggestion, my dear fellow,' returned Palfrey, with an acquiescent bow, 'I must insist that you retain the quilt. I am more than content to avail myself of the remaining blankets.'

'Not at all, sir!' exclaimed Gibbons. 'The quilt is yours—these fine blankets will do me just proud!'

Seeing that another argument between the disparate pair seemed about to ensue, Sophie, throwing up her hands in despair at their ludicrous behaviour, turned on her heel and hurriedly left the room, having come to the conclusion that any further intervention on her part would be pointless.

Just as she was closing the door behind her, however, she came upon Mrs Webster, who was just on the point of exiting the Lucans' room.

'Any further progress in that direction?' she enquired of the landlady, in a low voice.

'Slow goin', I'm afraid,' whispered Mrs Webster, with a pensive shake of her head. 'My guess is that the poor lass will be some little while yet—not that I've any great experience in these matters, only havin' had the one myself, you understand.'

'Then we must just hope and pray that this appalling weather improves sufficiently for us to summon the local midwife to help us out,' declared Sophie bracingly, as she followed her elderly hostess down the stairs. 'How is Mr Webster faring, after that nasty fall?'

'Well enough in the circumstances, thank you, miss,' replied Mrs Webster, pushing open the kitchen door. 'Although how on earth we are going to manage without his help, I can't begin to—great heavens above!'

The landlady having stopped dead in her tracks at the doorway, Sophie found herself obliged to peer over the woman's shoulder in order to discover the cause of her astonishment—only to find herself equally taken aback at the extraordinary scene that met her eyes.

There at the kitchen table stood Marcus Wolfe, his shirtsleeves rolled up to his elbows and minus his neckcloth, unconcernedly ladling milk out of a wooden pail into a large blue-and-white-striped pottery jug. A quick look across at the cheery flames leaping up between the bars of the range's firebox soon ascertained that he had fulfilled his pledge to replenish the supply of logs. Hesitating for only the barest moment, Sophie, her eyes agleam with amusement, raised her hand and, whipping off the lace cap, stuffed the offending article into her apron pocket before following Mrs Webster into the room.

At the sound of their entry, Helstone looked up and smiled, his lips curving to an even greater extent as he registered the lack of covering on Sophie's now slightly tousled chestnut tresses.

'Mrs Webster, I presume?' he said, laying aside the ladle and sketching the landlady a brief bow. 'Marcus Wolfe, at your service. No doubt your husband has already informed you that he was obliged to offer me shelter last evening. I trust that he has not suffered serious hurt from his unfortunate fall?'

'Just twisted his back slightly, sir,' returned the woman, staring at the milk pail in some confusion. 'You've been out and milked our Daisy, sir? How very good of you to put yourself to so much bother!'

Helstone raised a disaffected shoulder and indicated the jug of freshly made coffee simmering gently on the top of the kitchen range. 'Had to be done, if we were to have milk in our coffee.'

It having been a good many years since he had been anywhere near a cow, let alone milked one, Marcus's initial attempts at the activity had met with little success. Daisy had greeted his nervous fumblings with considerable mistrust, jostling him off the stool and kicking away the pail in her impatience to rid herself of his decidedly amateur ministrations. It had taken sheer bloody-mindedness—along with the virtual ruination of a perfectly good pair of leather riding breeches—to finally persuade the recalcitrant animal to succumb to his advances, but once he had managed to get back into the swing of things the old memories had come quickly flooding back.

Milking cows, collecting eggs, haymaking, picking apples and chopping logs—there had been very few activities in which the Viscount had not involved himself during his boyhood on the family estate. Sadly, his ongoing feud with his father had brought about an instant demise of any undertaking that smacked even vaguely of husbandry, in whatever shape or form it might have appeared. Indeed, for the past six years or so he had resolutely refused to involve himself in all matters that had to do with the running of the family estate—to his own detriment, more often than not, as his recent unexpectedly pleasurable activities were now starting to bring home to him.

It had been while he was splitting the logs into a more convenient size that it had begun to occur to him that he actually enjoyed involving himself in this sort of manual labour. Even as the snow had continued to fall in gusting billows all around him, its icy wetness gradually penetrating the fine wool of his expensive riding jacket, he had not been able to help but feel that there was something infinitely wholesome about expending one's energy for the benefit of others—a feeling of healthy satisfaction that even several hours spent in Gentleman Jackson's salon or at the fencing parlour failed to emulate. Sophie's unspoken message that the entire well-being of a handful of total strangers might well devolve upon his being able to keep the house supplied with firewood had brought about the first real sense of purpose that he had experienced for many years. Indeed, just the thought of finding himself the recipient of another of her devastatingly captivating smiles was more than enough incentive to have him attacking even the largest of logs with considerable relish.

And as to the milking! It was beyond thought that he was ever going to allow a mere animal to get the better of him! Aside from which, he was quite determined not to set a foot back inside that blessed kitchen without bearing a reasonable quantity of milk—he'd have that confounded cap off the saucy little madam's head if it was the last thing he did!

His dark eyes gleaming with satisfaction, he now considered Sophie's greatly improved appearance. Freed from the constriction of the cap, several strands of her hair—the colour of which he could only liken to that of ripe chestnuts—fell about her neck in a teasing tangle, instilling in him a sudden urge to rip out the confining pins of the remains of her bundled chignon just to see if the total effect was truly as glorious as his alcohol-fuelled fantasy of the previous night had imagined it to be.

Drawing in a deep breath, in order to steady his rapidly increasing pulse rate, he turned his attention back to the landlady, who had been marvelling at the huge pile of logs stacked beside the chimneypiece.

'There's a good bit more just inside the door of the taproom, ma'am,' he said, jerking his head in the direction of the saloon bar. 'I took the liberty of piling it there, since I doubt that any of your regular clients will be likely to pay us a visit during the next couple of days or so.'

'Still no sign of a let-up, then?' queried Sophie, as she collected three bowls from the dresser and doled out a healthy serving of porridge into each of them.

'Sadly not,' he replied, taking a seat at the table. 'That driver of yours seems to be of the opinion that we're stuck here for the duration. Having very sensibly taken the precaution of pulling the carriage into the barn as soon as they arrived, he and the guard have made themselves up a couple of very comfortable looking beds on the squabs. Organised themselves quite a cosy little set-up out there, they have—even got a brazier burning in the middle of the barn.'

'It sounds as though they must have been soldiers at one time.' Sophie laughed. 'Many's the time my little brother and I were obliged to bed down in such a manner.' Then, stealing an impish look at him, she went on, 'I dare say you must quite envy the pair of them, given your own rather Spartan accommodation.'

Mrs Webster gave a quick nod. 'Yes, we must see if we can't do something about that, young man,' she declared. 'There are a couple of cushioned settles in the tap room—not ideal, certainly, but a sight better than what you had to put up with last night, I feel sure!'

'Oh, I've known worse, I assure you!' he said, flashing a mischievous smile at the now somewhat rosy-cheeked Sophie. 'Nevertheless, I daresay another cushion or two would be most welcome—I'll bring them into the parlour after I've eaten, if I may—although I rather fear that my being obliged to commandeer the room for my own personal use will disadvantage your other guests to some extent.'

'Can't be helped,' retorted Mrs Webster, getting to her feet and moving towards the pantry. 'Needs must, as they say—now, what do the pair of you say to a nice dish of bacon and scrambled eggs?'

'I say yes, please, and thank you very much,' replied Marcus with a quick nod of his head, as he spooned the last of his porridge into his mouth. 'Best porridge I've tasted in years,' he then averred, fixing Sophie with another of his slightly lopsided grins and causing her to experience all sorts of problems with her breathing processes. 'Although I feel bound to confess that I haven't touched the stuff since I was in leading-reins!'

'It's amazing what one will eat if one is hungry!' she returned somewhat distractedly, gripping her hands tightly together under the table in an effort to still the frightening rapidity of her heartbeat. 'My brother and I were often obliged to eat all manner of strange concoctions during our years with the military—but it certainly taught us to appreciate good food when it was offered to us.'

'I appreciated every mouthful, I promise you,' he assured her quickly, his sharp eyes not having missed the rather forlorn look that had suddenly crept across her face as she spoke of her past. 'However, I cannot help but wonder about these strange concoctions of which you spoke. Pray enlighten me.'

Pushing back her chair, she stood up, affecting an airy little laugh. 'Best not to describe such delicacies in detail, I assure you, and certainly not while you are about to eat Mrs Webster's delicious breakfast!' she said, determinedly busying herself with the collecting up of the empty bowls before carrying them over to the kitchen sink.

His eyes following her progress across the room, Marcus's lips curved in appreciative recall of the softly rounded curves that dwelt beneath the ill-fitting grey gown she wore, the memory of which brought about the all too familiar clenching of his gut followed by the usual pulsating throb of his loins. Gritting his teeth, he forced himself to concentrate his attention on the very appetising-looking meal that Mrs Webster had placed before him, ruefully reflecting that any sort of casual dalliance with the comely governess in these present conditions looked to be very much against the odds. Not only had it transpired that Miss Flint was sharing her room with her young charge, but—even given that his chances of persuading her to venture there a second time were probably a hundred to one against—his own accommodation hardly lent itself to the sort of activity he had in mind.

Heaving back a sigh of regret, he did his best to dismiss the several enticing images that were beginning to crowd his brain and, reaching for his knife and fork, endeavoured to apply his concentration to the heaped platter of eggs and bacon in front of him, being very careful to avoid looking directly at the object of his lustful thoughts when she returned to the table and took her place opposite him.

'At least the pump hasn't frozen,' she remarked cheerfully, as she reached across the table and helped herself to one of Mrs Webster's hastily cooked griddle scones. 'I was afraid that we might have to resort to melting buckets of snow for our water!'

'Lor' bless you, no, Miss!' chortled the landlady. 'That's one thing we won't have to worry about, thanks to the fellow who built this place originally. Comes up from the well right next to the back wall, the water does. We have to wrap the outside pipe with a bit of sheepskin every winter to be on the safe side, of course, but apart from that we've never had a hap'orth of trouble.'

'I dare say you've been obliged to do that as well,' remarked the Viscount, chancing a quick look at Sophie.

She looked puzzled. 'Wrap pipes with sheepskin, you mean?'

He shook his head and a reluctant grin crept across his face. 'No, I was referring to your reference to the melting of buckets full of snow—I assumed that you must have been involved in such an activity during your days with the military.'

'Once or twice.' She nodded, her face clearing. 'It can get very cold in the mountain areas of Spain and Portugal.' She paused, as a little furrow creased her brow. 'I take it that you chose not to volunteer your own services?'

There was a moment's silence, then, 'I had my reasons,' returned Marcus curtly, as he pushed back his chair and rose from the table, his meal scarcely half finished. 'If you will excuse me? I really ought to go and check my horse over.'

'Touched a sore nerve there, it seems,' murmured Mrs Webster, after he had exited the room. 'Yon driver told me he'd fed and watered all the horses first thing, before him and his mate cleared the yard. Our Mr Wolfe looks to be sufferin' from a bit of a guilty conscience, if you want my opinion.'

'Probably just not cut out for that sort of life, Mrs

Webster,' said Sophie. 'Judging from the quality of his
boots and the cut of his jacket, I should imagine that Mr
Wolfe spends most of his time lounging in the high-class
drawing rooms of the rich and famous—although I feel
bound to admit that his undoubted expertise with the
axe did come as somewhat of a surprise to me.'

'And may the heavens be thanked for it,' returned the
landlady, with a slight shake of her head. 'Where we
would have been without the lad, the Lord only knows.
Your old driver and his mate have been workin' nineteen
to the dozen keepin' the yard clear of snow, as well as
seein' to the horses, but I doubt if either of them could
chop up a log to save his life. Even my Walter would
be hard put to it these days—our potboy usually deals
with the likes of that sort of thing!'

'Well, we definitely shan't go cold, at any rate,' said
Sophie, rising to her feet and beginning to gather up the
dirty dishes. 'And, thanks to your excellent housekeep-
ing, it seems unlikely that any of us will starve. Shall
we take a peek into your larder and see what we can
conjure up for dinner between us?'

'I've a nice leg of ham hanging there,' began Mrs
Webster, as she made her way across the room towards
the storeroom. 'I had thought of keepin' it for…'

The rest of her sentence was cut off as the sound of
running footsteps on the stairs heralded the arrival of
a white-faced Mr Lucan, who burst into the kitchen,
calling out for immediate assistance.

'My wife!' he gasped, as he clutched at the doorjamb
to steady himself. 'She thinks the babe is on its way!
Somebody help her, I beg of you! *Please!*'

Whipping off her soiled apron, Sophie started for
the door, only to find herself being pulled back by Mrs
Webster.

'Not you, my dear,' cautioned the landlady. 'This sort of thing is not at all suitable for a young unmarried lady such as yourself. I'm not exactly up to the mark myself, but I shall do what I can. You stay here and see to the dinner.'

'Nonsense!' averred Sophie cheerfully. 'I've helped deliver dozens of babies—midwives were few and far between on the Peninsula, I assure you!'

Turning to Lucan, she bade him to calm down and then instructed him to make himself useful by filling all the pots he could find with water and putting them on to boil.

'Why ever 'ave you set 'im to doing that?' whispered the mystified Mrs Webster, as the two of them hastened up the stairs in the direction of the plaintive wails issuing from within the Lucans' bedroom. 'I disremember anyone doin' any such thing when my Jamie was born.'

'Just gives the poor fellow something to occupy his mind,' replied Sophie, with a slight chuckle. 'Expectant fathers are known to become somewhat beside themselves at such times—we always found it better to keep them well out of the way until the worst of the business was over and done with. Speaking of which—do you have some old sheets we could use?'

Chapter Four

Having spent the best part of the past hour exchanging ribald jokes and anecdotes with Driver Lapworthy and his guard, Marcus was in a far better frame of mind when he eventually returned to the kitchen, only to find himself confronted by the sight of a white-faced Jack Lucan, anxiously pacing the floor of the room, quite oblivious to the argument going on between the Reverend Palfrey and Captain Gibbons who, having finally ousted themselves from their bed, had come down to the kitchen in the expectation of finding a meal waiting for them. Finding no one available to serve their needs, they had raided the larder and were now noisily debating the merits of frying eggs as opposed to scrambling them.

'Do you actually have any idea how to scramble eggs?' demanded Gibbons scathingly, as he attempted to extricate the skillet from the parson's hands. 'At least I've fried a good few in my time!'

'And nasty greasy things they were too, I'll be bound,' retorted Palfrey, determinedly clinging to the pan. 'A lightly scrambled egg is far better for a delicate stomach.'

'Well, my stomach ain't in the least bit delicate,' roared the Captain, having finally managed to wrench the utensil out of the weaker man's grasp. 'It's just grumbling from lack of sustenance!'

'Please, please, gentlemen,' interposed the distraught Lucan. 'Have a little consideration for my poor wife in her hour of need.'

Casting sullen looks at one another, the two elderly squabblers ceased their wrangling and did their utmost to appear suitably chastened at his appeal.

Stepping forward, Marcus reached across and relieved Gibbons of his recently acquired trophy.

'Since there appear to be at least half a dozen cooking pots readily available,' he commented sagely, 'it would seem sensible for each of you to have his eggs in whichever way suits him best. If you would care to sit yourselves down at the table, gentlemen, I am sure I can attend to both your requirements.' Then, turning to Lucan, he added, 'You too, my good sir, if you please— from your agitated demeanour I must assume that your wife is at this moment doing her best to provide you with an heir. I hasten to point out that you will do the young lady no favours by collapsing at her bedside for want of an egg or two.'

Although he cast a somewhat piteous look in his direction, the young father-to-be obeyed the Viscount without comment, reluctantly sitting himself down at the table while Marcus proceeded to break three eggs into the already sizzling frying pan, before turning his attention to the whipping up of several more prior to tipping them into a butter-laced pot.

What an extraordinary day this is turning into! he

mused, as he stirred the eggs in one pan and flipped the others over in the skillet. *Chopping logs, milking cows and now—by all that's marvellous—acting as kitchen maid to as big a set of nincompoops as I've ever come across! Damned lucky I spent so much time down in the kitchens at Bradfield when I was a lad. What next, I wonder? Just so long as they don't expect me to deliver the blessed baby!*

At this thought he frowned, having suddenly realised that the continued absence of both Sophie and Mrs Webster seemed to indicate that the two of them were engaged in that very task. *Hardly a suitable occupation for an unmarried girl, surely?* Although, from what he had already gathered from her earlier remarks, it would seem that there were few things at which that particular young lady would demur from attempting, if the need arose.

His lips twisted as Sophie's query as to his involvement in the country's recent hostilities returned to haunt him, and, as always, a hot surge of resentment ran through him as he recalled his father's absolute obduracy over the matter throughout the past six years. Although why it should now concern him what conclusion a virtual stranger might have reached over his apparent lack of participation, he was hard put to fathom. Yet for some unknown reason it did.

The faint smell of singeing alerted him back to the task in hand. Hastily he slid the pan of frying eggs away from the hotplate before any real damage was done, and skilfully tipped the contents on to Captain Gibbons's plate, then returning to the range to collect the pot of scrambled eggs, which he placed on the table and exhorted the other two men to 'dig in' while his offering was still at its best.

Sadly enough, Mr Lucan had barely dipped his fork into the minute portion of the creamy mixture to which he had helped himself before the passage door sprang open and a laughing-eyed Sophie was informing the assembled company of the safe arrival of one Master John Henry Lucan.

'I believe your wife would like to see you now, sir,' she said, shooting the new father a mischievous smile. 'She is rather tired, of course, but has asked if you could manage to spare her a few moments of your time…?'

Dropping his fork, Lucan was on his feet in a flash, had dashed through the doorway and was halfway up the stairs before any of his table companions could even draw breath to offer him their congratulations.

Heaving a deep sigh, the now slightly tearful Sophie turned to look at the coffee-pot, simmering at the back of the range. 'I believe I have earned a cup of that, if one of you gentlemen would be good enough to pour it for me,' she murmured, as she lowered herself into Mrs Webster's fireside chair and, leaning her head back against the cushions, closed her eyes.

Marcus had sprung to attention before either of the other two men had even registered her words, and in no time at all he was at her side, offering the requested refreshment.

Having reluctantly managed to pry her eyelids apart, Sophie was startled to find herself immediately confronted with Marcus's dark brown gaze, only inches from her face. For a moment it seemed that her heart had stopped beating and her entire body seemed to be flooding with the oddest sensations, the like of which she had never before experienced. An inexplicable feeling of panic ran through her, causing her to shoot bolt upright, and it was only Marcus's quick reaction to her sudden movement that prevented her from being deluged with the scalding contents of the cup he held in his hand.

'Whoa, steady, there!' he cautioned, as he laid the cup down on the hearth. 'A breath of fresh air is what you really need, you know,' he said, frowning in concern as he took in the faint shadows beneath her eyes. 'I believe it stopped snowing some time ago. If you would care to step outside for a few moments, I should be more than happy to keep you company.'

Sophie rose to her feet, desperately trying to control the violent wave of trembling that still beset her.

'I—I'll just get my pelisse—it should be dry by now—Mrs Webster kindly hung it on the drying frame for me…'

She had the distinct feeling that she was talking gibberish but could not seem to get a grip on herself. Before she could even attempt to extricate her pelisse from the overhead frame, Marcus had reached up and unhooked it and was, even now, coaxing her into sliding her arms through the sleeves. Ignoring her muted protests, he proceeded, in the most matter-of-fact way, to pull the coat-fronts together and fasten the buttons, before standing back and regarding her with a quizzical frown.

'Not exactly the warmest coat I've ever come across,' he observed, with a crooked smile. 'You had better have my scarf.'

Tucking her arm into his elbow, he led her across to the back door where, after collecting his thick red woollen scarf from the hook on the wall, he wrapped it firmly over her head and around her neck before opening the door and leading her out into the stableyard.

'Oh, goodness me!' she gasped, stepping back as the cold air hit her. 'I'm not sure I wouldn't rather have stayed by the fire!'

'A little bit of exercise will soon get the blood flowing,' he teased and, bending down, he picked up a small handful of snow, compressed it into a ball and gently tossed it towards her, taking great care to avoid actually hitting her.

'Why, you…!'

Filling her hands with snow, she balled it and flung it at him, missing him by several feet. Stooping to gather up more ammunition, she found herself obliged to dodge the hail of missiles that Marcus had seemed able to conjure up before she had managed to collect even the one—although she quickly came to the conclusion that his aim was no better than hers since very few of his snowballs ever made real contact with her person. Nevertheless, dashing from one side of the stableyard to the other soon had her feeling warmed from the tip of her nose right down to her toes, and it was not long before she was obliged to seek refuge against the cowshed wall where she held up her hands and laughingly begged him for mercy.

'Only if you pay the time-honoured forfeit.'

He walked towards her, his lips curved and eyes gleaming with unsuppressed amusement. Standing directly in front of her, he reached out his hands and began busying himself with a purposeful rearrangement of her head covering, which had gone somewhat adrift during their boisterous frolic.

'F-forfeit?'

Sophie cast a wary glance upward and then wished she had not done so, for the look in his eyes as he stared down at her was more than enough to have her heart doing that very same stop/start dance that had brought her out here in the first place. She was almost certain that he was about to kiss her and she was not at all sure if that was such a good idea. She had been kissed before, it was true—swift, daring pecks on the cheek by bashful sub-lieutenants, for the most part, as her upbringing, though irregular, had been somewhat meticulous in certain respects. But, given what she had experienced the previous night, coupled with the strangely disturbing feelings that he seemed to engender within her simply by catching her eye, she could not help feeling that allowing herself to be kissed by Marcus Wolfe would prove to be a very big mistake.

Carefully easing one hand behind Sophie's neck, the Viscount, hardly daring to breathe lest he broke the spell that he had succeeded in conjuring up, bent his head to claim his much-desired forfeit.

Quick as a flash, Sophie ducked beneath his arm and spun out of reach, only to find herself suddenly sliding sideways across the snow-covered ground in the most inelegant fashion. With a startled oath Marcus grabbed at her falling figure, whereupon he too found himself sliding on the ice. Concerted cries of dismay emanated from the pair as, wildly clutching at each other and powerless to prevent their descent, they fell headlong into a nearby snowdrift.

'Deuce take it, woman!' gasped Marcus, when he had recovered sufficiently to take a breath. 'What in God's name was that all about?'

With the full weight of his body on top of her, Sophie was finding it impossible to concentrate her mind on the whys and wherefores of her precipitate action, but, as the melting snow began to make its presence felt through the thin fabric of her pelisse, the need to extricate herself became paramount. 'Kindly remove yourself!' she grated through clenched teeth. 'The snow is soaking through my coat.'

'Hardly surprising,' he snapped, as he clambered to his feet and reached down to haul her out of the drift. The whole experience had left him feeling decidedly irritated. Hardly had he had time to react to Sophie's unexpected rejection of his advances before he had found himself pitched ignominiously into a heap of snow where, to his everlasting shame and annoyance, he been unable to control his all too swift reaction to the soft imprint of her curves as they pressed against his body. The powerful sensations that had swept through him had left him in a state of stunned bewilderment which had, somehow or other, exacerbated his feelings of umbrage towards the wet and shivering creature standing in front of him. 'You really need to furnish yourself with a much more suitable outfit, my dear, if you will insist on long-distance travel at this time of year,' he ground out tersely.

Now thoroughly chilled to the bone, Sophie was in no mood for such high-handed observations from someone who clearly had no notion of how it might feel to be inadequately clad and all but penniless.

'Some of us have little choice in the matter of what we are obliged to wear,' she flashed back, doing her level best to stop her teeth from chattering. 'We don't all have fat purses and wardrobes full of furs!'

He stilled, staring down at her, a mental picture of her sprawled across his bed draped in white furs suddenly filling his imagination. 'You could have all of that and more if you really wanted it,' he said huskily, his fingertips reaching across to caress her damp cheek. 'I have the neatest little cottage in Chelsea—'

'How dare you, sir?'

An ice-cold hand hard across the side of his face brought the trembling Viscount swiftly to his senses.

Good God, he thought, aghast, *was I really about to offer a* carte blanche *to an impoverished governess? I must be losing my mind!*

Shaking with a curious combination of heart-wrenching desolation coupled with out-and-out fury, Sophie angrily divested herself of the Viscount's scarf and, after flinging the offending article at him, started back towards the inn, taking very careful steps across the now visibly melting snow. She had almost gained the back door when the faint but unmistakable jingle of horses' traces reached her ears. She stopped, straining hard to identify the sound. Yes, there it was again! There was traffic moving on the road above. Her eyes shining, she whirled round to face the still rigidly motionless Viscount.

'There!' she cried. 'Do you hear it? The road must be passable again. We must all set to and dig out a passageway for the coach. We could be away first thing tomorrow if we put our backs into it!'

'Dig out a passageway?' returned the Viscount, with a disdainful curl of his lip. 'Who? You, me and those two old has-beens in the stable, I suppose? It would take us until a week next Friday to clear that amount of snow!'

She stared at him in disbelief, then shook her head. 'You can take it from me that neither Lapworthy nor Hastings will be so faint-hearted when they hear that the road is open,' she said, before adding disparagingly, 'It's little wonder that you chose not to join the military. I doubt that you would have even survived the Channel crossing!'

Clenching his fists, Marcus took a single step forward, then stopped.

'Had you been a man, you would have paid dearly

for that insult,' he ground out. 'Let me assure you that you'll get your passageway, Miss Flint—even if I have to carve it out with my bare hands. Might I suggest that you take yourself off and devote your efforts to attending to the needs of those who clearly appreciate your company more than I do?'

With that, he turned on his heel and stalked towards the door of the stable, from which were already emerging the elderly coach driver and his guard, each of them carrying an assortment of tools.

'Did you hear it?' called the guard, as he rolled up his sleeves and started to shovel at the softening snow. 'That be the four o'clock mail out of Bath, sure as my name's Gus Hastings. Trifle tardy, to be sure, but they allus keeps the mails runnin', no matter what! Bit o' fierce diggin' and we'll be out of here before the cat can spit!' Then, turning to the Viscount, he added, 'How's about it, sir? You'll be up for it, I'm sure.'

'Lead on, Macduff,' murmured Marcus resignedly, as he divested himself of both his greatcoat and jacket, at once revealing the hefty muscles in his arms and thighs, courtesy of his many hours spent in Jackson's parlour, sparring against the great man himself. 'At a guess, I'd say it's about fifty or sixty yards to the turnpike.'

With a brief nod, the driver screwed up his eyes and stared across the snow-covered terrain in front of them. 'Uphill, too,' he said tersely, as he gathered together his chosen implements. 'We'll be slippin' an' sliding all the way—puts me in mind o' that winter when we was holed up in Lisbon, Gus. Do you recall?'

'Hard to forget!' came his companion's cheerful reply. 'Still, at least we don't 'ave to cross a flooded Douro on this occasion!'

Laughing together, the pair set to, but it soon occurred

to Sophie, who had been unable to drag herself away from the scene, that the advanced ages of the driver and his guard would eventually tell against them, for in spite of their obvious courage and determination it was clearly all they could do to stay abreast of Marcus, who was shovelling away as though his very life depended on it. Which, in the terms of bolstering up his dented pride and filling him with a much-needed sense of achievement, perhaps it did.

'*I'll show the cold-hearted shrew,*' he muttered to himself, as he tossed yet another hefty shovelful of snow to one side. '*I'll have her out of here by morning, if it's the last thing I do!*'

The sight of the damp shirt clinging to his rippling muscles was more than enough for Sophie to begin to regret her earlier outburst, for it was becoming increasingly clear that Marcus Wolfe was hardly the chicken-hearted poltroon that she had all but accused him of being. After watching him for some minutes she turned away and, with hot tears pricking at the back of her eyes, re-entered the inn to do as he had suggested and concentrate her attentions on the needs of the three invalids—at least they seemed to appreciate her efforts, she thought as, with a plaintive sniff, she wiped away the unbidden tears.

The snow-clearing operation continued well into the evening, when the lack of light brought such proceedings to a halt. Even Lucan had insisted upon taking his turn, and had done sterling work for almost an hour, despite the fact that neither he nor his wife were likely to be in any position to complete their own journey for some days. Even the doughty Captain managed a couple of feet or so, before a violent bout of coughing sent him back into the welcoming warmth of the inn's kitchen.

Throughout the entire range of shift-changing, however, Marcus pressed on, oblivious to the various recommendations that he should stop and take a well-earned rest. Sheer dogged determination drove him on—to give up now would be to admit defeat, and there was no way he was going to allow Sophie to witness failure at this stage of the game!

In the end, however, despite the fact that the ever-cheerful Gus Hastings had brought out a lantern to help the Viscount carve his way through the waist-deep drifts that had formed throughout the previous night and earlier part of the day, the growing darkness finally overcame even his obdurate resolution.

'Best jack it in now, mate,' advised the guard. 'A good night's sleep and we can 'ave at it again come first light—less than twenty yards to go now, by my reckonin'.'

Utterly spent, and with every muscle in his body crying out for reprieve, Marcus at last agreed that it was time to quit, and, after virtually dragging himself back to the sanctuary of the kitchen, he collapsed into the chair by the fireside and thankfully accepted Mrs Webster's offer of a hot toddy.

'I'll take myself off to my bed now, if you have no objections,' he croaked wearily, after he had downed half of the spicy mixture. 'If you could manage to dry my shirt by morning, I'd be most grateful.'

'No problem at all, sir,' Mrs Webster assured him, as she draped a large towel over his heaving shoulders. 'I've put extra rugs and cushions on the settle, so you should get a fairly decent sleep tonight. Just pass me out your shirt and I'll have it clean and ready for you when you need it.'

Ignoring the rest of the assembled company, the

Viscount headed for his makeshift bed in the parlour, unbuttoning his soaking wet shirt as he went. Once inside his room, he peeled it off and passed it out to the waiting landlady, bidding her a weary goodnight as he closed the door.

'Young fool was practically killing himself out there,' observed the Captain, with a concerned shake of his head. 'Must be desperate keen to get on his way.'

Desperately keen to get away from me, more likely, was Sophie's forlorn thought, as she finished drying the last of the supper dishes. Having been watching Marcus out of the corner of her eye, in the vain hope of seeing some sign of conciliation from him, it had been made clear to her that he had no intention of giving her any chance to apologise for her recklessly hurtful remarks, the constant memory of which now filled her with a burning sense of self-recrimination. She found herself thinking that even the fact that he appeared to have been about to suggest that living under his protection might be preferable to the penury of her present position could not really be regarded as ample justification for the unbridled discourtesy of her response. Her six-month tenure with the Crayfords had left her with few illusions as to how the so-called *haut monde* conducted their lives. Indeed, she had soon learned that many females in circumstances similar to her own would have been only too glad to jump at such a generous offer especially—as she found herself obliged to admit, albeit with a some-what rueful sigh—from so personable a man as Marcus Wolfe!

But then, she reasoned, as she lifted her chin and squared her shoulders in preparation to bidding her fellow travellers goodnight and quitting the room, her parents had brought her up to place a high regard on her self-respect, and, although it was true that her situation within the Crayford family was far from ideal, she was not yet reduced to selling herself in order to survive!

This spirited resolve was doomed to falter slightly as she made her way past the door to Marcus's sleeping quarters and was unable to prevent herself from conjuring up a picture of his bronzed and muscular torso—shirtless now, of course—only to find herself then wondering if he slept in those thigh-hugging leather breeches or…!

Pulling herself up sharp, she all but fled up the stairs to her own bedchamber, where she was more than pleased to find that her young charge, having been liberally dosed with Mrs Webster's willow-bark powders throughout the day, was now almost back to her normal petulant self. So much so that she was quite adamant in her refusal to allow her governess to borrow one of her many nightgowns, forcing Sophie to spend yet another night in her flimsy shift.

Rolling off his cushioned settle well before any sensible-minded lark would even consider the possibility of rising, Marcus flexed his aching muscles, pulled on his breeches and opened his bedroom door—to find there on the floor, just as promised, his shirt, newly washed and ironed. Even the hardly surprising discovery that none of the other stalwart navigators had yet risen from their beds did not deter the Viscount from rescuing his discarded shovel from where he had tossed it the previous evening and applying himself once more to his gruelling self-appointed task.

Having spent much of the night doing his best to dismiss all thoughts of Sophie from his mind, he had found himself racked with an unfathomable remorse at having treated her in such a cavalier manner. *What in God's name could I have been thinking of?* he had asked himself over and over again. With two perfectly satisfactory mistresses already at his disposal and any number of bored young matrons indicating their willingness to make themselves available to him, his needs in that particular direction were more than adequately served. So what it was about this chestnut-haired, startlingly blue-eyed nobody that had managed to get under his skin he was hard pressed to comprehend. It was true that he had been without a woman for almost a week now, but surely, he thought savagely, as he dug his shovel into the snow, his sexual proclivities were not so all-consuming that he needed to latch on to the first pretty wench that he came across after a mere seven days? If so, heaven help him! He must really be turning into the godforsaken wastrel that his father had dubbed him! At that thought he could not help but let out a deep chuckle. If the old man could but see him now—knee-deep in a snowdrift! Knee-deep? He paused, leant on his shovel and stared at the blanketed terrain around him, suddenly realising that the snow's depth, which had been well over three feet down at the lower part of the dig, was now down to less than two the closer he got to the highway. In just a couple of yards it would be possible to simply scrape it to one side to allow the carriage free access.

And so it was that, shortly after ten o'clock that same morning, the three other men having applied themselves to the task with extra vigour once they realised that their goal was no longer as insurmountable as it had seemed eighteen hours earlier, the passage was pronounced navigable. A hasty breakfast was gulped down as quickly as was humanly possible by those intending to travel, and by eleven o'clock the horses were poled up, the luggage strapped on to the roof and the driver declared the coach ready to depart.

With her four shillings and ninepence still intact—Mrs Webster having waved away all attempts at any sort of payment from her, on the grounds that she had achieved far more in the past two days than the absent local girl usually managed in a week—Sophie climbed into the carriage and took one of the window seats, with the well-wrapped-up Lydia at her side and Gibbons and Palfrey seated opposite. The Lucans, of course, would not be travelling to the Maidenhead post with them, but Sophie had promised to get a message to Mrs Lucan's anxiously waiting mother, in order that that lady might set about organising her family's safe removal from the little inn.

Looking out of the window, she could see that Jack Lucan and Marcus were standing ready to apply their shoulders to the rear of the vehicle, should the precipitous slope prove difficult to negotiate. She tried focussing her gaze on the back of Marcus's head, desperately willing him to turn and look in her direction so that she could at least wave him farewell, but to no avail.

After two failed attempts to chivvy the lead horses up the slope, the coach at last began to move, and with Gus Hastings encouraging the horses at the front, and Marcus and Lucan hefting their backs at the rear, the ancient vehicle gradually began to lumber slowly through the man-made passageway.

Once on the turnpike, however, it was clear that the going had been made easier by the passage of several other vehicles already. Added to which, the sun had finally come out from behind the clouds and the snow was now beginning to melt quite rapidly. By midafternoon, Marcus hazarded, as he stood at the top of the incline trying to get his breath back, most of it would in all likelihood have disappeared completely, leaving him with nothing but a few painful memories that he could well do without. Time to saddle Jupiter and continue his own interrupted journey, he reminded himself dismally. On to London, his original destination, or back to Bradfield to try and make peace with his father? At this point, he had no real idea of what he wanted to do.

Heaving a deep sigh, he turned to watch Gus climbing up on to the box next to Lapworthy. In doing so, he was unable to prevent himself casting a quick glance towards where Sophie was sitting, next to the carriage's already misted-up window. Having made up his mind to avoid all contact with her since their altercation in the yard, he had not even joined in the round of farewells that had taken place when the travellers were ready to depart, electing instead to busy himself with the strapping on of the luggage. But now, as his eyes made contact with hers, his heart stopped, his stomach seemed to turn over and a sudden disquieting panic threatened to overwhelm him.

Barely stopping to think, he stepped forward, wrenched open the door of the carriage and, dipping his hand into his jacket pocket, extracted one of his calling cards. Thrusting it into the startled Sophie's hand, he exhorted her to contact him should she ever require his help, then, slamming the door shut before she could deny him, he stepped away from the vehicle just as the driver gave the lead horse the office to move on.

A heartening surge of relief seemed to flood through his veins as he stood back and watched as the coach pulled away. Now, at least, she was not lost to him for ever. By giving Sophie his card he had made it possible for him to call on her in the socially accepted manner. After that—well, who knew what Fate might have in store for them? But even as the Viscount sought to console himself with this comforting thought, the cold trickle of impending disaster proceeded to sweep it abruptly away as all at once it came to him that he had not the slightest idea of Sophie's place of residence—nor did he even know the name of the people who employed her! Any thoughts that he might have had about contacting her within the next few days were clearly doomed to failure!

Letting out a loud groan of dismay, he started after the carriage, though he was well aware that, with a team of frisky horses having been cooped up for two days at its head, his chances of catching up with the now swiftly moving vehicle were somewhat less than nil. After a fruitless dash of some fifty yards or so, he dragged to a gasping halt, his shoulders slumped in despair, and, disconsolately retracing his steps, he made his way back to the inn, hoping against hope that Mrs Webster could furnish him with the information he needed—information that had, for some inexplicable reason, suddenly become a most vital necessity!

Chapter Five

'I still fail to understand why finding this blessed female is of such vital importance to you. Have you fallen in love with her, or what?'

'Don't talk rot!'

Strolling with his brother Giles down Oxford Street's wide thoroughfare, Marcus let out a dismissive bark of laughter. Two weeks had passed since his return to the capital and he was still no further forward in his search. The tavern's landlady having informed him that she knew very little about Sophie's personal history, other than the fact that her father had been killed in action at Waterloo and that she had a younger brother who was away at school somewhere, Marcus had been reduced to enlisting his brother's help. The Major, in his capacity of Chief Intelligence Officer at the Home Office, was equipped with the necessary seniority of rank to pull all sorts of strings that were unavailable to the Viscount himself. So far, however, it would seem that even Giles's investigations had drawn a blank.

'Well, as I've already told you, the only Flints that I've been able to get any leads on are a young rifleman from the ninety-forth and a Scottish Colour Sergeant, neither of whom were married with children. There was one other—for what it's worth—but he was a highly decorated Lieutenant-Colonel, name of Pendleton-Flint. Can't see that he would fit your—where in the hell are you off to now?'

Left standing speechless as he watched his brother tear across the road, dodging in and out of the heavy press of traffic and taking his life in his hands, Giles was set to wondering—and not for the first time during the past fourteen days—whether Marcus had suffered some sort of weird brainstorm when he had been benighted by that freak blizzard. That the Viscount had been acting rather oddly since that time would be something of an understatement, to say the least, especially in regard to the puzzling rekindling of his once close relationship with his brother Giles, from whose side Marcus had hardly strayed since his arrival back in town. No all-night drinking and gambling sessions, no mad escapades with those equally notorious associates of his and, somewhat more disturbing, not a single minute spent in the company of either of his rather comely mistresses! Instead, an apparently single-minded dedication applied to the task of uncovering the whereabouts of some mysterious governess—a task to which he had also managed to persuade Major Wolfe to devote not only his expertise but quite a significant portion of the manpower at his disposal, in addition.

With a groan of dismay, Giles heaved in a choking gasp of despair as he witnessed his brother narrowly managing to avoid being crushed under the wheels of a heavily loaded brewer's dray before leaping up on to the pavement opposite, where he skidded to a breathless halt in front of the rather drab-looking wench who was walking amongst the press of people there.

'Mr Wolfe!'

Although her eyes had widened with delight at the unexpected pleasure of seeing Marcus again, Sophie's cheeks immediately flushed scarlet as she realised how she had addressed him. 'I do beg your pardon, my lord,' she substituted hurriedly. 'H-how nice to see you! H-how are you keeping? Well, I trust?'

The mere sight of him had reduced her to talking gibberish again, and she knew it. A fortnight of sleepless nights, tossing about on her hard, lumpy mattress, doing her best to put all thoughts of Marcus Wolfe out of her mind, had done little to improve her appearance. Her hair was, once again, encased in the dreaded lace cap, and both her nondescript bonnet and pelisse were as grey and as shabby as they had ever been. Since her shocked discovery that plain Mr Wolfe was—as indicated by the card that he had thrust into her hand at their parting—none other than Viscount Helstone, heir to the Bradfield earldom, and, according to what she had overheard of the servants' chatter, more generally referred to as 'Hellcat Helstone' in the gossip columns of the popular press—she had alternated between thanking her lucky stars that their acquaintanceship had been cut short so precipitately and ruefully wondering how it might have developed had she been bold enough to accept his outrageous offer.

Mrs Crayford having held her personally responsible for Lydia's severe cold on their belated return to the capital, the quality of her life in the Lennox Gardens residence had continued to deteriorate and, since there had been no snow in or around the centre of London at the time, her employer had refused to concede that the weather could have been so bad as to prevent their return at the pre-arranged time. This had not been helped by her daughter's input that 'There really didn't seem to be that much snow about, as far as I could recall'—an unsurprising evaluation of the situation, given that the girl had spent the whole of the two days in bed, being waited on by her luckless companion.

Added to which, the young Arthur Crayford, his objective having been made only too clear on any number of previous occasions, had recently taken to waylaying Sophie in some deserted part of the house or other and pressing his lubricious attentions on her—a rather taxing situation that was beginning to cause her real concern.

Marcus, gazing down at her pale drawn face, could not help observing that she seemed to have lost weight since their last meeting, and as the possibility that she might be being deprived of food invaded his mind he found himself beset by a hot flood of rage.

'I'm fine,' he said, in reply to her garbled question. 'How about you?'

'Very well, thank you,' came her automatic response, which might have caused the Viscount to laugh out loud, had his attention not been drawn to the dark shadows under her eyes.

By this time Giles had managed to cross the road and was standing to one side, waiting for his brother to introduce him to the waif-like creature in the shabby attire.

At his discreet cough, Marcus flushed, as he belatedly
remembered his manners.

'My brother—Major Wolfe,' he said, not taking his
eyes from Sophie's stricken face as he waved a careless
hand in Giles's direction. 'This lady is my Miss Flint,
Giles.'

'Good God!'

Marcus's use of the possessive pronoun, followed so
swiftly by his brother's explosive epithet of astonishment, brought yet another rosy flush to Sophie's cheeks,
but on this occasion it was a flush of indignation. Raising her chin, she stared pointedly at Giles, favouring
him with an example of one of the chilling glances that
generally had the effect of putting even the most recalcitrant of her charges firmly in their place.

It worked, rendering the Major duly admonished.

'I beg your pardon, ma'am,' he stuttered as, casting a
furious glare at Marcus and registering the unrepentant
gleam of amusement in his brother's eyes, he collected
himself sufficiently to execute an elegant bow.

Before Sophie was able to respond to the Major's
gallant gesture, however, she felt herself being shunted
forward as someone barged into her from behind, throwing her completely off balance. Letting out a cry of
dismay, she would certainly have fallen to the ground
had not Marcus, uttering an angry curse, thrown out
his hands to grab at her and pulled her quickly towards
him. For an instant the sudden surge of joy that cascaded
through her at finding herself wrapped in the Viscount's
arms once more wiped all vestige of sense from Sophie's
mind, filling her entire being with a wholly primitive
need to return the unexpected embrace. Almost of their
own volition her hands reached up, and might well have
attained their goal had she not suddenly become aware

of the fact that her small beaded reticule, which normally dangled by its chain at her wrist, was no longer in its accustomed place.

Groaning in exasperation, she hauled herself away from Marcus, crying, 'Oh, not again! My purse—it has been stolen!'

Pushing the bewildered Viscount to one side, she quickly took stock of the crowds milling all about them. Then, with an angry cry, she pointed to the raggedy barefoot youth she had spotted fleeing towards a nearby side alley. 'There!' she cried. 'See? That little devil has it in his hand!'

'Leave it to me!' responded Giles, and, taking off with all speed, he made after the fingersmith, leaving his brother to comfort the now highly irate Sophie.

'You had better come and sit down,' he urged, catching hold of her hand and directing her towards a nearby tea shop. 'You are shaking all over.'

Once inside, he signalled to a waiter and ordered tea. 'Best thing for shock,' he said, casting a concerned eye over Sophie's white-set features. 'Or so I have been told.'

'I'm not suffering from shock,' she retorted, through clenched teeth. 'What kind of a weak-kneed creature do you think I am? I'm just so utterly furious!'

'I can see that you must be,' sympathised the Viscount. 'I'm just glad that you weren't hurt. These young sneak thieves are getting more audacious by the day.'

Still frowning, Sophie did not reply.

'Did you lose a great deal?' he then asked, recalling the pitifully small cache of coins that she had had with her at the inn.

She gave a slight shrug of her shoulders. 'Do I really look as if I'm worth robbing?' she demanded, hurriedly blinking back the angry tears that threatened. 'Three shillings and sixpence and my last good handkerchief, if you really must know. All the rest went with my other purse yesterday morning.'

'You're not telling me that the same thing happened to you yesterday, too?' exclaimed Marcus, with a shocked expression.

Sophie gave him a weary nod. 'While I was taking my charges for their afternoon walk in the square gardens—I would have gone after the little devil, but of course I was unable to leave the children.'

'What truly damnable luck. You won't allow me to reimburse you, I dare say?'

She stared across at him, exasperation plain on her face. 'Certainly not! I thought I had made my position perfectly clear in that respect at our last meeting.'

'Well, yes, you did rather,' replied Marcus, his lips curving slightly as he lifted his fingers and patted the cheek she had slapped. 'This, however, is a somewhat different matter. I wouldn't care to think of you going without, for the sake of a few shillings on my part.'

Sophie shook her head. 'I shan't go without,' she assured him. 'It was money I had set aside for a book— an atlas I am in need of—I was on my way to the book-shop to enquire after it when we met.'

Leaning closer, he stretched out his hand and laid it on hers. 'Then at least let me purchase the book for you,' he said eagerly. 'Surely you must agree that it would be quite unexceptional for you to accept so mundane a gift from a friend?'

At his touch, Sophie's heart-rate shot up by several notches and, raising her teacup to her lips in order to hide her confusion, it was all she could do to prevent her hand from shaking. 'Thank you, my lord, but that really isn't necessary, I promise you,' she eventually managed and then, having struggled to get her emotions under control, added, 'In any event, I need to have words with the bookseller. I still have not received the book he promised to find for me, yet he has sent me the most ridiculous bill of sale. It's just fortunate that I was carrying it in my coat pocket; otherwise I would have lost that, too.'

A wide grin crept over Marcus's face. 'Well, I've often heard of bills being referred to as irritating, but "ridiculous"? That's certainly a new one on me!'

'Well, this one *is* ridiculous, I assure you,' retorted Sophie and, dipping her fingers into the pocket of her pelisse, she withdrew a folded sheet of paper and spread it out on the table in front of him. 'As you will see for yourself, if you care to examine it.'

At first, as far as the Viscount could see, the document looked like any other bill of sale, until he realised that, although it had 'Miss S. Flint' and—to his secret delight—Sophie's full Lennox Gardens address written clearly on the reverse of the sheet, the bill itself was, in fact, invoiced to a Mr Matthew Nyne.

'A simple misdirection, I'd say.' He smiled, handing it back to her.

'Yes, that's what I thought, at first,' she said, staring down at the missive. 'If it weren't for the fact that the arithmetic is quite bizarre. Look more closely, my lord, if you would.'

Although he was finding Sophie's continual use of his title somewhat jarring, Marcus thought it best to refrain from commenting on the matter. Reaching for the proffered document, he proceeded to give it his full attention.

Urgent Attn. Matthew Nyne

	£ : s : d
To Items	9 : 5
.. ..	5 : 4
.. ..	2 : 1
.. ..	2 : 2
To Items	2 : 4
.. ..	3 : 7
.. ..	5 : 4
To Items	5 : 1
.. ..	5 : 11
.. ..	2 : 2
.. ..	2 : 1
.. ..	3 : 8
Balance	£7 : 13 : 5

'Good grief!' he exclaimed eventually. 'Your book-seller clearly needs a few lessons in accountancy! Here! Take a look at this, Giles!'

This last was to his brother who, having failed in his pursuit of the guttersnipe who had made off with Sophie's reticule, had just this moment peered into the tearooms, in search of the missing pair.

'Tea! Good—oh!' he said, eyeing the teapot with satisfaction as he joined them. Then, catching sight of the piece of paper in Marcus's hand, he queried, 'What's to do? Not got behind in settling up your debts, have you, bro?'

After giving the Major's ankle a swift but harmless kick under the table, Marcus grinned and shoved the bill under his brother's nose while Sophie busied herself with the tea things. 'What do you make of that, then?' he asked.

Giles cast a cursory glance over the figures, and his

expression was at first quite indifferent. Then, stiffening, he shot a quick sideways look at Sophie and said quietly, 'May I ask how you came by this document, Miss Flint?'

'It was delivered along with yesterday morning's post,' she replied, somewhat taken aback at his abrupt manner. 'Why do you ask?'

'You were expecting an invoice from this Mr Broomfield?'

'In a manner of speaking, yes, but my bill would only have been for three shillings and sixpence, and as you see…'

'Yes. Quite.' Giles nodded, continuing to stare at Sophie in the most searching manner.

'Steady on, Giles!' protested Marcus, laughing. 'Why the interrogation? Miss Flint is not the one who has got her sums wrong!'

'Yes, I am aware of that,' said the Major abruptly, shooting his brother an exasperated glance before turning once more to Sophie and asking, 'Would it be possible for me to borrow this invoice for a day or so, I wonder? I would like to have one of my men take a copy, if you have no objection.'

'Take a copy!' exclaimed Sophie in astonishment, while Marcus simply looked at his brother in dumbfounded incredulity. 'Whatever for? Surely Mr Broomfield just needs to tell his clerk to sharpen up his ideas?'

'Possibly,' replied Giles briskly, rising to his feet, his tea still untasted. Folding the bill of sale carefully, he raised his eyebrows questioningly at Sophie and, at her mystified nod, tucked it into his jacket pocket, bowed neatly and bade them both farewell, before exiting the tea shop in considerable haste.

'Well, I'll be well and truly damned!' muttered Marcus under his breath, as he glared at his brother's departing figure in mystified disbelief.

Her sharp ears having caught his nonchalant profanity, Sophie was all at once put in mind of the scurrilous tales she had heard the servants whispering about the notorious Viscount, causing her to ask herself what on earth she thought she was doing, sitting in a public tea shop with so infamous a character as Hellcat Helstone. 'Oh, I do hope not,' she murmured softly, as she allowed her eyes to drink in the never to be forgotten contours of his features.

He, not having missed her words, stared across at her, a sardonic smile tugging at his lips.

'It would appear that your earlier opinion of me has undergone little alteration since our last encounter,' he sighed. 'Doubtless you have spent the past two weeks perusing the gossip columns—might I venture to suggest that I'm not actually as black as I have been frequently painted?'

A sudden flush covered her cheeks as she recalled her previous ruthless assessment of his worth.

'I seldom have the opportunity to read gossip columns,' she said, carefully avoiding his eyes. 'I usually prefer to make up my own mind about people.'

She paused, her brows furrowing slightly as she searched for the words. 'I am, however, sometimes a little too swift to reach conclusions,' she added, albeit somewhat reluctantly. 'My father was often obliged to remind me never to judge people on first appearance.'

His pulse quickening, the Viscount leant forward eagerly, finding himself inexplicably keen to learn whether her former opinion of him had changed.

'And so, after due consideration,' he said, hiding his

innermost feelings behind the light bantering tone that he was wont to employ when he was not entirely in command of the situation, 'may I be so bold as to enquire what conclusion you have now reached in regard to my reprehensible character?'

Frowning, Sophie gave a quick shake of her head. 'I have decided that I really don't know you well enough to have formed any worthwhile opinion, my lord,' she replied carefully. 'And, whilst your sterling efforts back at the tavern were certainly more than enough to revise my original view of you, I still do not understand why you felt it necessary to hide your true identity from all of us there—were you afraid that someone might try to take advantage of your lofty position?'

Shifting uncomfortably, the Viscount gave a non-committal shrug. 'It has been known,' he replied. 'But I have to say that on that particular occasion it all came about rather by accident. I supplied my name—which *is* Marcus Wolfe, as it happens—and merely failed to qualify my title. Besides which…' Here he gave a rueful grin, before continuing. 'Following my behaviour towards you on the previous evening, I judged that it might be more circumspect to remain relatively anonymous for the duration of my stay there—I fear my reputation in that particular direction has the habit of preceding me.'

'Yes, I imagine that it must,' returned Sophie in a somewhat distracted tone of voice, unable to prevent her colour heightening as the well-remembered sensations of that encounter once again flooded through her being. But then, as she observed the almost imperceptible slump of his shoulders, her heart turned over, causing her to add gently, 'That being so, I have to say that, whilst you may not be quite as black as rumour seems to have painted you, you do appear to be verging on a rather dark shade of grey!'

At this, Marcus tipped back his head, letting out a sudden shout of laughter that reverberated across the room, causing several of the other customers to turn and cast disapproving frowns in their direction.

Still grinning, he then rose to his feet and held out his hand to her. 'Thoroughly hoist, then, I would say!' he chuckled. 'Let us hie ourselves off to your bookshop, then—it seems clear that I am desperately in need of a tome on moral rectitude, and you, my dear Miss Flint, seem to be the very person to point me in the proper direction.'

'But I no longer have the bill of sale to take to Mr Broomfield,' protested Sophie, as she got to her feet and began to pull on her gloves. 'What am I to say to him?'

'There is no need for you to mention anything about it—the fellow's not to know that you received the wrong invoice. The other note—the one that this Mr Nyne is now very likely in possession of—was probably to tell you that the book you had asked about had arrived. That being so, it will be perfectly in order for you to call into the shop and enquire after it.'

Yes, she could do that, thought Sophie, her eyes brightening at the notion of extending this chance meeting for a further half hour or so. Having given up all expectation of ever setting eyes on Marcus again—especially once she had been made aware of his true identity—there was no way on earth that she was even going to consider rejecting such an opportunity. Besides which, she reasoned, surely there was little need for her to concern herself with all those unproven rumours of the Viscount's less than perfect reputation since, after today's out-of-the-blue reunion, the chances of the pair of them ever crossing each other's paths again were extremely unlikely. That being so, the mere idea of spending even just a few more precious minutes in his company was far too tempting an offer on which she was prepared to turn her back. Regrettably, however, there was still that one troublesome drawback to consider...

'But if Mr Broomfield should happen to have my atlas in stock,' she felt constrained to point out, 'he will be expecting me to pay for it there and then, and—'

'Let's not cross that particular bridge until we get to it, shall we?' retorted Marcus, cutting her off before she had a chance to remind him of her lack of finances. 'I merely wanted a plausible excuse to take a quick peek at this numbskull clerk of his. My brother seemed extraordinarily interested in that invoice of yours—maybe this bookshop of yours is the hub of some shady goings-on and this Mr Broomfield is some sort of master criminal!'

Taking hold of her elbow, he manoeuvred her across the tea shop's threshold and out into the busy street where, on a sudden impulse, he beckoned over a nearby flower-seller and selected a large bunch of violets from her tray. Dividing the bunch into two halves, he drew Sophie towards him, and before she had any idea of his intent he had tucked one small posy into the top buttonhole of her threadbare pelisse.

Smiling down at her, a mischievous glint in his eye, he held the remaining flowers out towards her, allowing their delicate fragrance to waft into the air.

'I believe I have already earned the right to relieve you of that confounded cap, but if milking a cow is what it takes, I dare say I could prevail upon one of the milkmaids in the park to allow me to manhandle one of her charges!'

'Oh, but I couldn't possibly—' she began, uncomfortably aware of the crowds milling all about her, but then,
as the powerful look of entreaty in the Viscount's eyes
threatened to stop her breath entirely, a soft flush covered
her cheeks and she began shakily to unravel the bow of
her shabby grey bonnet, saying, 'I really cannot imagine
what it is about the poor thing that annoys you so!'

'Apart from it being quite hideous in its own right,'
he retorted softly, as he reached across and whipped
the offending article from her head, before stuffing it
into his jacket pocket, 'it makes you look about a hundred and five. But, more to the point, it has the damned
effrontery to cover up your glorious hair.'

And then, before she was even aware of what he was
about, he had tucked the stems of the remaining violets
under the top ribbon of her bonnet, settled it back on to
her head and was busily engrossed in retying the bow.

'Well, really, my lord!' exclaimed Sophie in stupefied
amazement as, stepping back, the smiling Viscount gave
a satisfied nod. Even though she was thoroughly aston-
ished at his quite audacious behaviour, she could hardly
help but feel secretly delighted at his rather gratifying
comments regarding her hair, for, as she well remembered, her father had always considered her bright chestnut locks to be her crowning glory. It had been only as a
result of Arthur Crayford's insidious pestering that she
had taken to covering up what she had decided must act
as some sort of catalyst to his repulsive conduct. Not that
her actions appeared to have dissuaded the youth to any
great extent, she was obliged to remind herself. But then,
as Marcus, an oddly intent expression in his eyes, reached
out and fingered a wayward curl that had escaped its
confinement, all thoughts of Crayford and his irritating
ways were wiped immediately from her mind.

Chapter Six

'So where exactly are we heading?' enquired Marcus, as he skilfully steered her through the heavy throng of Saturday afternoon promenaders. 'I thought I knew all the book emporiums in this part of town but I don't recall ever seeing a Broomfields.'

'His establishment is in an alley off Gilbert Street,' explained Sophie, somewhat guardedly. 'It is not a very grand place, but one of the assistants at Hatchards was good enough to recommend it to me as a possible source of the atlas for which I was searching.'

He looked down at her, his curiosity fired. 'And what's so special about this particular atlas?' he asked.

'It has some rather nice sketches in it, making it more suitable for younger children.'

'And Hatchards don't stock it?' The Viscount sounded surprised. 'They are usually pretty well up to snuff with that sort of thing, if my memory serves me aright.'

'As a matter of fact they did have several copies in stock,' replied Sophie, after some slight hesitation. 'But they were priced at three guineas each, and I—well—as you know—'

His face clearing, Marcus nodded. 'Ah! Now I begin to see! I take it that your Mr Broomfield is more of what we might term a *"used"* bookseller? May I ask how much he is asking for his copy?'

'Just three shillings and sixpence.' She sighed, uncomfortably aware of the fact that she no longer had such wherewithal available. 'He told me that he was sure that he had one somewhere in his stock—it really is most vexing!'

'I still don't understand why you feel it necessary to purchase the book yourself. Surely that sort of thing falls within your employer's domain? I should have thought that any household capable of employing a governess would be equipped with an adequate supply of necessary textbooks.'

'That's probably because you never have to involve yourself with people like the Crayfords,' muttered Sophie under her breath, but then, having reminded herself that this unexpected bonus of an hour or so in the Viscount's company was far too precious to be marred by petty grievances about her daily life, she tipped back her head and awarded him one of her most brilliant smiles—the effect of which was to cause Marcus to veer awkwardly into the path of an extremely stout gentleman who was struggling under the weight of a large assortment of boxes and packets.

'I say! Have a care, young fellow!' yelped the man, clutching at his mound of parcels.

Inwardly cursing, Marcus stooped to retrieve the lone packet that had fallen from the pile, before returning it to its former position with a bow and an apologetic smile. *No second-hand books for this extravagantly dressed figure of fun,* he thought bleakly, having instantly recognised Hatchards' distinctive wrapping paper on the neatly packaged item.

All of a sudden the fact that Sophie should feel obliged to make do with someone else's cast-off reading matter filled him with a red-hot fury the like of which he had never before experienced. That her employers were clutch-fisted upstarts was becoming increasingly clear to him, and to think of her having to live her life in so penurious a manner was becoming almost more than he could bear. He was consumed with an overpowering desire to sweep her up into his arms and carry her off to some secluded retreat where he could lavish upon her every luxury at his disposal—silks, satins, jewels, furs, perfumes—whatsoever she might wish for. He would be only too happy to see her every desire fulfilled—not to mention one or two of his own! Not that there was the least likelihood of being able to persuade the lady in question to even consider such a plan, he was obliged to remind himself as, with a painful jolt, the realisation that they had finally reached their intended destination brought him swiftly back to earth.

Still, he mused, standing back and allowing himself to drink in the reflection of Sophie's lovely features as she peered through the bottle-glass window of the bookseller's cluttered-looking premises, *hope springs eternal, as they say, and in the meantime the odd little gentle nudge in the right direction can't do any harm!* For now that he had finally managed to run his chestnut-haired temptress to ground, the Viscount had no intention of allowing her to slip through his fingers again. *It's high time my sweet Sophie started to learn that I can be quite as intractable as she is*, he thought, carefully hiding a self-satisfied smile as he pushed open the door to allow her to precede him into the shop.

'Good afternoon, sir, and what may I have the pleasure of doing for you?'

The small, bespectacled, bald-headed man who was peering out at them from behind a huge pile of books located on a desk to one side of the shop being the only creature in sight, Marcus could only suppose that this was, indeed, Sophie's Mr Broomfield.

'I believe that you are keeping a copy of an illustrated atlas for Miss Flint here?' he said, motioning Sophie forward.

Casting her a condescending glance, the bookseller gave a deprecating nod before turning to rummage in a nearby box for several moments. Finally extracting a decidedly tattered-looking version of a map book—one that Marcus had little difficulty recognising as having been one of his own childhood favourites many years back—he slapped it down on the desk in front of the Viscount. 'Three shillings and sixpence!' he announced, holding out his hand.

'Is that the best copy you have available?' asked Marcus stiffly.

'It's the cheapest I could find,' returned the shop-keeper with a careless shrug. 'The young lady was quite firm on that point, as I recall.'

Conscious of a slight tug at his elbow, Marcus turned, only to be confronted with an expression of earnest entreaty in Sophie's eyes. Heaving back a sigh, he bent his head in her direction.

'This book is perfectly adequate for my purpose,' she murmured into his ear. 'If you would be so good as to advance me the money, you have my promise that I will very soon find the means to reimburse you.'

At the thought of her being obliged to skimp and scrape to gather together such a pitiful outlay, Marcus felt his anger deepen and, turning back to the waiting Broomfield, he curtly ordered him to have the book wrapped.

'Bargain books don't usually warrant—' began the man, but, catching sight of the steely glint in the Viscount's eye, he gave a quick nod and, picking up the atlas, began to make his way to the rear of the shop.

'You stay here for a moment,' Marcus directed Sophie as he made after the shopkeeper. 'I just want to take a quick peek at that clerk of his.'

Although she was finding it well nigh impossible to comprehend how merely looking at the fellow could possibly determine his ability to add and subtract figures correctly, Sophie gave the Viscount a brief acquiescent smile and sat herself down on Broomfield's rather rickety-looking chair to await further developments.

'No need for you to come along, sir,' protested the shopkeeper as he observed Marcus's intention.

'Just want to see that you do the job properly,' came the Viscount's reply. 'Wouldn't do for Miss Flint's parcel to fall apart while I was carrying it, now, would it?'

Mumbling crossly to himself, Broomfield pushed open the door to the tiny back room that served as an office. Seated before a high desk, his head bent in deep concentration as he carefully inscribed a row of figures on one of the bookshop's bills of sale, was a sharp-nosed gangly youth of possibly sixteen or seventeen summers. *Not exactly the stuff of subterfuge or other under-the-counter deeds of derring-do,* thought Marcus, as he stepped across the room's threshold and studied the clerk. *Easy to understand the accounting errors, though!*

* * *

Emerging from the office some few minutes later, he found Sophie immersed in a book of Shakespeare's sonnets.

'Would you care to have that too?' he asked, smiling down at her.

'Oh, no!' She laughed, jumping up and placing the book carefully back on its pile. 'I already have my own copy—I was just enjoying reading them again, that's all.' Eying the neatly wrapped volume under his arm, she then observed, 'It was very good of you to go to so much trouble on my behalf.'

'No trouble at all,' he assured her, as the now surprisingly compliant Broomfield stepped forward and cheerily ushered them both out of the shop. 'My pleasure entirely.'

'You do seem to have quite a remarkable habit of winning people around,' she said, the shopkeeper's *volte-face* having thoroughly confounded her. 'I suppose it comes with being born with the proverbial silver spoon in your mouth?'

'Shouldn't be surprised,' replied Helstone nonchalantly, as he raised his hand to signal an approaching hackney carriage.

Realising his intention, Sophie immediately let go of his arm and stepped away from him. 'Oh, I'm not at all sure that I can agree to this,' she said pensively. It had temporarily slipped her mind that her very agreeable companion was still none other than the notorious Hell-cat Helstone, and, while sitting in a public tea shop with him and strolling along London's busy thoroughfares whilst surrounded by scores of other shoppers might be considered quite unremarkable, climbing into a hackney carriage with so infamous a character might be regarded in a somewhat different light.

Raising his eyebrows at her uneasy expression, the Viscount let out a soft chuckle. 'My days of seducing females in carriages are long gone, I assure you,' he twinkled, as he unceremoniously bundled her up into the cab. 'Decidedly uncomfortable business it was too, as I recall! I just figured that we might avoid the inevitable battering experience if we resorted to wheels for our return journey?'

In point of fact, being closeted in such a confined space with so charismatic an individual as Marcus was showing himself to be was turning out to be the icing on the cake as far as Sophie's afternoon was concerned. Throughout the whole of the journey from Gilbert Street to Lennox Gardens the Viscount had no difficulty keeping her fully entertained with his charming and witty observations. At least now she would have plenty to fill her dreams in the coming lonely days and nights, she thought, mentally hugging herself with delight as she gazed across the carriage at the Viscount's smiling countenance. Although on the other side of the same coin was the painful realisation that this short afternoon spent in his company could only serve to bring her greater heartache when the inevitable parting finally came. And come it must, she was forced to concede, given the wide disparity of their respective circumstances.

'I do hope that my employers don't see me arriving home in a hackney,' she ventured, with a nervous laugh. 'They will begin to think that they are paying me too high a salary!'

Having spent the whole of the past fifteen minutes or so fighting off a rapidly growing desire to haul her into his arms and feast his lips on hers, this disagreeable reminder of Sophie's disadvantaged situation was too much for Marcus to bear.

All at once he was at her side as, with a despairing groan, he pulled her towards him, murmuring huskily, 'Accept my offer, then, why don't you? How can you think of going back to humiliations of that sort when I could give you everything your heart desires!'

And then, before Sophie had either the wit or sense to prevent him, he had captured her lips with his and her whole world seemed to explode into a million sparkling fragments. Every single fibre of her being suddenly leapt into life as he trailed the tip of his tongue across the contours of her lips before finally forcing entry and deepening the kiss. Her entire body was awash with such indescribable feelings of rapture that the temptation to give in to his request was almost too much for Sophie to resist. The thought of never again having to bite back a stinging retort to one of Mrs Crayford's constant put-downs, never again having to grapple with Arthur Crayford in unexpected corners of the house, having a home of her own—with a fire in every room, should she so desire it, a well-stocked larder and wardrobes full of the most fashionable wear imaginable. Why, mother and Roger would—

At that sudden thought she froze and, wrenching herself away from his grasp, shunted to the far end of the seat, crying, 'How could you? You led me to believe that you would not attempt anything of that nature! Can it be that you truly are as black as you are painted?'

His jaw set, the Viscount flinched visibly at her accusation and, his body still aching with unfulfilled desire, sank back against the squabs, struggling to catch his breath as he tried to come to terms with his inexplicable behaviour.

What the hell is happening to me? he thought, as he stared across the carriage at Sophie's dumbfounded, wide-eyed expression. *Have I lost my wits entirely? Am I really reduced to behaving like an unfledged stripling on his first outing?*

'Please accept my apologies,' he managed eventually, desperately trying to summon up his customary air of insouciance. 'I really had not intended that to happen—some sort of fleeting aberration appears to have overruled my better judgement.' Summoning up a smile, he held out his hand. 'Come,' he said. 'It won't happen again, I promise you. Please don't let us part as enemies.'

Having had all her newly formed dreams so violently fractured, it was as much as Sophie could do to shake her head and wriggle herself more securely into her corner, and, since she was conscious of the carriage slowing down, she kept her eyes firmly fixed on the door handle, ready to make as speedy an exit as possible the minute the vehicle stopped.

But then, to Marcus's bewilderment, just as she leant forward to wrench open the carriage door, upon raising her eyes to peer out of the window she slumped back into her corner, her fingers to her lips, and uttered a moan of dismay.

Leaning across and staring through the glass in order to ascertain what it was that could have caused her such unease, the Viscount could see nothing amiss. The hackney driver had pulled his vehicle up outside number twelve, as instructed, and apart from the rather flashily dressed young man who was in the process of mounting the steps to the front door of the house there was no one else about.

Somewhat perplexed, he sat down again and studied

her, a frown forming on his brow as he registered her apprehension.

'What is it, my dear?' he said, leaning forward. 'It is perfectly safe to alight, I promise you. I saw no signs of curtains twitching or anything of that nature.'

Suddenly straightening herself, Sophie seemed to flare into life. 'My cap!' she ordered him. 'You have it in your pocket. Please give it back to me!'

Still mystified, the Viscount shrugged, drew out the requested article and handed it to her, watching in growing confusion as she hastily dragged off her bonnet before proceeding to stuff the abundant coils of her hair back into their former confinement. Glancing down at her bonnet, prior to replacing it, she caught sight of the tiny bunch of violets that Marcus had tucked into the ribbon just an hour or so earlier. She hesitated, a soft sigh escaping her lips, but then without further ado plucked them from their place, did likewise with those in the buttonhole of her pelisse. She stuffed the now badly crushed blossoms into her pocket and, leaning forward again, reached for the door handle.

But Marcus, his face clearing now that he had at last begun to fathom out what was troubling her, was ahead of her. *Now, this I can do something about,* he thought in satisfaction as, thrusting open the door, he leapt nimbly out on to the pavement and held out his hand, giving Sophie no opportunity to do other than accept his proffered assistance.

Having heard the carriage, the young Crayford had turned to see who might be visiting his home at such an unusual hour for calling. His expression, when he witnessed his younger siblings' governess being handed out of a vehicle and escorted up the steps by one of the Town's most notorious rakes, was something to behold.

'L-Lord Helstone?' he stammered in disbelief, half paralysed with nerves as, tugging at his cravat, he made the Viscount an exaggerated leg.

'Ah, Mr Crayford, I believe,' drawled Marcus, eyeing the youngster gravely. 'I have been wanting to have a word with you, if you could spare me a few moments of your time?'

That such an out-and-out Corinthian was even prepared to stop and pass the time of day with him, let alone engage him in any sort of conversation, was almost too much for Crayford to comprehend.

'You wish to have words with me?' he squeaked, the hue of his cheeks glowing even more brightly than the strawberry-pink brocade of his waistcoat.

'If you would be so good as to open the door for Miss Flint?'

Without sparing Sophie even the briefest of glances, Crayford at once sprang to attention, applying the knocker with such vigour that its strident clanging reverberated halfway down the street.

Whilst it was perfectly clear to both Sophie and the Viscount that the elderly manservant who opened the door was decidedly unimpressed with his young master's peremptory use of the knocker, Crayford was too far up in the boughs to notice the man's barely disguised expression of contempt.

'Ah, Hawkins, there you are,' babbled the youngster, almost pushing an unresisting Sophie through the entrance, before turning to Marcus and asking eagerly, 'Would you care to come into the library, my lord? My father has a halfway decent sherry I can offer you.'

'Thank you, but no,' replied Marcus, pausing only to

flash an encouraging smile at the somewhat distracted Sophie, as the manservant offered him a courteous bow before finally closing the door. 'What I have to say to you won't take long.'

Then, reaching out, he grasped hold of Crayford's neckcloth and pulled the startled youngster towards him, his tone unmistakably menacing as he murmured, 'If I should hear that you have dared to lay a finger on so much as a single hair of Miss Flint's head ever again, I will make it my business to have both you and your father barred from every club in Town. Do I make myself clear?'

Satisfied that the youngster's petrified gurgle was intended to signal some sort of assent, the Viscount nodded and released his hold.

'Very well—now, here is my card,' he continued, almost conversationally, and he took out his card case and extracted the pasteboard rectangle that held his noble details. 'You may inform your mother that I have called, and will be doing so again at some time in the very near future.'

From what he had been able to gather from Sophie's occasional references to her employer, the Viscount was reasonably certain that the parsimonious Mrs Crayford would turn out to be a social climber of the very worst sort. He had little doubt that within hours news of his visit would be circulating like wildfire amongst her cronies. Dissolute reprobate though he was considered to be, as the wealthy heir apparent to a long-established earldom he could hardly help being aware that there were few members of the *Ton* who would not give their eye teeth to have him grace their functions with his presence.

Society hostesses were known to go to extraordinary

lengths in their endeavours to secure his attendance at their balls and soirees, and not merely for the fact of his undoubtedly compelling charm, for he was, after all, an extremely eligible bachelor. This being so, he judged that it was fairly safe to assume that not a single member of the Crayford family would be likely to take issue with Sophie if they received the impression that their humble governess was someone he held in high regard.

His lips twisting in distaste as he recalled the damage that he had already done to that otherwise gratifyingly blossoming friendship, he passed his card to the still quivering stripling on the doorstep, inclined his head briefly, and sauntered casually down the steps before climbing into the still waiting hackney carriage.

Chapter Seven

Having managed to reach her attic bedroom without further intervention, Sophie, wanting nothing more than to throw herself onto her bed and sob her eyes out, thrust open the door and stepped inside—only to be met by the heartstopping sight of every single one of her precious possessions strewn in haphazard fashion across the bare floorboards, with the now empty drawers of her chest tossed into a careless heap in the room's far corner.

Collapsing onto the bed and staring at the jumbled mess with disbelieving eyes, she began to suppose that she must be living in some sort of ghastly nightmare. As though having been relieved of both of her purses, her one comb, two handkerchiefs and the bulk of her hard-earned savings in the space of twenty-four hours were not enough to endure, this must surely be regarded as the crowning touch to one of the most disagreeable days she had had the misfortune of experiencing for quite some time.

Even what had started out to be a joyful reunion with

Marcus Wolfe—or Viscount Helstone of Bradfield, as
it had transpired—had ended in disastrous disappointment, when the libertine that he clearly was had finally
chosen to revert to his true colours.

Angrily brushing away the gathering tears, Sophie
dropped to her knees to make a start on returning her
possessions to some sort of order. *I should have listened
more carefully to what the servants were saying about
him,* she chastised herself. *It's all very well making gran-
diose statements about paying no attention to gossip
and arriving at one's own conclusions about people,
but, really, with all that information at my fingertips,
I must have been mad to allow myself be played on his
line like the veriest gudgeon!*

Yet those rapturous sensations that had all but overcome her resolve the moment his lips had touched hers
had been akin to a sort of madness, she was forced to
admit to herself. Another few moments and who knew
where such careless passion might have led? Thank
heavens that timely vision of her mother had prevented
her from forgetting herself entirely.

At the thought of her mother, a sudden frisson of
alarm ran through Sophie, and, her hands shaking with
panic, she began a feverish search through the heaps of
articles that the disrespectful Henry—it *had* to be that
beastly little devil, Sophie was almost certain, for no
one else but the eight-year-old mischief-maker would
think to harass her in such a petty manner—had tossed
so carelessly about the room.

When at last her eyes lit upon the sleeveless flannel
spencer that her mother had insisted on tucking into her
travelling-box 'in case the weather turns cold', Sophie
grabbed at the garment and ran her fingers hurriedly
along its lower hem where, with a sob of relief, she

discovered that the two crowns she had slid into the jacket's hem for safe-keeping were still there. She tossed up a prayer of thanksgiving for her mother's sensible teachings during the family's years with the military that, should the possibility of sudden evacuation ever occur—which it had frequently done—such a hidden source of money might serve to save their lives. Ever since those days, it had been Sophie's habit to tuck all of her loose change into the hem of the never-likely-to-be-worn flannel jacket. As it happened, the ten shillings that she had put aside from her quarterly salary of three pounds was intended to bolster up the meagre pension awarded to her mother by the War Office, in recognition of the late Lieutenant-Colonel's services to his country. On glancing up from her position on the floor, however, Sophie chanced to see the splendidly wrapped package that lay on her bed, and she realised, to her sorrow, that she would be obliged to ask her mother to make do with only five shillings on this occasion, since paying Helstone back his three shillings and sixpence had now become more a point of honour than a matter of principle.

Getting to her feet, she sat down on the bed and began to unravel the string that surrounded the parcel, ruefully recalling the vibrant joy she had felt at simply being in the Viscount's company. Was it possible that one could love someone and yet dislike them in almost equal measure at one and the same time? she wondered, as she unwrapped the package, only to find as the wrapping paper fell from her fingers that the book that now lay on her knees was not the tattered version that Mr Broomfield had offered to her in his bookshop but an almost pristine edition of the same work!

She stared down at the book, a mixture of wild fury

and disbelief coursing through her veins. It seemed that the duplicitous Helstone had hoodwinked her yet again, in the certain knowledge that she did not have the resources to fulfil so great a debt! For one awestruck moment she was not certain whether she wanted to laugh hysterically or scream her anger to the four walls.

In the event, a sharp tap at her door prevented her from venting her aggravation in either fashion, and as one of the maids poked her head around the door with the message that the mistress required her presence downstairs on the instant, Sophie could only suppose that the day's misfortunes had not yet reached their pinnacle. Evidently, it would seem, Arthur Crayford had informed his mother of her arrival in a hackney carriage in the company of one of the Town's most notorious rakes. Instant dismissal was clearly on the cards yet again, she thought, as she made her way down to the drawing room to confront her employer, dismally conscious of the fact that this threat dropped from Mrs Crayford's lips with monotonous regularity, wherever and whenever things failed to go exactly as she had planned them.

To her surprise, however, Mrs Crayford stood up and moved forward to greet her on her entry into the room, saying, 'My dear Miss Flint! How nice to see you looking so well. You enjoyed your afternoon off, I trust?'

Considerably taken aback at her employer's over-effusive welcome, Sophie glanced suspiciously at the young Mr Crayford who, skulking nervously behind his parent, seemed reluctant to meet her gaze.

'Do sit down, my dear. I have just rung for tea.'

Motioning her to the chair nearest to her own, Mrs Crayford reseated herself and regarded Sophie with what the startled governess surmised was meant to be a look of affection.

'Arthur tells me that you came home in the company of Viscount Helstone,' she then gushed, before leaning across and tapping Sophie playfully on the knee with her fan. 'You really should have mentioned that you were acquainted with the gentleman, you naughty girl! What must he think of us for having failed to invite him to the various soirees and musical evenings that we have given during these past few weeks? Clearly we must see to it that such a grievous omission is rectified without delay—is that not so, dear child?'

Still finding herself to be in a state of shocked disbelief, Sophie was unable to summon up a suitable reply. Not that one was necessary, it appeared, since Mrs Crayford then proceeded to outline some of her ill-thought-out schemes for entertaining the Viscount during the coming months, barely stopping to take a breath as she set off on a wild flight of fancy that included such things as ice sculptures, chocolate fountains and the like.

Sliding her glance across to where Arthur Crayford was sitting, nervously fingering his cravat and staring back at her in an apprehensive manner, Sophie was struck with the oddest impression that he was expecting her to leap up and attack him at any minute.

Suddenly the reason for all this ingratiating obsequiousness became horrifyingly apparent. Having marked her agitation when she had caught sight of the young man on the doorstep, Helstone had obviously drawn his own conclusions as to her uneasiness and, as soon as the front door had closed, must have set about intimidating Crayford in some way or another—which would explain the youngster's conspicuously edgy demeanour. And, whilst Sophie was decidedly annoyed at finding herself presented with yet another example of the Viscount's high-handed interference in her life, she could not help but experience a warm ripple of pleasure at the thought of him having gone to such trouble on her behalf.

Mrs Crayford's wildly extravagant plans, on the other hand, were another matter entirely, and Sophie knew that she had to find some way of putting a stop to them before they got out of hand. The mere thought of Helstone being invited to come and go as he pleased—as seemed to be her employer's heartfelt ambition—was enough to send her senses skittering in all directions. Even worse, it now appeared, when she had surfaced sufficiently to take in yet more of Mrs Crayford's revised plans for the Season, that she herself was to be included in all this jollification!

'But I do not have a suitable wardrobe to wear on such occasions,' she interjected in dismay, the minute Mrs Crayford at last paused to draw breath.

'Not to worry, my dear,' declared her employer, waving a dismissive hand. 'Lydia has more gowns than she can possibly wear—she shall loan you some of hers. You are of a size, I believe. The child can scarcely object, after all,' she went on, her eyes glowing in anticipation. 'With so noble a patron, the possibilities for her are endless!'

Biting at the inside of her lip in an effort not to burst out laughing at the thought of so infamous a rake as Helstone being persuaded to sponsor the Crayford's seventeen-year-old daughter into Society, Sophie was obliged to concentrate her attention on the slightly faded patterning of the room's Aubusson rug.

'So, that's settled then,' declared her employer, in a satisfied tone, as she rose to her feet. 'I shall write to his lordship at once and invite him to take dinner with us on Tuesday next—that will give Mrs Hawkins ample time to have all the glass and silverware polished to perfection.'

'Oh, no! I fear that won't do at all,' cried Sophie, clutching at straws. 'I believe his lordship mentioned that he would be out of town all next week—possibly longer,' she added, in desperation.

'Hmm.' Pausing in her tracks, Mrs Crayford swung round to frown at her son. 'Did you not tell me that the Viscount said that it was his intention to call upon us shortly?'

'Very near future, was what he said,' gabbled the youngster, standing up and clutching at the back of his chair for support. 'Took that to mean in the next day or so—but I couldn't swear—'

'Never mind,' interrupted his mother, turning back to face Sophie. 'You will just have to ascertain his lordship's movements for the coming weeks, so that I can plan my functions accordingly. I shouldn't care to find myself going to a host of trouble for nothing—we have to be sure of the dates that he will be available. You must write him a note straight away and I will have Fisher take it across.'

'Oh, but I couldn't possibly,' began Sophie, her eyes widening in dismay. How was she supposed to explain that the Viscount was merely a passing acquaintance when he had, it would seem, chosen to give Crayford the impression that he and she were close friends of a long standing. Telling the truth would merely serve to blacken her own character to such an extent that she really would be in danger of losing her position, and then where would she be? Realising that, unless some miracle should occur to prevent the inevitable revelation, there was nothing for it but to appear to go along with Mrs

Crayford's plans, she gave her employer a resigned nod of acquiescence and, at that lady's continued insistence, took her place at the escritoire, desperately wondering how best she might pen such a note.

Having divested himself of his jacket, waistcoat and boots, Marcus had taken up residence in one of the two leather fireside chairs that straddled the fireplace in the library of his Grosvenor Square mansion. His brother Giles, in similar garb, lounged wearily back in the other.

'Bit of luck you running into that Flint female this afternoon,' observed the Major, as he took a hefty swig of the brandy that his brother had just poured him. 'Finally managed to get one of my chaps to decipher these damned coded messages that have been causing us such difficulty these past couple of weeks.'

'Some devilment afoot somewhere, then?' enquired Marcus lazily, his brain more intent on conjuring up sweet visions of kissing Sophie than paying a great deal of attention to his brother's words.

'Another plot to assassinate old Hookey, by the looks of it,' returned Giles complacently. 'Must be at the least the sixth this year, by my reckoning.'

'Does it bother his grace—this new-found antagonism towards him after all that adulation of last year?'

'He says not.' The Major laughed, leaning forward to top up his glass from the brandy decanter positioned on the table between the two of them. 'Noticed that he's made a start on having railings erected round Apsley House, though—had a couple of rocks heaved through one of his windows the other day, apparently.'

'Teach him to stop mouthing off about the country's need for greater mechanisation. The last thing we want now is more riots, what with the number of unemployed men piling into the capital.'

'Good God, Marcus!' exclaimed his brother in astonishment. 'Don't tell me you're developing a social conscience at long last—the old man will never believe it when I tell him!'

'Then don't,' returned Marcus shortly, before taking another pensive swig of his drink. 'How is the old devil, by the way? Still cursing the day I was born, I imagine?'

'Not to my knowledge. As a matter of fact, he's not been too good this last week or so—ever since you rode off into that blizzard he's been surprisingly quiet on the subject of your descent into dissolution. You really ought to go down and make your peace with him, you know.'

Marcus nodded. 'Yes, I shall—as soon as—'

Stopping abruptly, he coloured and swiftly changed the subject. 'This code business, then—how did Miss Flint's bill of sale help solve the puzzle?'

'Pretty clever, really,' said Giles, leaning forward. 'We'd already intercepted a similar invoice to a Mr Luke Fower, and hadn't been able to make a great deal of sense out of it, but as soon as we got hold of the one addressed to Mr Matthew Nyne it all began to fall into place.'

'I'm not sure I follow your line of reasoning.'

'Quite simple. One of my newer chaps—part-time lay preacher, as it happens—finally twigged the connection. Luke Fower and Matthew Nyne! Get it?'

At his brother's continued expression of puzzlement, the Major, after a brief pause, proceeded to explain. 'Luke Four and Matthew Nine—books and chapters of the New Testament, old chum! Once our chaps had hit on that, of course, the rest was pretty plain sailing—just a matter of working on the whys and wherefores. The first number indicated a verse, the second a letter in that verse, so Miss Flint's invoice, when correctly deciphered, actually reads "BOW SWAN FINAL"—presumably signifying a final meeting of some sort at the Swan Inn at Bow. The invoice's erroneous total, cleverly spotted by that sharp-eyed little governess of yours, spells out the time and date of the meeting—hence seven pounds, thirteen shillings and fivepence translates as seven o'clock on the thirteenth of May—just two weeks away, as it happens.'

He sat back, looking extremely pleased with himself. 'I've got two men keeping an eye on the bookshop, in order to see exactly how Broomfield and his clerk might be involved, and with this new information at our fingertips we should have no difficulty in catching the beggars red-handed, so to speak. All thanks to your Miss Flint and that invoice of hers!'

'Which would explain why someone was so keen to get hold of the thing, then,' murmured Marcus, almost to himself. 'She told me that was the second of two purses she'd had stolen in as many days—I'd thought it was mere coincidence, but now—good Lord!'

Starting up, he reached forward and grasped his brother's arm.

'You realise what this means, of course?' he demanded and, at the Major's bewildered shake of the head, exclaimed, 'The fact that there is no such person as Matthew Nyne surely suggests that, had not Broomfield's clerk carelessly mixed up the addressees, the invoice that was delivered to Miss Flint must have been intended for one of the other occupants at the Crayford residence!'

His eyes sparkling with triumph, he sat back. 'It just

remains for you to find who got hers and you'll have your man!'

'That's not necessarily as simple as you might suppose,' remarked his brother dryly. 'Do you have any suggestions?'

Marcus shook his head. 'Ordinarily, my money would be on the odious Crayford junior, but from what I've seen of him I take leave to doubt that he's got the nous to involve himself in any sort of political activism—all puff and no blow, if you get my meaning!'

'I wouldn't be too sure of that, if I were you,' returned Giles, with a pensive frown. 'In my experience it's often the most unlikely seeming character who turns out to be the villain of the piece!'

'Oh, I can't imagine the little toad—good grief!' The Viscount shot his brother a startled look. 'Are you saying that wretched performance of his could just be a clever blind?'

At the Major's nod, Marcus's face paled visibly. 'Merciful heavens!' he groaned. 'Here am I, getting slowly foxed, when that poor sweet creature might be in who knows what sort of danger from that foul swine!'

Leaping to his feet, he swayed violently before being obliged to sit down again, landing back in his seat with a heavy thump. 'Dammit!' he exclaimed angrily. 'She was quite right! Fat lot of use I'd be in an emergency!'

Frowning in concern, his brother reached over and removed the almost empty glass from his grasp. 'This young woman is really getting to you, isn't she, bro? I can't recall ever having seen you working yourself into such a state over a female since that time when you were about sixteen and swore that you were going to elope with one of the dairymaids. The customary treatment soon put paid to your over-excessive enthusiasm, if I remember rightly. I take it that you haven't managed to work your usual magic spell on this one?'

'Go to hell!' rasped Marcus, and he snatched up his glass from the table and refilled it, tossing back half of its contents before sinking into a morass of brooding silence.

Shaking his head in bafflement at his brother's decidedly out-of-character behaviour, Giles got to his feet and began to prise himself back into his snug-fitting military jacket, hazarding a guess that there was likely to be little further sensible conversation from his brother on this occasion. That being so, he decided, with another quick look at his uncommunicative sibling, he might just as well go back to his own apartment and carry on with his investigations into that other rather interesting matter that he had been working on.

On exiting from the library, however, he narrowly missed colliding with one of Marcus's footmen, who had been just on the point of tapping on the door to announce a lately delivered missive for his master.

'Just arrived, sir,' he said, nodding his head to indicate the presence of a second liveried person standing in the hall. 'Been told to wait for an answer.'

'He'll be lucky!' muttered the Major, as he picked up the letter from the tray and began to retrace his steps. Tapping Marcus briskly on the shoulder, he bade him open his eyes. 'Urgent message, old chap,' he announced, while giving his brother another vigorous prod. 'Looks like a female hand—might be from that new lady-love of yours!'

As Giles's laughing words began to penetrate his befogged brain, the Viscount heaved himself upright, grabbed at the missive and, his fingers trembling with impatience, ripped it open—only to find the words swimming blearily across the page.

> *My lord. You must excuse my presumption in writing to you like this, but your earlier actions have left me with an unfortunate predicament. My employer is now labouring under the misconception that we are closely acquainted and has insisted that I obtain your agreement to attend some of her forthcoming functions. I apologise for this intrusion, but wonder if it would be possible for you to write to her and explain that you have other commitments which will prevent you from accepting any of her invitations? I would be most grateful for your co-operation in this matter.*
> *Yours &c.*
> *S.F.*

Swiping his hand across his eyes, Marcus had to concentrate hard to keep the neat script in focus. Even so, it took him three attempts before the meaning of the words finally sank in. 'Not mine, unfortunately,' he growled, as he let the paper slip from his fingers before slumping back into his seat. 'And not nearly as grateful as I would like her to be!'

Grabbing at the missive before it floated into the fire, Giles cast a quick glance over the words, but was unable to make sense of their content. 'Seems the lady needs your help,' he said, somewhat awkwardly, since he had no idea what sort of brouhaha his brother had got himself into this time. 'Messenger's waiting for a reply.'

Muttering scabrous imprecations, Marcus stumbled to his feet again, staggered over to the nearby bureau, snatched up a piece of crested writing-paper and, after stabbing a quill into the inkstand a couple of times, shakily scrawled '*3 p.m. tomorrow. M.H.*' across the sheet. Folding the paper with careful precision, he picked up a stick of sealing wax and stared down at it in some confusion.

'Might be better if you left that to me, old boy,' came his brother's gentle voice from behind him.

With a weary nod, the Viscount passed the sealing wax to Giles and, blinking rapidly, watched as the Major lit a candle, melted the wax and sealed the letter.

'Pass me your ring!' commanded Giles, holding out his hand.

Easing the crested band from his finger, Marcus slid it across the desk towards his brother who, wordlessly retrieving the item, proceeded to press its raised design into the blob of wax, leaving on its hardening surface the clear imprint of an upright lance along with the ancient family motto—*nunquam cesseris*—*never give in!*

Pulling the missive towards him, Marcus stared dumbly down at the inscription for some moments, before his lips twisted in a wry grimace. Then, straightening his shoulders, he lifted his chin and rose cautiously to his feet.

'I can do this,' he muttered, his teeth clenched tightly together as he eased himself around to face the library door. 'I *can* do this.'

Then, to Giles's amazement, he proceeded to cross the room with barely the faintest hint of having over-indulged himself. Swinging open the door, the Viscount then poked out his head, beckoned to the still waiting messenger and pressed his reply into the man's hand, along with the requisite shilling.

It was only after the visiting footman had bowed and

taken his leave that the flash of an incomplete memory leapt into Marcus's still somewhat befuddled brain. He was sure that it was connected to something he had seen in the bookshop, but he was damned if he could call it to mind.

Returning to the fireplace, he pulled at the bellrope to summon his butler. 'Sorry about that pathetic display, Giles,' he said with an awkward grin. 'A large jug of black coffee seems to be in order. It's high time I started making a few much-needed changes to my life, I believe.'

Chapter Eight

Even though her living conditions seemed about to take a turn for the better following Mrs Crayford's wrongful assumption of her relationship with Helstone, Sophie was not at all sure that she cared for such a change, since it appeared that from now on she was expected to join the family at dinner, instead of taking the meal with the two younger Crayford children in the nursery parlour, as had previously been required of her.

Nor did it add to her sense of wellbeing to have Lydia march into her room the following morning and deposit a huge pile of miscellaneous articles of clothing onto her bed, with the words, 'You may have these—I no longer have any use for them!' before letting out a barely disguised snort of laughter, clapping her fingers to her lips and running from the room.

Even the discovery that several of the garments appeared never to have been worn before was of no great consolation to Sophie, since it was clear that every single item had been designed for someone a good few years younger than her own three and twenty, in both fashion and colour scheme. But even as she stared down in dismay at the pale pastel-shaded gowns, every one of them complete with more than its fair share of frills, flounces and furbelows, she was well aware that, other than appearing at the table in one of the three service-able grey gowns that comprised her limited wardrobe, she had little choice but to comply with her employer's instruction that she wear one of Lydia's repugnant cast-offs that evening.

Neither had Helstone's message that he intended to present himself at three o'clock that afternoon brought her any solace. The fact that he had chosen to ignore her request had already cost her a sleepless night, as her exhausted brain endeavoured to fathom out his rea-sons for hounding her in this manner. By his impetuous actions he had made it very clear that he was attracted to her but, given that he was a man who could have the pick of the most beautiful women in Society—and probably already had, if the truth be known—his apparent deter-mination to add a provincial nobody to his list of con-quests had left Sophie feeling confused and ill-equipped to deal with any further onslaughts from him. For, as she was gradually being forced to admit to herself, the plain fact of the matter was that she was already more than halfway in love with the charismatic devil—a situation which only served to make his continued importuning of her all the more difficult to resist, when all she really wanted to do was to shout, *Yes! Yes! Yes! Hold me in your arms and kiss me to distraction!*

Not that she could ever imagine herself acting in such a wild and abandoned manner, she concluded with a disapproving grimace, as she stared at what she could see of her reflection in the pock-marked mirror that stood on her chest of drawers and ruefully contemplated the likely effect of the least offensive of Lydia's gowns when held up against her own rather more curvaceous figure. *Perhaps I am just more strait-laced than I had otherwise supposed?* was her next thought. *Although, whilst it is true that my upbringing might have been somewhat out of the ordinary, Mama was always quite strict in certain matters, and I am perfectly sure that she would never approve of me even considering such a shameful course of action!*

Heaving a sigh, she tossed the over-embellished pink-spotted muslin back on to the bed and selected another from the pile—pale green this time, and almost identical in design to the former, apart from a deep flounce of figured lace at its hem. *Hmm...* she then thought. *If I unpick all those ridiculous bows and folderols, this might well serve the purpose for this evening. Not that anyone will give a fig as to how I look—apart from the odious Arthur, of course—although, thanks to Helstone's timely intervention, the little creep does seem to have drawn in his horns somewhat. Oh, dear! I really must learn to count my blessings, as Mama is often wont to say!*

Unfortunately, unpicking the numerous bows and other unnecessary ornamentation on the gown took Sophie rather longer than she had expected, and as she reached for a clothes hanger upon which to hang the completed garment her eyes happened to fall on the little clock that stood on her bedside table. Good grief! It was a quarter to three already and she had barely left herself with enough time to wash her hands and brush her hair!

She was just in the process of stabbing the last hairpin into her hastily constructed chignon when a tap at her bedroom door heralded the appearance of the maidservant, bearing the message that the mistress wished to inform Miss Flint that Lord Helstone had arrived, and would she be so good as to join the family in the drawing room?

Brushing her fingers down the front of her grey cambric gown, in a vain attempt to smooth out the creases that had formed during her needlecraft activities, Sophie followed the girl down the stairs to the ground floor where, pausing outside the drawing room, she took a deep breath, stiffened her spine and pushed open the door.

'Ah, come in, my dear Miss Flint,' cried Mrs Crayford at her entry. 'As you can see, your cousin has kept his promise to call on us!'

Cousin! Great heavens! What other barefaced lies had the wicked devil been constructing during her absence?

It was all Sophie could do to stop herself from exclaiming out loud. Inwardly fuming that Helstone had had the audacity to claim a non-existent kinship with her, she dipped him the briefest of curtseys and refused to raise her eyes to meet his, knowing full well that they would be regarding her with their usual mischievous glint.

'It was good of you to come, my lord,' she managed, through partly clenched teeth.

Marcus bit back the grin that threatened. Sophie's indignant reaction to his spurious assertion was proving to be much as he had expected, but, having finally decided his course of action, he was quite prepared to make some sacrifices in order to achieve his intended goal. The past ten or more minutes spent engaged in pointless conversation with the inept and decidedly doddery Crayford senior, along with his unbelievably bourgeois and graceless wife, having been the first of such sacrifices, the Viscount was only just beginning to realise exactly how much of a challenge he had set himself. But then, as he was quick to remind himself, *to the victor the spoils*—or so the saying would have it.

Not that there was any real chance of him failing in his chosen pursuit, he thought complacently. There never was. Once he had set his sights on a particular target, it merely remained to find ways of persuading the object of his interest to succumb to his advances. This method had always served him perfectly well in the past, and the Viscount could see no reason why it should fail him on this occasion, having already reached the conclusion that the mounting ardour he felt for Sophie was simply some sort of adverse reaction to her continued refusal to accept his offer. The trouble was, as he was now obliged to admit as he sat back in his seat and covertly studied her set expression, he was just not used to being turned down—rather the reverse, in the majority of cases!

'His lordship has expressed the desire to take you for a drive in his curricle this afternoon,' gushed Mrs Crayford, coyly batting her eyelashes at the Viscount. 'In the ordinary way, of course, such a suggestion would be out of the question, but now that he has explained your relationship I see no reason to refuse his request—although I do think that you might prefer to go and change into one of your prettier gowns before you depart?'

This last was to Sophie, to whom her employer shot a fierce look of disapprobation—doubtless for her having chosen to appear before the noble guest dressed in her customary colourless fashion.

'I cannot think that his lordship would care to keep his horses standing any longer than absolutely necessary,' returned Sophie mutinously. Torn between wanting to reject Helstone's offer out of hand and a pressing need to take him to task for falsifying their relationship, she had opted for the latter. Nevertheless, she had no intention of primping herself in Lydia's outmoded cast-offs just to oblige Mrs Crayford's *déclassé* ideas of propriety. 'I will just go and collect my bonnet—if you will excuse me?'

Dipping another quick curtsey to no one in particular, she left the room before her employer could summon up an adequate reply.

'So impetuous—I sometimes find it quite difficult to keep up with the girl!' exclaimed Mrs Crayford gaily, in a failed attempt at merriment, as she feverishly applied her fan to her reddening cheeks. 'Do sit down again, my lord—another glass of sherry, perhaps?'

'Thank you, but no,' replied Marcus, bending to retrieve his hat and gloves from the arm of his chair. 'Miss—er—my cousin is quite correct in her assumption that my horses have been left standing quite long enough. I will take my leave of you now, if you will excuse me? Thank you both for your indulgence.'

'Oh, our pleasure entirely, my lord!'

Doing his utmost to construct a bow at the same time as reaching for the bell-pull in order to summon the butler to escort his esteemed visitor from the premises, the doddery Crayford senior lost his footing and all but tumbled into the fireplace. His ungainly recovery brought forth a barely suppressed snigger from his son, whose apprehension over the Viscount had rendered him virtually speechless throughout the entire visit. A questioning glance from Helstone, however, soon put him firmly back in his place. A bright flush crept across his cheeks as, mortified once more, he hunched up his shoulders and did his best to appear invisible, mentally swearing eternal damnation to Helstone and all his kind.

Blissfully oblivious of the vicious maledictions being cast against his person, Marcus strode out into the hallway just as Sophie stepped off the bottom stair. Hurrying across to meet her, he felt his heart execute the same extraordinary somersault that it had done at every other one of their meetings. Catching his breath as he offered her his hand, he could only put the inexplicable sensation down to his recent over-indulgence of liquor which, he was forced to admit, seemed to have increased out of all proportion of late—a matter that clearly needed addressing.

Tucking her gloved hand into the crook of his elbow, he led her out of the house and into the late April sunshine, glancing down at the fine woollen shawl on her shoulders.

'Are you sure that scrap of stuff is going to be warm enough?' he asked in concern as he handed her up into his curricle, before taking the reins from his tiger and climbing into his own seat. 'The breeze will tend to feel quite brisk once we're on the move.'

'I trust that you are not about to give forth with one of your usual panegyrics regarding the supremacy of the fur stole over the humble woollen shawl,' said Sophie wearily, and she attempted to edge herself further along the seat, away from Helstone's impossibly charismatic masculinity. 'After spouting that inexcusable falsehood, I wonder that you have the audacity to face me at all!'

'Needs must.' He laughed, nodding to the tiger to let go the horses' heads. 'How else was I supposed to get you out of the house? That old cat of an employer of yours is a sight too inquisitive for my liking. I was obliged to invent all manner of relatives to satisfy her curiosity. I'm still not entirely sure that she trusts me to return you in one piece!'

'Then your reputation has clearly preceded you,' retorted Sophie tartly, clutching at the side rail of the highly sprung vehicle as it swung sharply around a bend in the road, while secretly in awe of the way the Viscount's strong, shapely hands manipulated the reins to control his team. Hands that had held her so firmly against his chest—

'Do you have to drive so fast?' she gasped, desperately trying to banish that oft recurring image from her mind. 'You will have me tipped over the side if you're not careful! Where are we going, anyway? This isn't the way to the park.'

'Too busy, and too many prying eyes for my liking.'

A frisson of unease shot through her. 'I trust you aren't thinking of attempting to repeat yesterday's sordid activity?' she challenged him.

His eyes gleaming with laughter, Marcus shook his head. 'Don't worry. Your virtue is quite safe this time, I promise you. Besides which,' he added, jerking his head over his shoulder, 'Kimble is here to see that you come to no harm—isn't that so, Kim?'

'Whatever you say, guv,' returned the tiger, with a nonchalant shrug.

'Very confidence-inspiring, I'm sure!' muttered Sophie. 'I dare say you pay him extra for helping you abduct helpless maidens!'

'Not my style,' retorted the Viscount, shooting her a sideways glance. 'Besides which, I've never thought of you as particularly helpless—you had little trouble fighting me off, as I recall.'

'Probably because your conscience got the better of you!' she flashed back at him.

'Conscience!'

Letting out a scornful hoot, Marcus tightened his hands on the reins, signalling to his team to slow down to a trot. 'I can't imagine what has given you the impression that I have any sort of a conscience.'

'Everyone has a conscience if they dig deeply enough,' she replied smugly.

When he did not answer, she glanced across at him. Though his eyes were fixed on the road ahead, he had a frown on his face, and as she watched a small tic appeared at the side of his lower lip. She opened her mouth to ask him if something was wrong, but then, thinking the better of it, remained silent.

Eventually he spoke, with a slight grate to his voice. 'Did you really mean it when you described my kissing you as "sordid"?'

'I—I—!'

Her cheeks aflame, Sophie was temporarily lost for words.

'I had the distinct feeling that, for a moment or two at least, you were actually enjoying the whole experience quite as much as I was,' he continued, still concentrating his gaze to the front. Then, with a jerk, he pulled his team to a standstill and swung round to face her, his eyes boring into hers. 'In fact, I defy you to tell me that you didn't enjoy it!'

'I—I—that is—it was wrong of you to pounce on me like that!' she floundered, finding it totally impossible to withstand the blatant heat of his compelling gaze.

'That's not what I asked!' he rasped, ripping off his

glove before reaching out and cupping her cheek so as to prevent her turning her head away. 'Look me in the eye and tell me that you didn't enjoy it as much as I did!'

Endless minutes ticked slowly by, as the Viscount's unremitting gaze seemed to strip away every one of her defences and lay open her very soul, until at last, as a little sob escaped her lips, Sophie was forced to tear her eyes away from his with the broken whisper, 'I—I cannot—you know full well that I cannot!'

A hot flood of elation pulsed through him. *I knew it! I knew it!* Marcus told himself exultantly, clenching his fists and almost punching at the air in his utter delight at having forced the admission from her, but then, as his gleeful eyes turned once more to confront her, a bewildered frown furrowed his brow. Sophie's face was turned away from him, but there on her right cheek the slow trickle of a single tear was clearly visible. All of a sudden his heart seemed to stumble to a standstill, and what he had previously regarded as a resounding victory swiftly deteriorated into the most crippling of defeats.

Motioning to Kimble to get down and hold the horses' heads, the Viscount reached across and took hold of Sophie's hands, only to feel his heart lurch once more. Even through the thin fabric of her cheap cotton gloves the trembling of her fingers was marked.

'Don't,' he murmured hoarsely, as he gripped her hands tightly in his. 'Please don't—I'm so very sorry—I didn't mean to browbeat you so—I really cannot think what came over me to behave in such a way. I can't apologise enough—please tell me that you forgive me?'

Sniffing back her tears, Sophie tried her best to extricate herself from his hold. 'If you would be so good as to let go of my hands, I really would like to wipe my nose,' she mumbled crossly.

Although Helstone's ruthless badgering had undermined her confidence considerably, she was determined not to let him see the extent of her humiliation. She felt thoroughly wretched and was quite certain that the Viscount, despite his extensive apologies, must think her behaviour ridiculous. When all was said and done, it was hardly the end of the world to have been obliged to admit to having enjoyed his embrace—especially since she had thought of little else since it happened. Although, what had caused his lordship to get so fired up about the whole matter was a complete mystery to her. *He probably keeps a little black book of all his conquests, marking off the names whenever he achieves a success,* she concluded, giving another despondent sniff at the thought of having allowed herself to be just another ticked-off name on some well-practised womaniser's list.

Relief flooding his face at Sophie's return to normal, Marcus let go of her hands and, reaching into his jacket pocket, drew out his handkerchief and set about mopping up the damage her tears had done to her face. His gentle, ineffectual dabbings achieved so little success, however, that Sophie was obliged to relieve him of his handkerchief and complete the job to her own satisfaction.

'Am I forgiven?' he asked anxiously, when she finally sat motionless, her eyes fixed on the balled-up handkerchief in her gloved hands. 'Do we proceed or would you prefer that I took you back home?'

Home! The mere idea of the Crayfords' residence being described as 'home' was almost enough to reduce Sophie to tears once more. She and her family had never really had a home of their own—plenty of rented or even commandeered dwellings as they had travelled the continent, but nothing of any long standing. Even the little house in Dulwich that her mother had managed to acquire could hardly be classed as a home, since it was really too small to accommodate all three of them, especially now that two of the rooms had been rented out in order to help Mrs Flint make ends meet. It would seem that a place that Sophie could truly call "home" was forever to remain the "castle in the air" daydream it had always been, rendering the thought of a quick return to her attic bedroom in Lennox Gardens even less appealing than usual.

'We might just as well go on,' she said, stifling a sigh. 'Now that we've come this far—you presumably set out with a particular objective in mind?'

I did indeed, thought Marcus somewhat ruefully, as he now began to wonder whether he might not have been just a little too precipitate in his planning for this afternoon's excursion. Despite having woken up with the very devil of a headache, he had set about carrying out his previous evening's intention of wearing down Sophie's resistance with a series of delightful treats, having convinced himself that all that was required was a few tastes of the high life to make her rethink her stubborn refusal to put herself under his protection. He had spent much of the morning organising the delivery of champagne, hot-house strawberries and an unlimited number of baskets of all sorts of other luxury comestibles to his intended destination, and he had been hoping to overwhelm her with such bountiful largesse.

That the delightful cottage and grounds would speak for themselves he had little doubt, he himself having been thoroughly charmed with the tiny estate when he had first come across it some months ago. He owned several other properties, of course, including the two that presently housed his current mistresses, but neither

of them had received a visit from him for almost a full
month now—as certain parts of his body were only too
aware—due to his having allowed himself to become
thoroughly preoccupied with a chestnut-haired vision
who had inadvertently crept into his bedchamber in the
middle of a snowstorm!

Now, however, thanks to a careless lack of judgement on his part, it was beginning to look as though
his original plan might have to be postponed. Not that
that need prevent the two of them spending an idle hour
or so at the cottage, he thought, brightening. Indeed, it
would be a great shame to allow all that food to go to
waste, and after all Mrs Bellamy had been warned to
expect him, and had, in all probability, gone to a great
deal of trouble on his behalf…

'Just a little way beyond the next village,' he said,
having finally made up his mind, and, whistling for
Kimble to return to his perch, he took up the reins and
once more pointed his team in the direction of Laurel
Cottage.

Having been too engrossed to pay much attention
to the landscape during the earlier part of their journey, Sophie found herself wondering exactly where
they were. She vaguely recalled travelling along the
Knightsbridge Road and turning into Sloane Street, but
now that they were out in the country, with her limited
knowledge of London's environs, it was difficult for her
to guess where they might be—somewhere in the region
of Chelsea Village, she assumed.

Chelsea! Sitting bolt upright, she swivelled herself
round and fixed Helstone with a piercing glare.

'We wouldn't be heading for your "neat little cottage
in Chelsea" by any chance, would we, my lord?' she

asked, her voice dripping with sarcasm. 'Do you never give up?'

'In the blood, I'm afraid,' he replied, with a slightly self-conscious half-laugh. 'You need have no fear for your virtue on this occasion, however. The house comes fully equipped with as highly respectable a staff as you are ever likely to come across—the formidable Mrs Bellamy would doubtless have at me with a frying pan if I so much as lifted a finger in your direction!'

'I cannot suppose that that has ever prevented you from turning up with a succession of opera dancers and other such lightskirts,' she returned frostily.

'Not so,' he drawled, before skilfully swinging his equipage through an arched gateway and up an attractively curved driveway flanked by laurel bushes. 'I have never felt the need to associate with females of that sort and, much as it may surprise you to learn, you are the only lady of my acquaintance who has ever been invited to cross the threshold of this particular establishment. There!' As the carriage drew up outside the front door steps, he swept out his arm to encompass the surrounding vista. 'Tell me what you think.'

No sooner had her eyes lit upon the graceful lines of the simple but charming two-storeyed building, surrounded by a profusion of neatly stocked flowerbeds and set in a wide expanse of carefully tended lawn, than Sophie's throat started to contract painfully, making it impossible for her to take a full breath. For there in front of her, in all its splendid glory, stood her dream home, almost exactly as she had always pictured it.

Utterly lost for words, she could only sit and gaze about her in silent awe, causing Marcus to experience a sharp stab of disappointment when the expected words of approval failed to materialise, since he had already convinced himself that the peaceful beauty of the place would appeal to Sophie in much the same way that it had attracted him.

'I take it that you're not overly impressed, then,' he said abruptly as, tossing the reins to the already descended Kimble, he leapt lightly from the driving seat and walked around the carriage to help Sophie alight. Doggedly resisting the impulse to fasten both his hands about her waist and haul her down into a crushing embrace, he gritted his teeth and held out only the one hand, in the total expectation of Sophie's making use of its assistance to help her down from her seat. But no! It seemed that she was still so heavily engrossed in the view that she remained completely oblivious to both his words and his actions. A baffled frown appeared on his brow as he registered the thoroughly stunned and awed expression on her face.

Good Lord! he thought, as he let his arm fall limply to his side. *She is as entranced with the place as I had hoped she would be. Round one to me, it seems. It would appear that the lady is well and truly hooked!*

Filled with a deep sense of satisfaction, but well aware that the battle was not yet won, the Viscount, clearing his throat briskly, reached out his hand again and tapped Sophie gently on the arm.

'I hate to interrupt your reverie, my dear, but I fear that the horses are starting to get restive!'

At the unexpectedness of his touch, Sophie found herself jerked back to the far-from-dreamlike reality of her present situation. *How typical of the devil to have stumbled across the very place that might cause me to change my mind,* she thought crossly, as she placed her hand into Helstone's and allowed him to help her down from the carriage. *Nevertheless,* she vowed, *he*

*will soon find that I still have no intention of becoming
his paramour, no matter how impossibly perfect his
beastly cottage might be!*

Not that the idea was without a certain appeal, she
was obliged to concede, casting up a quick sideways
glance at the Viscount's handsome visage as he escorted
her up the front steps and through the cottage's already
opened door. *Would it really be so very wrong to agree
to his proposition in order to acquire the tenancy of
this splendid house?* she conjectured wistfully, as she
stepped inside the elegantly appointed hallway. But
even as she felt the heat of so enticing a notion coursing through her veins, she forced herself to thrust it
instantly away. To exchange a future lifetime of pain
and regret for a few months of vicarious pleasure could
in no way be considered any sort of a bargain, she cas-
tigated herself impatiently. For, despite having had a
rather limited acquaintance with the subject, she was
not so foolish that she did not understand that the sort of
liaison in which Helstone had suggested she might care
to involve herself was well known to have a somewhat
limited tenure. It was not difficult to fathom out what
might become of women in such situations once they
were cast aside—the very thought of which was enough
to make her own dreary existence seem almost palatable
by comparison!

'Good afternoon, my lord. I trust that you had a pleasant journey?'

Returning her thoughts to the reality of her present
situation, Sophie became aware that the Viscount was
being addressed by a tall, stately looking female of inde-
terminate years, clad in a black bombazine gown with
a neat frill of white lace at its neck. *Mrs Bellamy, the
housekeeper*, she supposed, doing her utmost to adopt

an air of detached nonchalance in the face of the house-keeper's expected attitude of disparagement. *Not that I should expect anything less from the poor creature,* she reminded herself. *Unaccompanied young ladies of good standing do not accept invitations to the secret love-nests of well-known libertines. The good woman has probably already formed her own opinion of my doubtful worth—especially since my mode of dress is likely to be somewhat dowdy when compared to that of his lordship's usual doxies!*

Lifting her chin, she stared defiantly at the house-keeper, daring the woman to show her disapproval.

'Pleasant enough, thank you, Mrs Bellamy—although a trifle more breezy than I had anticipated. Perhaps you would be so good as to direct Miss Flint to a chamber where she might wash her hands and tidy her hair?'

'But of course, sir—do come this way, ma'am.'

To Sophie's surprise, the housekeeper's tone was in no way starchy or censorious. In fact, as she led her up the broad staircase to the upper floor, Mrs Bellamy's face creased in a friendly smile. She showed her into a prettily decorated bedchamber and invited her to make use of its facilities.

'I shall have hot water sent up directly,' she said, directing Sophie's attention to the washstand beside a fully equipped dressing table. 'You will find combs and brushes there—they are all brand new, of course, so please do not be afraid to avail yourself of them. I was beginning to doubt that they would ever be used! His lordship has owned the property for well over six months now, and you are the very first visitor ever to have set foot inside it!' Pausing, she shot Sophie a somewhat shrewd glance, before going on to say, 'I do so hope that you approve of all the decorations and improvements that have been made.'

That the housekeeper should consider her opinion to be of any value came as something of a surprise to Sophie, given that she was just a casual visitor and hardly likely to come here again. But then it occurred to her that the woman was merely looking for some sort of acknowledgment for all the hard work that she and her staff had put in.

'I really cannot imagine that anyone would be able to find fault with a single thing, Mrs Bellamy,' she assured her earnestly. 'Everything looks so clean and bright—it's quite the loveliest cottage that I have ever seen, and the gardens, well, who could possibly ask for a more delightful view?'

Crossing over to the open window, she poked her head out, only to find her senses almost overwhelmed by the fragrant scent of the densely blossomed honeysuckle bush, whose branches had spread their tendrils right across the cottage wall just below the room's windowsill. And then, as her eyes travelled slowly across the neatly laid out gardens before her, they fell upon an arching rose arbour at the far end of the side garden, beyond which another glorious aspect threatened to take her breath away. There, with its gently sloping banks edged with aspen and willow trees—complete with all the obligatory bulrushes, water lilies, swans and assorted ducks of her childhood imaginings—lay a small but picturesque lake, its limpid waters sparkling invitingly in the afternoon sunshine. The entire prospect was so devastatingly awe-inspiring that she was rendered almost speechless.

'Perfect,' she breathed softly. 'Truly perfect.'

'I am so glad you approve, ma'am.' The housekeeper

beamed as she turned to leave the room. 'I have always thought it a most pleasant view, myself. And now, if you will excuse me, I must go and see about that hot water I promised you.'

Chapter Nine

Tentatively retracing her steps down the stairs some ten minutes later, Sophie was well on the way to convincing herself that Viscount Helstone must be something of a mind-reading magician for, having brought her to this delightful cottage, presumably with the sole intention of persuading her to accept his offer, he seemed to have managed to conjure up almost every one of the wild and wonderful fantasies that she had held dear for most of her childhood years and beyond. *How Mama would love all this,* she thought dreamily, as she ran her fingers over the smooth, lovingly polished surface of the mahogany banister rail. *And what an incredible place for Roger to come home to in the holidays! All those trees, just waiting to be climbed, and the lake—how he would revel in fishing there—possibly he could even have a boat of his own! We could have picnics by the lakeside, and in the winter, when the water froze…*

'A penny for them, Miss Flint!'

The sound of Helstone's deep voice at her elbow

wrenched her from her daydream. With a gasp of dismay, she spun round, her cheeks aflame. *What could she have been thinking, to let her imagination run away with her in such a foolish manner? To accept Helstone's offer would mean totally cutting herself off from her family, just as her father had done from his all those years ago. There would be no way on earth that she would ever see her mama strolling across these lawns twirling her parasol, and her brother would most likely never be allowed to speak to her again, let alone climb the apple trees in Laurel Cottage's orchard!*

'Hardly a sufficient offer, perhaps?' continued the Viscount, easing himself away from the doorframe against which he had been leaning while watching Sophie's preoccupied descent of the stairs. 'I have the feeling that your thoughts were worth a good deal more than that—but I shan't press you, so your secrets are perfectly safe, I promise you.'

Which is probably just as well, thought Sophie, steadfastly refusing to look at him. *If he had the slightest inkling of where my thoughts were leading me, I cannot begin to imagine what his reaction would be!*

'Come,' he said, holding out his hand. 'Mrs Bellamy tells me that she has laid tea in the pavilion—it seems a pity not to take advantage of the sun while it is still shining.'

A pavilion too? Sophie could hardly believe it. Was the man supernatural?

'I didn't see a pavilion when I was looking out of the window,' she said, as she tucked her hand into the crook of his arm and allowed him to lead her out of a side door onto a path that led through the abundantly stocked flower gardens down towards the lake.

'No, you wouldn't,' he explained. 'It is hidden away

on the other side of the rose arbour—I found that the trellising helps to ward off the wind.'

'You designed all this yourself?' Sophie could not conceal her astonishment.

'Not all,' he replied, a soft smile tugging at his lips as he registered her incredulous expression. 'Just a few minor improvements here and there. Do you approve?'

'I'm utterly overwhelmed—it would be difficult to imagine anything more perfect. It is so kind of you to allow me to see it all.'

Kind! Marcus blanched. Kindness had been the last thing on his mind when he had drummed up this idea. Total seduction of Sophie's senses had been his original intention, followed by…

Grimacing, as the only too familiar ache in his groin assailed him once again, he bit back a groan. *Take it easy,* he rebuked himself. *Slowly does it—it wouldn't do to frighten the lady away entirely!* Apart from which, he found himself admitting there was something oddly refreshing about Sophie's refusal to bend herself to his will—a distinct change from his many past conquests, who had been only too eager to bestow whatever favours he required in exchange for some paltry bauble or other. Sophie, on the other hand, had even made a point of turning down his offer to pay for that damned atlas of hers, insisting that she would somehow find the money and reimburse him! Having managed to scotch that plan by getting Broomfield to exchange the tattered copy for a much newer version, Marcus was surprised that Sophie had not yet tackled him over that particular subterfuge. *Probably saving it up to attack me with it when I least expect it,* he concluded ruefully, as he attempted to ply her with the various sumptuous dishes that Mrs Bellamy had laid out for them.

'But there is far too much food here for just the two of us!' she protested, laughingly waving away his offerings. 'I couldn't possibly eat that amount of veal pie—you must cut that slice in half, at the very least!'

'But you've taken scarcely enough to feed a kitten,' he complained. 'Do try some of this chicken. It is utterly delicious, I swear. We can't have Cook thinking that we don't appreciate her culinary arts—good cooks are very hard to come by.'

'Well, just a little, perhaps,' conceded Sophie, holding out her plate in order that he could serve her a slice of the succulent meat. 'But I really need to save a little space for those delicious-looking strawberries—I can't remember the last time I had any and I do enjoy them so.'

In fact, her enjoyment of the whole afternoon was such that she had all but ceased to be chary of him. After all the deprivation that she had suffered during the past few months, she was finding the Viscount's dedicated attention to her every need so very heart-warming. Not only that, but the sheer beauty of her surroundings was threatening to dazzle her entirely, making her uncomfortably aware of the fact that, should Helstone happen to choose this particular moment to launch another one of his amorous assaults on her, she very much doubted that she would be able to find either the strength or the willpower to resist his advances.

Fortunately for her peace of mind, the Viscount's thoughts appeared to be elsewhere.

'You've led a most unusual life, haven't you?' he asked, reaching forward to pass her a generous helping of the ripe red fruits. Then, repositioning himself comfortably against the stone bench's fat cushions, so that he could indulge himself in witnessing Sophie's sheer delight in what was, to her, yet another unexpected luxury, he murmured, 'Care to tell me about it?'

'Our life was no different from any other family who chose to follow their loved ones to war,' replied Sophie, somewhat evasively. 'My mother travelled with my father when his unit was sent to Ireland back in ninety-two, and we always accompanied him thereafter—that is,' she amended, 'Mama and I did. Roger, my brother, was sent away to school when he was eight. When Papa was killed, of course...' Her voice trailed away and her eyes were suddenly filled with desolation. Biting back the tears that threatened, she attempted a mocking laugh. 'The rest you know—lack of finance required me to seek some sort of position, but, since I had nothing to show in the way of references, I was obliged to settle for the Crayfords' offer.'

Although he was tempted to remind her that his own proposition far outweighed the Crayfords' in terms of generosity, Marcus held his tongue, having just recalled the chance remark made by his brother the previous day.

'Your father,' he said, leaning forward. 'He must have been an officer to have been allowed to have his family travel with him. What rank was he, may I ask?'

'He was a Lieutenant-Colonel,' responded Sophie instantly, her chin held high. 'He died attempting to move his unit to higher ground and was awarded for his bravery—not that such an accolade is a great deal of help to us now,' she added bitterly. 'But I am still immensely proud of him, nevertheless.'

'And rightly so,' returned the Viscount, much moved. 'He was clearly a credit to his country.' He paused, slightly unsure of how to phrase his next question. 'My brother once spoke to me of a Lieutenant-Colonel Pendleton-Flint,' he then said. 'He wouldn't have been your father, by any chance?'

'Yes, he was,' she replied dully. 'And if you are wondering why I do not use my full name just ask yourself how many people would wish to employ a companion or governess with a double-barrelled name. The employment agency advised me to discard the Pendleton, on the grounds that it might give prospective employers the idea that I had ideas above my station!'

'But that's nonsense!' protested Marcus angrily. 'Surely everyone is entitled to use their given name, no matter what their walk of life?'

'It would appear not, my lord,' rebutted Sophie, as she rose from her seat. 'Needless to say, I would appreciate your discretion in this matter—I already have enough with which to contend after your claiming to be a cousin of mine, without having to explain my reasons for not using my full name.'

She paused and then, fixing him with an angry glare, went on, 'Which reminds me—I believe I am in your debt for an even greater amount than the three shillings and sixpence we originally agreed upon. Perhaps you would let me know the exact figure and I will do my best to see that you—'

'Heaven preserve me from idiotish females!' exploded Marcus, jumping to his feet and cutting her short. 'You know perfectly well that you haven't a hope in hell of being able to pay me back this side of Judgement Day, so will you kindly desist from mentioning the subject again?'

Sophie's face whitened. 'Was the book so very expensive then?' she persisted, quite resolute in her determination to refund the Viscount the full amount of her indebtedness, regardless of how long it might take.

'What does it matter what the damned thing cost?' he cried, clapping his hand to his brow. 'I shan't accept a single penny from you and that's final! No!' he ordered, as she opened her mouth to protest. 'I won't hear another word on the subject! If you imagine that I'm going to stand here arguing over a paltry ten shillings, you are— oh, damn it to hell!'

As the sound of Sophie's barely suppressed chuckle filled the air, a rueful smile spread across Helstone's face. 'Rolled up, lock, stock and barrel!' he groaned, as he threw himself back onto his seat.

'Don't fret, my lord,' cooed Sophie gleefully, reaching forward and patting him on the hand. 'I was bound to have found out eventually—I had it in mind to ask Mr Broomfield had you refused to tell me!'

Marcus stared at her, shaking his head in self-disgust. Then, as the seed of an idea planted itself in his brain, 'How much do these Crayfords actually pay you, then, Miss Moneybags?' he asked carelessly.

'Twelve pounds a year, all found,' replied Sophie, caught off guard by his casual tone.

'Good God!' The Viscount was visibly shocked. 'The miserable skinflints—even my sister's governess gets twenty pounds a year and her husband is the most tight-fisted clutch-purse known to man! How, in God's name, do you manage on such a pittance?'

'There are plenty of people who survive on a good deal less,' she retorted dryly. 'I have more than enough for my own needs and I even manage to put a little aside every quarter to send to my mother.'

'And you would rather live like that than…?' he

asked, eying her wonderingly. 'Hardly the most flattering thing I've ever been told!'

Sophie shrugged. 'It's just a question of self-respect, my lord. That and—' She stopped, her cheeks flaming.

'And what?' he prompted, impatient to know her true reasons for continually turning him down.

Blinking rapidly, she turned away, so that the Viscount could not see her face.

'I've always supposed that I would—give myself to someone that I loved and who loved me in return,' she said, in a low voice. 'And, even though marriage is denied me, I see no reason to relinquish my principles.'

Marcus stilled, his eyes focussed on her back. Then, 'In what way is marriage denied you?' he demanded hoarsely. 'You are quite lovely.'

Turning to face him, she gestured impatiently. 'I am a dowerless, impoverished governess, and the only gentlemen who cross my path are those whose inclinations are as far removed from thoughts of marriage as are your own, sir!'

He stiffened as hot colour mounted his cheeks, struck silent by her damning words and heavily conscious of the fact that the charge was impossible to deny. In fact, no one knew better than he that his recent behaviour in regard to this chestnut-haired siren had been well outside his normal code of conduct, and the disquieting awareness of which, it had to be said, had caused the Viscount a good many sleepless nights of late. From the very first moment he had set eyes on her, he had felt himself drawn to her in a way that was both compelling and yet at the same time quite mystifying. Sophie's departure from the tavern had left him feeling so bereft that he had, unaccountably, badgered his brother into helping him search for her, and now that he had found her again he knew that his life meant nothing unless she agreed to be part of it. Now, however, since she had made it quite clear that the final objective was to be denied him, regardless of anything he might say or do, any attempt on his part to continue with his carefully thought-out plans to persuade her to succumb to his desires now seemed totally pointless.

Apart from an offer of marriage, of course, he allowed, with an inward grimace, supremely confident in the knowledge that should he, as heir to the Bradfield earldom, ever care to cast his hat into that particular ring, he would have the pick of the Season's debutantes scrambling to take up his offer. *Should I be mad enough to venture into that hornets' nest!* thought Marcus scathingly. *No, thank you! I'm more than happy to leave the question of succession to Giles—let him put his head into the parson's mousetrap, if he must. Marriage is most definitely not on the cards, as far as I'm concerned!*

At his continued silence, Sophie returned to the table and, holding back a disconsolate sigh, picked up her discarded napkin and proceeded to fill it with random scraps of food.

'With your permission, I shall go and feed the ducks,' she said, casting a questioning glance at the Viscount's scowling visage.

'As you wish,' returned Marcus, with a careless shrug. He was beginning to regret his decision to bring Sophie to Laurel Cottage. From now on this peaceful bolt-hole would be forever tainted with tantalising images of her walking down the stairs, strolling through the gardens admiring his designs, daintily sipping champagne in the pavilion—his very favourite spot of all—and now...

Against his better judgement, he let his eyes drift over to where Sophie now stood at the water's edge. Having leaned forward to toss a handful of crumbs towards the flock of ducks now heading swiftly in her direction, she had let out a loud peal of laughter and was clapping her hands in delight as the comical antics of the noisy jostling birds captured the whole of her attention.

At the sight of her laughing face Marcus felt his stomach give a violent lurch, and it was all he could do to stop from hurling himself across the grass and dragging her into his arms. His entire body ached to feel the soft roundness of her curves pressed against him and to taste the incredible sweetness of her lips again. *God, but it's going to be difficult to give her up!* He groaned inwardly, steeling himself to descend the pavilion steps and walk towards the water's edge with a modicum of dignified composure.

'Watch out for the swans,' he advised, as he approached. 'They are apt to go for the hand, if one isn't careful.'

'Oh, what a pity!' she said, turning her attention to the far side of the lake, from which she could see two majestic-looking swans making a graceful approach. 'I didn't think that they would come while there were so many ducks squabbling for my offerings and now it has all gone!'

Rising to her feet, she shook the final few crumbs into the water, setting off another clamour, as the flapping, squawking waterfowl jostled one another witlessly in their frenzied attempts to get at the offerings.

'There's plenty more back there,' offered Marcus with a light laugh, jerking his head towards the plates full of untouched delicacies still sitting on the table in the pavilion. 'Enough to satisfy even the most voracious of their appetites, I should think.'

'Thank you, but I fear that I really ought to be thinking of leaving now,' returned Sophie, casting a last regretful look at the swans, now drifting in aimless circles in search of long-gone provender. 'Mrs Crayford distinctly said "afternoon drive", as I recall, and it must be getting close to five o'clock by now, I should think.'

'A quarter to,' supplied the Viscount, after pulling out his watch and flipping open its lid to check the hour. 'I'll have the carriage brought round.'

Probably for the best, he told himself sternly as Sophie gave a swift nod and turned to make her way back to the house. *I'll just have to accept the fact that she means what she says and let her go to get on with her own life.*

'I trust that you've had no further attacks on your person since our last meeting?' he then added, as if by afterthought.

'No, of course not,' she replied, with a vehement shake of her head. 'I should have mentioned it had I done so. Apart from having to clear up my room after all the mess that my dear pupil caused, my life has gone on much as usual.'

'Your pupil ransacked your room?' Marcus bit back his anger. 'When did this happen?'

'I discovered it upon my return yesterday afternoon,' she said in reply. 'I must confess that I found it a trifle dispiriting at the time.'

Hardly surprising, reflected the Viscount, with a wry grimace. *Coming on top of my boorish behaviour as it did! The perfect ending to a perfect day!*

'Does the boy make a habit of that sort of thing?' he asked.

'Not as such.' She sighed. 'He did set a host of frogs free in my room shortly after I arrived, and is inclined to be somewhat insolent at times, but he has never before gone to such a spiteful extreme.'

'You administered a suitable punishment, I imagine?'

'No, I refuse to give him the gratification of thinking that it bothered me. I have learned that, in Henry's case, at least, children are apt not to repeat things that fail to have the effect they had hoped for. He won't do it again.'

'You're quite certain that the lad was the culprit, I suppose?'

Faced with this latest piece of information, Marcus was seriously beginning to doubt that Sophie's errant pupil had been to blame for the ransacking of her room. Since the unwitting governess had already been the unfortunate victim of two-bag snatches in a matter of hours, it was hardly a long shot for him to infer that the retrieval of the misdirected cipher had been the real purpose for each of these robberies. If so, and rather more to the point as far as Marcus was concerned, it was not difficult to deduce that the ransacking of her room could be laid squarely at the feet of whoever had been responsible for the bag snatching. A cold trickle of unease ran through him as it then became clear that what he had vaguely suspected all along was no longer open to any doubt. *One or other member of the Crayford household was behind all three attacks!* And, much as the Viscount would have taken great pleasure in being the one to apprehend the craven individual and teach him a much needed lesson in civility, he had sufficient sense to appreciate that such things were best left in the more competent hands of Giles and his team of experts. He could only thank God that Sophie no longer had the damned invoice in her possession!

A slight furrow appeared on Sophie's brow as she pondered his question.

'Reasonably so,' she replied cautiously. 'I admit that I did, at first, suspect Arthur Crayford, but, having seen him leave the house just before I myself left, I was obliged to discount him. Apart from which,' she added, her tone more scathing, 'I cannot imagine him going to so much trouble for so little return—his methods are far more confrontational.'

Not any more, they aren't, reflected Marcus with a certain amount of satisfaction. But then, bearing in mind his brother's remarks regarding the sometimes dual personalities of hardened criminals, he realised that it might be unwise to dismiss the coxcomb entirely.

'You always keep your bedroom door locked, I imagine?' he then asked, as they were about to re-enter the house. 'An open door is often regarded as an open invitation, in certain quarters.'

Giving him a reassuring smile, Sophie replied, 'I hadn't always done so—except at night, of course. But I shall be sure to do so from now on.'

'Very wise,' agreed the Viscount somewhat inattentively, since his mind had instantly latched on to Sophie's veiled reference to the nightly locking of her door. *That evil toad Crayford at his tricks again*, he supposed, harnessing his fury at the thought of Sophie having been obliged to endure such iniquitous harassment. Hopefully, yesterday's warning should have put a stop to the noxious little swine's activities, but, if not, Marcus was in no doubt that he would soon find a way of dissuading the young wretch in some other, possibly less gentlemanly fashion.

Not that Sophie's future well-being was really any concern of his, he was at pains to remind himself. Now that she had made her intentions clear, it merely remained for him to see her safely home, put in a cursory appearance at the Crayford soiree and simply put the whole sorry business out of his mind as though none of it had ever happened.

If only life were that simple…

Chapter Ten

An open curricle, as Mrs Bellamy had been swift to
point out upon their departure, was not, perhaps, an ideal
mode of transport for what was to be a somewhat chill-
ier journey back to Town, but to Sophie's undisguised
delight Helstone had already thought to cater for such
an eventuality. Having equipped himself with one of the
soft woollen rugs that were draped over the backs of the
sofas in the cottage's parlour, he had tucked it behind
his driving seat, in the event of an emergency.

At the first sign of Sophie's shivering, he swung his
equipage over to the side of the road and, pulling out the
rug, draped it neatly about her shoulders saying, with a
somewhat wry smile, 'Since you insist upon denying me
the pleasure of lavishing you with furs, at least allow me
the privilege of ensuring your comfort for the duration
of this trip.'

Snuggling blissfully into the cosy warmth, Sophie
gave a contented sigh. 'You are very kind, my lord, and
I really must thank you for a most enjoyable afternoon.'

Pausing, she then cast him an uneasy glance before continuing. 'I'm truly sorry that we failed to see eye to eye over—um—a certain matter, but I feel sure that, once you have had a chance to review the situation, you will agree that it is really for the best that we do not continue to see each other.'

Whilst it cost her a great deal to make this pronouncement, Sophie was convinced that it was the right and proper thing to do. She already had an inkling that the Viscount had accepted the fact that she was never going to agree to become his mistress, and, that being so, there could be no further need for him to remain in touch with her. She would go her way and he, no doubt, would continue to go his. He would never know the true extent of her feelings for him and she would have to learn to live with the knowledge of what she might have had, had she been a little more courageous or even a little less prideful, perhaps!

'That might prove a little difficult,' replied Marcus, in response to her ultimatum. 'I have already accepted an invitation to attend this function that the Crayfords are holding on Tuesday evening. I feel that it would be rather discourteous of me to default at this stage.' Not that he really gave a tinker's cuss as to what the Crayfords might think or feel about his failure to attend their pathetic little soirée, but, even though his carefully laid plans had failed to tempt Sophie away from her chosen path of virtue, the Viscount still had every intention of finding some way of persuading her employers to treat their governess with a little more respect than hitherto.

Unable to think up an adequate reason as to why Helstone should not fulfil his commitment, Sophie remained silent, although her thoughts were chaotic. The Viscount's having agreed to put in an appearance at the Crayfords' rout would mean that she too would be obliged to attend the hastily arranged function, occasioning even more time in his company—a situation that she was desperately keen to avoid, well aware that every minute spent in such close proximity with him took her yet another step closer to her eventual undoing.

As the carriage swung sharply around a bend in the road, she could feel the warmth of Helstone's disturbingly muscular thigh pressing hard against hers, causing a hot spiral of longing to course throughout her entire body. Desperately trying to edge herself away from his enticing nearness, Sophie racked her brains for some topic of conversation that might help take her mind off the all too alluring images that her thoughts were presently conjuring up.

'You don't happen to know what your brother did with my bill of sale, I suppose?' she asked.

'He used it to help him solve some puzzle or other,' replied Marcus off-handedly, achingly aware of her presence next to him. Sophie's vain attempts to put more space between them had not passed him by, but had merely served to underline what he could only suppose was her growing antipathy towards him. Despite this rather dispiriting conclusion, however, he still had every intention of carrying out the task he had set himself. By the time he had finished with the Crayfords, he vowed, they would be blessing the day that Sophie had chosen to cross their threshold. With a surfeit of friends and acquaintances who owed him enough favours to serve his purpose, he intended to call in those favours by way of obliging several highborn members of the *Ton* to show their faces at some of the ghastly-sounding functions that the socially inept Mrs Crayford had spoken of in their earlier conversation. That should ensure that her indomitable governess slept safe in her bed at nights, if nothing else, he thought to himself in satisfaction.

'Puzzle?' ventured Sophie, breaking into his reverie.

'Apparently, the thing was in code,' he replied, hastily returning his attention to the subject in hand. 'Seems there's some sort of a plot afoot to do away with the Duke of Wellington, and your invoice unravelled the mystery as to the gang's next meeting place.'

'But that's appalling!' she cried, turning towards him, her fists clenched and her clear blue eyes alight with anger. 'His Grace is a national hero! Why, only a few months ago the crowds were pelting his carriage with flowers as he drove down Pall Mall. My father thought him the greatest general our country has ever known. Why would anyone wish to harm him now, after all he has done?'

Unwilling to share his brother's concerns regarding the growing unrest in the country, Marcus thought it best to change the subject.

'Probably just a few crack pots trying to stir up trouble,' he said, doing his best to adopt his normal blasé manner. 'I should put it out of my mind, if I were you. I'm sure that my brother has it all in hand, thanks to that invoice of yours.'

Sophie was silent for a moment or two, apparently digesting this advice, but then, turning to face him once more, she said, 'But surely your brother cannot suspect that decrepit old bookseller of being involved in such a plot?'

'Probably not,' conceded the Viscount, who was now devoting the majority of his attention to negotiating the sharp turn out of Sloane Street into Lennox Gardens. Having brought his carriage neatly to a halt outside the

Crayford residence, he then looked across at her to add, somewhat mischievously, 'But I'm bound to say that clerk of his looked decidedly shifty when I went into the back office to have your atlas wrapped.'

'*Your* atlas, you mean!' she retaliated at once, just as he had known that she would. '*My* atlas is still in the shop!'

'As you please,' he replied, giving her another of his lop-sided grins, before leaping down from his seat and skirting around the vehicle in order to be ready to offer her his assistance.

But instead of holding out his hand, as she had expected, the Viscount reached forward and, placing both hands firmly at her waist, swung her out of her seat to deposit her neatly on to the pavement.

Thoroughly taken aback by his unanticipated manoeuvre, Sophie stood in breathless bewilderment as she waited for Helstone to release his hold on her. When he did not immediately do so, however, her eyes flew up to his face, questioningly.

Helstone's expression, she discovered, was quite incomprehensible; his eyes, as they looked searchingly into hers, seemed to bore deep down into her very soul, setting up such a violent trembling within her that, had his hands not still been at her waist, she would have sworn that her knees were ready to give way beneath her. Her mind in complete disarray, she had almost convinced herself that the Viscount was about to kiss her... out here in the street...in full view of anyone who might be watching...when, with a sudden start, he blinked and, hurriedly releasing his hold, stepped away from her, a perplexed frown on his forehead.

Then, just as if the incident had never taken place, he drew in a deep breath, offered the thoroughly shaken

Sophie his arm and escorted her up the short flight of steps that led to the Crayfords' front door.

Any thoughts that she might have had regarding his strange behaviour were wiped completely from her mind by the fact that, even before the Viscount had reached out his hand to raise the knocker, the front door was opened by none other than Mrs Crayford herself, albeit that the highly indignant features of Hawkins the butler could be seen at his mistress's elbow.

'Ah, there you are, your lordship,' gushed Mrs Crayford, as she hurriedly reversed to allow the pair to enter the hallway. 'We were beginning to fear that you had met with some dreadful accident. How very naughty of Miss Flint to have kept you out for so long—you must be quite exhausted. You will come in and take a little refreshment, I trust?'

'It is exceedingly kind of you to offer,' returned Marcus, affecting an extravagant bow in order to hide his expression of utter disgust. 'However, Miss Flint and I have already dined and, as to our being late, I was unaware that any particular time of arrival had been specified. I was under the impression that my cousin's Sunday afternoons were hers to do with as she pleases.'

'Why, yes, of course,' replied the now highly flustered matron, braving the steely glint in the Viscount's eye to add, with a slight hint of defiance, 'After the children have attended the morning church service, Miss Flint's time is her own.'

'As I surmised,' observed the Viscount smoothly. 'My sister, the Duchess of Marchmont, practises a very similar arrangement with her children's governess.'

Marcus's casual reference to one of Society's most admired hostesses at once claimed Mrs Crayford's entire attention, as had been his intention. That he had then gone on to liken her domestic arrangements to those of the illustrious Duchess was almost enough to deprive the coarse vulgarian of her power of speech.

'One tries to be fair,' she eventually managed, vigorously fanning her reddening cheeks with her handkerchief, while Sophie did her best to control the expression of sheer disbelief that threatened.

In point of fact, not a single Sunday afternoon had passed since Sophie's arrival without Mrs Crayford having plied her with some secretarial chore or other. At the very start of her employment Sophie had been far too grateful to have been accepted for the position to even consider putting up any sort of resistance to this continual encroachment into what was meant to be her free time, as a result of which her employer now seemed to take it for granted that her children's governess would be prepared to make herself available to her as and whenever her services were called upon. Especially since Sophie's non-complaining lack of resistance obviated the need for Mrs Crayford to employ a secretary, thereby allowing her employer to put the generous quarterage that she received from her husband to cover the household expenses to what she considered far better use—namely, her own self-adornment.

Having done his best to raise Sophie's stock a little higher, Marcus made ready to leave. Executing another elegant bow in Mrs Crayford's direction, he turned to bid farewell to Sophie, but just as he did so his eyes chanced to fall on the footman who was waiting to open the door. Recognising him at once as the fellow who had delivered Sophie's message to him the previous evening, the Viscount was again beset by the feeling that he had come across the man before, in some other capacity.

'What's that chap's name?' he murmured under his breath, as he lifted Sophie's hand to brush his lips across the tips of her fingers. 'I keep getting the feeling that I know him from somewhere.'

Although she was quite startled at being questioned in such a covert manner, Sophie strove to maintain an impassive mien. Dipping his lordship a quick curtsey, she mouthed the word 'Fisher' at him, before straightening up and offering him her grateful thanks for 'a most delightful afternoon'.

'My pleasure entirely, dear coz,' he said, as he stepped away from her. 'We must endeavour to repeat the experience in the very near future.'

Ignoring her reproachful frown, he tossed another brief nod at her employer before turning smartly on his heel and striding towards the front door, still racking his brains as to why the footman's features should seem so familiar to him.

Before he was halfway out of the door, however, Mrs Crayford, suddenly galvanised into action, dashed across the hallway and grasped at his arm.

'You haven't forgotten our little soiree on Tuesday evening, have you, my lord?' she gasped anxiously.

Steeling himself not to rip her clutching fingers from his coat-sleeve, the Viscount forced a smile to his lips, saying, 'I shall be here, ma'am—you have my word.'

Then, without further ado, he ran lightly down the steps, hoisted himself up into his driving seat and, after signalling Kimble to let go the horses' heads, flicked the reins and headed towards his Grosvenor Square establishment.

Having come to the conclusion that there was little point in bemoaning the afternoon's lack of success in the seduction stakes, he set his mind to concentrating on the recurring puzzle that the footman's appearance had set him.

A pasty-looking, sharp-featured individual...eyes set too close together...distinctively pointed nose...

His unanticipated jerk of the reins had Kimble almost out of his seat as the two grey thoroughbreds skidded to an abrupt halt.

'Have a heart, guv!' protested the tiger, ruefully massaging his bruised knee. 'Nearly had me under that there coal wagon.'

'Teach you not to fall asleep on the job,' retorted Marcus. 'Hop down and help me head 'em back up towards Bond Street.'

'Thought we was going home,' muttered the aggrieved Kimble, reluctantly doing as he had been bidden. 'Took me eyes off the road for the barest mo, only to find meself hanging on to me perch for dear life—a bit of notice wouldn't have gone amiss!'

'Sorry about that,' returned the Viscount, shooting his groom an unrepentant grin as the man wheeled the greys around until the entire equipage faced in the opposite direction. 'I give you leave to drown your sorrows in the King's Arms—I find I need to have an urgent word with the Major.'

Having been unable to fathom Helstone's untoward interest in the Crayfords' footman, Sophie found herself casting the manservant a surreptitious glance—only to find Fisher regarding her in an equally disquieting manner. Hurriedly dropping her eyes, she made for the stairs, but was immediately forestalled by Mrs Crayford's sharp insistence that she should join the family in the drawing room.

'For I'm sure we are all agog to hear how the pair

of you spent your afternoon. And fancy his lordship choosing to take you out to dine—you simply must come along and tell us all about it.'

Groaning inwardly, since she was not at all disposed to sharing a single minute of her enchanting afternoon with her invidiously prying employer, Sophie made up her mind to ignore the implicit command.

'Thank you, but since I still have tomorrow's lessons to prepare I really ought to get on,' she said, lifting her foot in readiness to mount the stairs.

Unfortunately, Mrs Crayford refused to be denied.

'Oh, but that can wait a few more minutes, I am sure,' she said, waving a dismissive hand. 'Mr Crayford and myself are really most eager to hear about your trip.'

Very much doubting that Mrs Crayford's elderly, timorous spouse was in the least bit interested in the comings and goings of his children's governess, Sophie curbed the facetious retort that hovered on the tip of her tongue and then, conscious that her employer had left her with very little option but to comply with her demands, felt obliged to concede.

'As you wish,' she replied dispiritedly. 'But, I daresay you will excuse me for a moment or two while I take my things to my room and tidy my hair.'

'Well, if you really must,' pouted Mrs Crayford, eying with disfavour the prim grey gown Sophie had insisted upon wearing, despite her mistress's very clear objections to the contrary. 'And, while you're at it, you might care to change into one of those very pretty gowns that Lydia was so kind as to pass on to you—I really cannot understand why you felt it necessary to accompany his lordship in your workaday clothes when you have so many other lovely dresses to choose from!'

Her lips clamped firmly together, in order to prevent

the inadvertent emission of some choice but highly unladylike profanity regarding the loveliness or otherwise of the aforementioned offerings, Sophie sensibly demurred from making any reply and, her whole body seething with tightly suppressed fury, proceeded to climb the three flights of stairs that led up to her attic bedroom. On reaching the second floor, however, she was startled to find herself waylaid by none other than the footman, Fisher, who emerged from the entrance to the servants' stairway just as she was about to pass.

'A word, Miss Flint, if you please,' he hissed, his sharp eyes darting anxiously hither and thither in order to satisfy himself that his clandestine apprehension of the governess had remained unobserved.

Unfortunately, Sophie's recent unsatisfactory encounter with Mrs Crayford had left her in no mood to deal with what she considered to be an overly theatrical performance on the part of the footman. 'I'm sorry, Fisher,' she said, as she skirted past him and continued on her way. 'I'm afraid I don't have time to stop and chat with you just at the moment. The Crayfords are waiting for me.'

'But I have something…' he began, digging his hand into his pocket and withdrawing a tightly folded piece of paper. 'There was a mistake in the direction…'

Suddenly alert, Sophie came to a halt and, spinning on her heel, she stared down at the servant in wide-eyed incredulity.

'You have my invoice?' she cried, starting back down the stairs and holding out her hand.

But instead of handing her the missive, as she had expected, Fisher thrust his hand behind him. 'You'll get it back as soon as you return the one that was intended for me,' he grunted.

'But I don't—' began Sophie, but then, having suddenly realised that the orchestrator of all the ills that had befallen her over the past two days was standing here in front of her, did a swift rethink and went on, considering her words with a good deal more care. 'Unfortunately, I don't have it on me at the moment—I will bring it down to the servants' hall later. Now, I really must get on before I incur Mrs Crayford's wrath.'

With that, she turned on her heel once more and ran up the remaining stairs to the upper floor, reasonably confident that, since both the purse-snatching and the ransacking of her room could now clearly be laid at Fisher's door, the manservant might well think twice before attempting to follow her up onto the attic floor.

Not so. He stared up at her for only the briefest moment, before an uncouth grin spread slowly across his face and he started to climb the stairs after her— only to be suddenly halted in his tracks as the sound of a nearby door opening echoed down the passageway.

'Ah, Fisher—just the man.'

Never in her whole life could Sophie have imagined that she would actually be glad to see the loathsome son of the house hove into view. Fisher, muttering a crude imprecation, hastily regained his former position on the landing and quickly bent down, in order to give the approaching Crayford junior the impression that he had merely paused to tie up his bootlace.

''Fraid I've just kicked over my chamber pot—made a bit of a mess—get someone to see to it, there's a good chap,' called Crayford over his shoulder, as he unconcernedly continued on his way along the corridor and down the stairs.

Taking this opportunity to make good her escape, Sophie scuttled quickly to her chamber where, after dashing inside, she hurriedly locked the door. Not that this fairly basic precaution would necessarily keep her free from harm, she realised, since not only did Mrs Dixon, the housekeeper, possess a full set of keys to every room in the house, but there was also the spare set which hung inside the butler's pantry, in the event of a fire or other emergency. Meaning that just about anyone in the household was free to invade her privacy whenever they might choose to do so.

Gasping for breath and collapsing on her bed, she could not help wondering whether the plodding continuance of her formerly uneventful existence had not been a sight more preferable to the ongoing turmoil of the past couple of days. Not that this unexpected hiatus was likely to last for very much longer, she reminded herself brusquely. Not beyond Tuesday evening, at any rate. Having finally made her attitude clear to him, there was nothing else for her to do but wait and see whether Helstone would have the sense to cease his ridiculous pursuit of her and walk away, leaving her to her own devices. But even as she contemplated the prospect of so bleak a future the haunting image of his very perceptive glances swam into her thoughts and a sudden shiver rippled through her. It would be so very easy to allow herself to succumb to his persuasive entreaties and simply agree to his demands, she thought, as she closed her eyes and endeavoured to recapture the unbelievable thrill of that first breathtaking moment when the Viscount's firm, warm lips had finally made contact with her own. It had been as though every one of her recent dreams had come to fruition, only to find themselves suddenly dashed into a million irreparable fragments and cast to the four winds.

With a soft sigh, she rose to her feet and began to

undo the buttons of her gown. The die, it seemed, was well and truly cast, for had not she herself been the one to cast it? She had made her decision and all that remained was for his lordship to abide by his agreement to respect her wishes. Provided that she held fast to her resolve for the next forty-eight hours or so, she could see no reason why her life should not slide back to its former mundane tenure.

In the meantime, there was still the problem of Fisher to be addressed, but, since the footman was also entrusted with the house messages, it was difficult to see how she was going to manage to get word to the Viscount to inform him of her recent discovery. Even if she were able to persuade young Monks the Boots to take a note, she doubted that she could do so without drawing Fisher's attention to the fact. The problem, it seemed, looked to be insurmountable.

Chapter Eleven

Marcus stared at his brother in disbelief.

'Are you telling me that you have been aware of this Fisher chap's involvement all along?' he demanded, slamming down his glass and rising to his feet in a fury.

'Steady on, old son,' entreated Giles, as he hurriedly thrust out his hand to prevent the still full glass from tipping its contents over the edge of the table. 'The information was passed to me scarcely an hour or so ago. Once we'd got hold of Miss Flint's invoice I deemed it necessary to check out everyone in the Crayford household—I'd already put two men to watching the bookshop, as I told you. Anyway, as soon as it was learned that the footman and the clerk shared the same surname, it was not difficult to put two and two together.'

'And yet you've still not done a thing about it!' Marcus was incensed. 'Soph—Miss Flint's life might well be in danger and you're prepared to sit back and allow that fiend to run loose in the house!'

'Well, I didn't know about the lady's room having been ransacked until you informed me of that fact less than five minutes ago,' returned his brother, in his own defence. 'That sort of information does tend to put a different complexion on the matter.'

'But, if you are sure that these two are your men, why haven't you already had them both taken in charge?'

'Because we don't want to scare off the entire gang, that's why. It would be difficult to arrest the clerk without word getting out, thereby sending the whole bunch of them to earth. Additionally, we have reason to believe that the recipients of the coded message are group leaders—possibly running cells of four or five contacts each—which would explain Fisher's anxiety to get hold of his list of instructions.'

'Which Miss Flint no longer has in her possession!' pointed out Marcus, in some irritation. 'What if he decides to confront her head on? No one in that establishment is going to rush to her defence. I can assure you of that! The son is lily-livered; the woman is a self-centred sycophant and the husband appears to have the wits of a four-year-old!'

'Crayford senior is somewhat advanced in years, that's true.' The Major nodded. 'The blonde pea-goose is his second wife, I'm reliably informed.'

'Yet another fine example of married bliss, I dare say,' grunted Marcus, getting to his feet and glaring down at his brother. 'More than enough to put a fellow off for life! But enough of this chit-chat. Do you mean to sort out this Fisher chap or do I have to deal with the devious swine myself?'

'I think you had best leave the apprehension of felons to the experts, old son,' returned Giles briskly, as he leaned across and reached for the bell-rope. 'It is true that I had hoped to have returned the lady's invoice before matters reached such a crucial stage in the proceedings, but it now appears that I could have been just a little more incisive in my planning—ah, come in, Peters. It would seem that we might have some sort of crisis on our hands.'

Thus it was that, barely five minutes into Mrs Crayford's fervent cross-examination of Sophie, a wide-eyed Hawkins thrust open the drawing room door and stumbled inside, bearing the shocking news that two constables had invaded his kitchen and were now in the process of arresting the footman! At which point the mistress of the house promptly dissolved into one of her habitual vapourish fits and the elderly master of the house seemed unable to do anything other than shake his head at the thoroughly discomposed butler while murmuring, 'Well, 'pon my soul—two constables—in the kitchen—well, 'pon my soul, whatever is the world coming to?'

Since both Arthur and Lydia appeared to be similarly mesmerised by Hawkins's astonishing declaration, Sophie, mentally counting her blessings, realised that some sort of decisive action was required.

'Pray do not distress yourself, Hawkins,' she advised the still clearly shocked butler. 'No fault can be laid at your door, of that I'm sure. Nevertheless, do you not think that it might be wise to return to the kitchen in order to ascertain exactly what is happening? Added to which, I do feel that Mrs Crayford's maid ought to be informed of her mistress's apparent need of her *sal volatile* bottle.'

Then, getting to her feet, she approached Crayford senior and laid her hand on his arm. 'I imagine that you will wish to speak to the constables, sir,' she said gently.

'What—me? Oh, no, I couldn't possibly—Eleanor's the one—she'll sort it all out.'

His bottom lip trembling, he shook his head, refusing to meet her eyes.

'But Mrs Crayford is not well, sir. Hawkins has gone to fetch her maid.'

Receiving no response to her observation, Sophie gave a frustrated sigh and turned her attention towards the other two members of the family, who were now regarding her movements in a fascinated silence.

'Do try to rally your father, Arthur,' she urged him. 'Surely you can see that the poor man is in a considerable state of shock—the constables will be upon us shortly and might well want to ask questions.'

'Why should they want to question us?' returned the youth belligerently. 'We haven't done anything wrong!'

'Do you suppose he has murdered someone?' breathed Lydia, clutching at her brother's arm, her eyes wide with excitement. 'Slit their throat with a carving knife or stabbed them in the back, perhaps?'

'Who? Pa?' exclaimed Crayford junior, impatiently shrugging himself away from her. 'Don't be so stupid! You read far too many of those paltry Minerva mysteries!'

'I was referring to Fisher, you great clunkhead!' retorted the girl crossly. 'And I shall tell Mama what you just said to me.'

'Mama has perfectly good hearing of her own, thank you very much,' came Mrs Crayford's weakly rejoinder, as she thrust herself up into a sitting position. Having discovered that her performance had failed to achieve the effect that it usually commanded, she was not about to allow her governess to take centre stage. 'Help me to my feet, Miss Flint. I need to see what's going on in my kitchen.'

'I have sent for Capstan, ma'am,' said Sophie, hurrying forward. 'Perhaps you ought to wait and take a little *sal volatile* before you involve yourself in anything too energetic?'

'Nonsense!' Mrs Crayford was already on her feet. 'It's clear that the man must have been helping himself to our property—I need to take an immediate inventory of all our valuables in order to see what might have gone missing. Come along, Miss Flint, you can take down the list.'

Raising her eyes to the ceiling, Sophie gave a disbelieving shrug and prepared to follow her employer, only too aware that the exercise in which they were now about to involve themselves was going to prove a total waste of time. 'Might it not be better to go down to the kitchen first and hear what the constables have to say?' she ventured, as soon as they had reached the hallway. 'Perhaps Fisher's misdemeanour has nothing to do with his employment here?'

'Just as long as the dreaded constabulary hasn't advertised its presence to the entire neighbourhood,' moaned her mistress. 'What if that wicked creature has been raiding houses up and down the street? I shall never be able to hold up my head in public again!'

She did, however, agree to visit the kitchen prior to starting on her inventory and by the time they reached the basement Sophie was beginning to feel almost sorry for the footman, whose crimes, in Mrs Crayford's imagination, ranged from petty thievery all the way up to organised crime on the grandest of scales.

* * *

'Sedition?' repeated her employer, staring at one of the constables in some confusion, after he had acquainted her with the charges against Fisher. 'I'm not sure I...'

'Sort of treason, ma'am,' put in the constable helpfully. 'Incitement to riot and all that sort of thing.'

'Not stealing, then?'

Keeping her eyes carefully averted from the spectacle of her only footman standing heavily manacled at the back door, Mrs Crayford sank slowly into the chair that Sophie had had the good sense to position at her rear. 'Thank God it's nothing serious, then,' she murmured, as she clung on to the table-edge. 'But how on earth we are expected to manage without a footman to serve at table defies even my imagination. Why couldn't the selfish creature have put off his stupid sediting until later in the week, I ask you? I can hardly bear to contemplate what his lordship will think of such shoddy service when he next visits us.'

'Oh, I'm sure Hawkins will be able to arrange a suitable replacement by tomorrow evening,' Sophie was quick to assure her, as she cast up a questioning look at the butler who, having recovered from the humiliation of having two burly men of law bursting into his kitchen and apprehending his footman, had managed to revert to his former dignified persona.

'As you say, miss,' he replied gravely. 'I was about to make a similar suggestion myself—I shall deal with the matter first thing in the morning.'

'Well, make sure that you don't get another seditor this time,' snapped Mrs Crayford crossly, as she rose to her feet and prepared to depart. 'You may take yourselves off now,' she added, waving a dismissive hand to the still waiting constables. 'And do try not to cause too much of a commotion outside when you leave. This is a very respectable neighbourhood, you know.'

'But we still have several questions that we need answers to,' insisted one of the men, edging his way forward. 'Where this fellow came from, how long he's worked for you and all that sort of thing.'

'Well, you can hardly expect me to know those sorts of details about people in my employ,' returned Mrs Crayford edgily. 'Hawkins deals with all that kind of thing. He'll tell you anything you need to know. And now, if you will excuse me, I have other far more important matters to attend to.'

The Crayford soiree looked well on the way to becoming quite a resounding success, thought Sophie in considerable surprise, as she took in the bustling scene that surrounded her. The level of noise had already reached ear-piercing proportions and there was scarcely an inch of space to spare in any direction, making the air in both this and the adjoining room decidedly oppressive. The whole event, it would seem, had every sign of turning out to be the sort of crush for which her employer had been craving much of her married life.

Having been the one to whom the task of writing out the fifty or so invitations had fallen, she had supposed that perhaps half of the illustrious personages invited might deign to attend such a lowly gathering. The sheer volume of numbers turning up on the front doorstep, however, had come as something of a shock even to Mrs Crayford, who had been obliged to keep pinching herself in order to convince herself that the whole thing was not some sort of wild, improbable dream.

'I really cannot recall having invited either the

Hetheringtons or the Liskeards,' she whispered to Sophie in awe, as still more guests from the upper echelons of Society continued to pour into the lower hallway. 'I can only think that they must be associates of his lordship's—I did tell him that he was welcome to bring along some of his friends if he wished.'

'Well, he certainly seems to have taken you at your word,' returned Sophie, biting back her irritation. All this, presumably, was another of Helstone's far-flung ideas of attempting to give the Crayfords the impression that she came from much more worthy stock than they had originally supposed. But, whilst it was certainly true that the family's attitude towards her had changed for the better since the Viscount's claim to be a distant cousin of hers, it was not hard to envisage the level of antagonism that would be directed towards her when his assertations were found to be untrue and his visits came to a halt—as they most surely would, once this evening's affair was over.

Craning her neck to seek out Helstone's distinctive dark head of hair, she scoured the room but could see no sign of him. Her heart sank at the thought that, after her unsatisfactory performance of Sunday afternoon, he might well have decided not to attend the soiree, after all.

'Looking for anyone in particular?' came the Viscount's deep drawl, from somewhere in the direction of her left ear.

Spinning around, the tell-tale flush still on her face, Sophie gasped, 'But how on earth did you manage to fight your way through that crush of people without me catching sight of you?'

'I had my driver drop me off as we passed the mews and I came in through the back garden,' he said, motioning her gently towards the nearby terrace doors. 'Nice to know that you were keeping a weather eye out for me.'

Taking in a much needed breath of fresh air as she stepped out on to the deserted terrace with him, Sophie gave a careless shrug.

'I merely wanted to ask you whether the extraordinary number of uninvited guests who have turned up this evening is any of your doing.'

'Well, I have to admit that I did call in a few favours,' he replied, with a somewhat sheepish grin that immediately had Sophie's heart executing violent somersaults. 'But I must confess that I didn't expect them all to be repaid on the one night. I trust that her greatness is suitably impressed?'

'Completely overwhelmed, I should imagine,' responded Sophie, letting out a little chuckle. 'Although I am given to understand that such an unforeseen increase in numbers has made considerable inroads into Mr Crayford's stock of champagne, as well as having put paid to Mrs Crayford's idea of setting up a dance area at the far end of the drawing room, as was her original intention.'

'Now, that *is* a pity,' sighed Marcus, who was finding it almost impossible to tear his eyes away from the tantalising sight of the soft swell of Sophie's bosom peeping teasingly above the low-cut neckline of her hastily redesigned evening gown. 'I'm bound to admit that the idea of holding you in my arms again has enormous appeal—even if it's only to whirl you around the room in time with the music.'

Her mind unable to erase the piquant image his words had conjured up, Sophie stepped away from him, doing her best to manufacture a frown of disapproval. 'You really must desist from making that sort of remark—I was under the impression that we had finally reached an agreement over that matter.'

Marcus offered her what was intended to be a penitent grin. 'You can't blame me if my baser instincts threaten to get the better of me whenever I am close to you.'

Her pulse ratcheting up another notch, Sophie took a steadying breath.

'If you refuse to behave yourself, sir, I shall just have to go back inside.'

'No, please don't.' Marcus caught at her hand. 'I shall try to be good, I promise.'

'You really shouldn't make promises that you have no intention of keeping,' she retorted shakily. 'You have already broken your word to me on two previous occasions. I had always been under the impression that a gentleman's word was supposed to be his bond.'

His eyes darkening in exasperation, Marcus stared down at her, frowning. 'I think you'll find that that much used adage generally applies to financial agreements made in gambling dens and other such unsavoury establishments.'

'And only between persons who number themselves gentlemen, presumably?'

'Goes without saying, I should have thought.'

Her eyes widening in indignation, Sophie drew in a sharp breath.

'Are you saying, then, that a promise given to a lady doesn't require to be treated with the same respect as one you might give to a fellow gambler?'

'Why, yes, of course it does,' he snapped, then, hesitating, began to run his fingers through his hair in a somewhat distracted manner. 'Well, not in the same way, perhaps—the two cases are somewhat different. The first is a matter of honour—no, that's not what I mean. They are both matters of honour, of course but—damn, it, woman! How can you expect me to think straight when you look at me in such a way?'

Then, powerless to prevent himself, he let out a deep groan and, reaching forward, pulled her into his arms, slanting his lips across hers. Caught off guard, Sophie melted into his embrace, moulding her curves into the hard contours of his supreme maleness. Her arms twined tightly around his neck, while every nerve in her body responded to the urgent demands of his lips.

Lost in the wonder of the moment, she felt her senses swim, and nothing else in the world seemed to matter but the wondrously exciting feel of Helstone's arms surrounding her and the hot, insistent pressure of his lips on hers.

'Come away with me, Sophie.' He gasped, pulling away from her just long enough to drag in a lungful of air. 'Come away now. I don't think I can stand another night without you.'

Like a dash of icy water down her spine, the sudden shock of his words shattered Sophie's trancelike state, leaving her stunned and shaken. Uttering a faint moan of distress, she tore herself away from the still heavily panting Viscount and clutched at the stone bulwarks of the terrace in an effort to support her quivering limbs.

'No more, please,' she whimpered. 'Must I beg you to leave me alone?'

'Sophie—sweetheart!'

Marcus, still struggling to master his unsated ardour, took an uncertain step towards her and held out his hand. 'You cannot think that I mean to hurt you, surely?' he asked in astonishment. 'You must know that I would sooner cut off my right hand than—'

Trembling with a mixture of rage and some other unidentifiable emotion that she refused to acknowledge, Sophie clapped both hands against her ears, determined not to listen to Helstone's hollow blandishments.

Incensed, the Viscount whipped out his hand and grabbed at her wrist, wresting her fingers away from her head and pulling her towards him. 'Now you're being foolish,' he growled into her ear. 'Next you'll be telling me that you don't enjoy kissing me, when I know damn well that you do—you couldn't respond in that way if you didn't feel as I do.'

Wrenching herself out of his grip, Sophie stepped back and pointed an accusing finger at him.

'You have shown yourself to be the very worst kind of cad, sir. I have rejected your offer on more than one occasion, yet still you persist in pursuing me. How many more times must I tell you that I do not desire your attentions? Please remove yourself and take your worthless promises with you. You are without morals—no better than that odious little reptile Crayford—and I swear I would rather starve on the streets than submit to your improper suggestions.'

His face paling visibly, Marcus stepped away from her, his dark eyes glittering with some unnamed emotion and his mouth curving in a mocking smile.

'That wish may be granted sooner than you think, if I know anything of your employer's tactics,' he ground out abruptly, before turning on his heel and thrusting his way through the terrace doors that led into the crowded reception room. Then, ignoring the concerted cries of protest from the closely packed mêlée, his lips compressed in fury, he proceeded to elbow his way through

their ranks before taking the stairs down to the hallway
three at a time where, ignoring the waiting butler, he
flung open the front door himself and stormed angrily
out of the house.

Eventually locating his own carriage some hundred
or so yards down the waiting line, he ejected both driver
and groom with a curt dismissal and, after hauling himself up onto the box, spat out, 'Get yourselves a hackney
home—I'll take them myself.'

Hobbes, the Viscount's driver of many years standing, having opened his mouth to protest at such cavalier
treatment, took one look at his master's pursed lips and
rigid expression and immediately thought better of it.

'He's in a rare old pelter,' he muttered to the groom,
as Helstone inched the team out of the line until the
landau was clear and then, cracking his whip at the
leader, set off down the road at breakneck speed. 'Can't
recall ever seeing him that mad before.'

Chapter Twelve

Letting out a sob of despair, Sophie sank back against the stone balustrade, her heart pounding and hot tears welling up into her eyes. How could she have allowed her temper to get the better of her in such a cruel, malicious manner? she asked herself wretchedly. Just because Helstone had failed to control his ardour, it was surely no reason for her to have reacted quite so imprudently?

Angrily dashing the tears from her cheeks with the back of her hand, she gave a trembling sigh, well aware that the real reason behind her hurtful attack on the Viscount's character had stemmed from the fact that he had spoken nothing but the truth—a truth that she had been fighting against ever since he had first walked into her life. A truth that brought about feelings of embarrassment, shame and anguish—hence her hysterical outburst. For, although the Viscount had been the one to bear the brunt of her resentment, she knew quite well that it was she herself with whom she was most angry—for having been so foolish as to allow herself to fall so desperately in love with a man whose dreams and aims were about as far removed from her own as it was possible to be. Yet, now that she had cast him out of her life for ever, she could not help being achingly aware that, when the tears had ceased and the heartache had finally faded away—if indeed it ever did—those sweet dreams would be all she would have left to see her through the dark and dismal days ahead.

'A most edifying scene, I'm sure—although I have to say that I don't care to hear myself being referred to in such a derogatory manner!'

Letting out a sharp gasp of dismay, Sophie whirled round and saw Arthur Crayford, his fleshy lips curved in a malicious smile, climbing the terrace steps towards her.

'You were eavesdropping!' she cried scornfully, turning away from the advancing youth and making for the doors into the reception room. 'How very contemptible!'

'Not as contemptible as your kissing cousin, it would seem,' he sneered, as he quickly stepped around in front of her, barring her way. 'I believe you owe me an apology. Something rather similar to that which you treated his lordship would serve nicely—at least to begin with!'

'Get away from me, you loathsome little beast!' she hissed, backing away from him. 'How many times must I tell you to keep your hands to yourself?'

'As many as you like, my sweet,' he retorted, as he shot out a hand and, grabbing at her wrist, jerked her viciously towards him. 'The more insults you hurl in my direction, the greater the number of penalties you will pay—so I can't really lose, can I? How about that kiss, for starters?'

A ripple of ice cold dread ran through Sophie's veins as she tried frantically to free herself from Crayford's clutching hands. Having dismissed calling out for assistance as a pointless exercise, given the high volume of noise emanating from the nearby reception room, she quickly realised that her only hope lay in trying to manoeuvre her attacker in the direction of the doors and praying that one or other of the guests might witness her predicament through the panes of glass and come to her aid.

Unfortunately, Crayford was already intent on forcing her into one of the darker recesses, well away from the pools of light that shone from the windows of the reception rooms out on to the terrace beyond. Her heart racing with apprehension, Sophie knew that her only option now was to feign weakness. Letting out a weak little moan, she bent her knees and allowed herself to slump forward, which sudden reversal of tactics had Crayford desperately trying to maintain his hold on her.

'Stand up, you stupid bitch!' he grunted, staggering backwards as he strove to pull her to her feet at the same time as trying to correct his own balance.

Quick as a flash, Sophie seized the opportunity and, ducking under his arm, twisted herself away from him and made a desperate leap for the terrace doors. At that exact same instant, the doors flew open to reveal a livid-faced Mrs Crayford, who charged on to the terrace as though all the devils in hell were in pursuit.

'The guests are leaving in droves!' she babbled almost incoherently, drops of her spittle flying in all directions as she prodded the startled Sophie with her furled-up fan. 'Hawkins tells me that Helstone almost had the front door off its hinges in his fury to quit the premises, and now it seems that the rest of his friends

and acquaintances cannot get away quickly enough.
They are all going—every single one of them! I shall
never live down the disgrace as long as I live! This has
to be all your fault, girl! What can you have said to your
cousin to put his lordship in such a dreadful taking?'

'She ain't his cousin, Ma,' interrupted her stepson,
stepping out of the shadows. 'She just happens to be one
of his current ladybirds.'

'Ladybirds?' Mrs Crayford recoiled in distaste, staring at him. 'Kindly explain yourself, Arthur.'

'I was down in the garden, enjoying a quiet blow,
when I just happened to overhear their conversation,'
he replied carelessly, his eyes gleaming with spite as he
cast Sophie a malicious grin. 'Seems our little governess
here is no more his lordship's cousin than I am. One of
his latest demi-reps, more like, judging by what the pair
of them were up to when I chanced upon them!'

Letting out a little snigger at his stepmother's gasp
of horror, he gave a quick nod before adding, 'Anyway,
seems that little bit of business led to them arguing the
toss over something that ended with our Miss Goody
Two-Shoes calling his lordship all the names under the
sun and him storming off in a rare old dudgeon.'

'But that's simply not—' began Sophie, determined
to stop the flow of Crayford's wicked inventions.

'You're not going to stand there and deny that you
called his lordship an immoral cad, I trust?' he interrupted her, a challenging flash in his eyes.

'Well, I—' Sophie said hotly, but then, as the full
gist of her angry outburst returned to her, her cheeks
flooded and she stopped. 'It's not at all how it seems,'
she finished lamely.

'Is Lord Helstone your cousin, or is he not?'

demanded Mrs Crayford, now quite beside herself with rage. 'Speak up, girl!'

Biting her lip, Sophie shook her head. She had known all along that this foolish assertion of Helstone's would lead to trouble eventually. 'He is not,' she replied dully. 'He is merely one of the travellers who were caught in that snowstorm last month.'

'And that was when the pair of you started this *affaire* of yours, I presume?' Icy contempt dripped from her employer's lips.

'We are not engaged in an *affaire*!' protested Sophie. 'His lordship is just a-a—' Racking her brain to find a suitable epithet to describe her relationship with Helstone, she concluded weakly. 'He's merely a casual acquaintance.'

'Well, you must hope that this "casual acquaintance-ship" you speak of extends to his helping you find other employment,' snapped Mrs Crayford. 'Between the pair of you, you have succeeded in turning me into a veritable laughing stock, and I refuse to have you in my house another moment. You will go straight to your room, pack up your belongings and take yourself out of my sight without further ado!'

'But it's after eleven,' returned Sophie in bewildered stupefaction. 'Where am I to go at this time of night?'

'That is hardly my problem, Miss Flint,' said her employer, with an indifferent shrug. 'Having put paid to all my carefully thought-out plans with your outrageous lies and subterfuge—not to mention ruining Lydia's entire future—I cannot imagine why you should think I would wish to concern myself over your welfare!'

'Well, I trust that you intend to pay me my outstanding wages,' retorted Sophie, somewhat defiantly. 'I believe I am owed something in the region of five and a half weeks.'

Raising one supercilious eyebrow, Mrs Crayford raked a contemptuous glance over the passed-on gown that Sophie had so diligently altered. 'And I believe that the value of the gown you are wearing will more than cover that amount—needless to say you will return everything else that my stepdaughter kindly volunteered on your behalf.'

Before Sophie could voice her thoughts regarding Lydia's kindness or otherwise, Crayford junior stepped forward, anxious to have his say.

Having remained more or less silent during the whole of the foregoing proceedings, it had slowly dawned on the youth that if Sophie were to be turned out immediately all chance of bedding her would be lost to him. Whereas if he could just persuade his stepmother to allow the governess to remain until the morning there was every possibility that he might be able to creep into her bedchamber and fulfil what had been a long-held ambition of his. *And wouldn't that be one in the eye for the high and mighty Helstone?* He grinned to himself. *Given that the Viscount seemed to be experiencing a certain amount of difficulty persuading the little lady to part with the goods!*

'Might be better if Miss Flint left first thing in the morning, Ma,' he interjected hastily. 'Wouldn't look too good with the neighbours, her leaving with all her baggage at this time of night—especially after all the guests quitting the place in such a tearing hurry. Plus there was that other unpleasant business with the constabulary on Sunday,' he reminded her, in an effort to add extra fillip to his suggestion.

Pursing her lips, Mrs Crayford considered her

stepson's words. 'You may well be right,' she said, giving
a reluctant nod. 'Very well, Miss Flint. You may stay
until first light—but I refuse to have you in my house a
moment longer!'

Sophie's lip curled in disgust as she registered Crayford's expression of smug complacency, for it hadn't
required a great deal of intelligence to work out what
the devious coxcomb really had in mind. While she was
relieved that his intervention might, in the one sense, be
regarded as something of a temporary salvation, insofar
as keeping her off the streets for the next few hours, it
was also clear that it was going to involve her in a long
and sleepless night, while she kept a tight and vigilant
watch on the doorknob to her room.

Shortly before five o'clock the following morning,
Sophie dragged her heavy hamper down the steps of
the Crayfords' residence and stood staring down at her
pitiful little pile of belongings: one basket, two bulging
valises and a couple of paper-wrapped packages—the
sum total of her worth, she thought grimly.

But as to how she was going to get her possessions to
the coaching station in Piccadilly she still had not the
vaguest idea, even though this particular problem had
been uppermost in her mind for most of the past few
hours.

Just as she had anticipated, young Crayford's attempts
at invading her privacy had started almost as soon as the
last servant had crept off to bed, but, having taken the
precaution of pushing her chest of drawers up against
the locked door, Sophie had been able to sit back and
enjoy listening to the thwarted youth's vicious imprecations as he twisted the doorknob first this way and
then that, in his continual efforts to gain entry to her

room. Those attempts had persisted at varying intervals through much of the night, culminating in what had been his final endeavour, and one that had caused Sophie several moments of real panic, since by this time her tormentor, almost out of his mind with a combination of rage and frustrated libido, had managed to get hold of one of the spare keys to her door. It had been due only to a last-minute brainwave on Sophie's part that this final effort was doomed to meet with a similar fate to his previous sorties.

Realising that it would not be long before his key managed to displace her own, she had hit on the idea of jamming a pencil into the aperture, which had had the desired effect of preventing him from pushing her key out and inserting his own. After spending some ten minutes or more involved in various fruitless attempts to dislodge the obstruction, Crayford had finally given up all hope of achieving his ambition and, cursing Sophie to high heaven, hefted one last violent kick at her door before taking himself off to the library, where he'd set about doing his damnedest to drown his disappointment by way of his father's best cognac.

By that time it had already been past four o'clock, and, heartsick and weary as she was, Sophie had known that sleep was out of the question. She was to be out of the house before the maidservants rose to clean the grates and light the fires, and that was less than an hour away.

After stuffing the last of her possessions into the wickerwork hamper that had been her travelling companion on so many other journeys in her life, she had sat back on her knees and given her mind over to the problem of how to get her belongings down to the front doorstep. In the normal way, a footman would have carried her boxes down the back stairs into the servants' hall and thence out through the basement. However, as she was well aware, the main staircase was the most direct route, and her heavy basket would be far easier to manoeuvre on the carpeting than it would on the rough stone steps that the servants were required to use. With the memory of Mrs Crayford's cruel refusal to pay her what she was owed still ringing in her ears, Sophie, setting her chin defiantly, had made up her mind to flout convention and elected to go for the route that suited her purpose best.

In point of fact, she had been obliged to make her chosen journey three times before her task was complete. Luckily, the resonant ticking of the long-case clock in the hallway, coupled with the sounds of Crayford's strident snoring issuing from behind the closed door of the adjacent library, had all but obscured the soft, steady thump-thump of her basket as she had finally dragged it down the three flights of stairs and into the hallway. Pausing momentarily to catch her breath, she had cast a quick look around to satisfy herself that no prying eyes were there to witness her departure and then, pulling back the bolts on the front door, had let herself out into the cool half-light of the new day.

Now that she was here, however, out on the pavement surrounded by her bags and boxes, she was at a loss to know what to do next. She needed to remove herself from the vicinity of the Crayford house with all possible speed, that much was certain, but how? That was the question.

She stared up and down the street, hoping for some inspiration to strike her, but the only movement she could perceive was that of the lamp-lighter, who was making his laborious way up the street extinguishing all the lamps.

A sudden tug on her skirt-hem caused her a moment or two's anxiety until, peering down through the basement railings below her, she found herself looking into the begrimed and anxious face of Monks, the boot boy.

'What are you—?' she began, but stopped the moment she saw him press his fingers against his lips, in an effort to get her to still her tongue.

'Mr 'awkins sent me to get you an 'ack, miss,' the boy whispered hoarsely, while climbing up the steps and out into the street. 'There's usually a few of 'em in the rank on the corner of Sloane Street—shan't be a tick.'

'But I can't afford a cab,' she cried softly, reaching out her hand to grab the boy before he took off. 'I have barely enough money for my coach fare to Dulwich.'

'Not to worry, miss,' replied Monks with a wide grin, as he delved into one of his pockets and produced a shilling piece. 'Mr 'awkins thought o' that, too. This'll get you as far as the Piccadilly stage, 'e said.'

Hot tears flooded Sophie's eyes as she watched the boot boy's skinny figure tearing down the pavement towards Pont Street. In her role as a governess she had been neither fish nor fowl, insofar as her position in the hierarchy of the household had been concerned, and although she had always treated her fellow employees with the utmost respect, she had continued to feel something of an interloper whenever she had had cause to venture into the servants' hall, as a consequence of which, she had elected to take her meals in the nursery wing, along with her two young pupils. So to discover that the butler had held her in such esteem that he was willing to go to these lengths on her behalf was almost unbelievable, and quite the most uplifting thing that had happened to her for some little while.

Within minutes a hackney carriage rounded the corner of Lennox Gardens and, with the boot boy's assistance, Sophie had little difficulty in stowing her belongings into the cab's luggage basket. When the time came for her to take her seat, however, her heart was so full that it was as much as she could do to stop herself from flinging her arms around the beaming youngster and kissing his grimy cheek.

'Oh, 'ang on a minute!' said the boy, grasping hold of the handle and pulling open the door again. 'Nearly forgot—Cook sent you this.' And, thrusting his hand into another of his pockets, he withdrew a neatly wrapped package. 'Thought you might get peckish on the journey,' he added. 'Seein' as 'ow you ain't 'ad any breakfast.' And then, after bestowing another of his cheery grins on her, he turned tail and scampered back down the basement steps, soon to disappear from her sight.

Brushing away her tears, Sophie leaned back against the squabs and closed her eyes, thinking how very sad it was to have learned of the kind-heartedness of her fellow employees at this late stage of their association. She prayed that their actions would remain undiscovered, for she was left with no illusions as to the way in which the vindictive Mrs Crayford's mind worked.

The fare, on her arrival at the Piccadilly coaching station, was exactly one shilling, just as the butler had predicted, and having found himself strangely moved to witness his passenger's distress on departing from her abode, the elderly jarvey even hauled himself down from his box and helped Sophie carry her baggage into the station's left luggage department, accepting her grateful thanks but brushing away her offer of the single groat that she had found in her pocket.

'You keep it, miss,' he said gruffly. 'Buy yourself a nice 'ot drink to steady them nerves.'

After thanking the driver once again, Sophie turned her attention towards the booking office. Having tied her four half-crowns carefully into a handkerchief, for she had no intention of being deprived of her wealth on this occasion, she had kept the handkerchief tucked safely inside her glove. The six mile journey from the staging post in Dulwich had cost three shillings when she had set out to take up her employment at the Crayfords' some months earlier, and she could only pray that the fares had not increased in that time. The baggage clerk had already informed her, on handing her a ticket, that it would cost her sixpence to retrieve her possessions, and she did so want to be able to hand over to her mother as much of what was left of her sadly depleted store as she possibly could.

She had just booked her seat on the midday coach—at an increased cost of three shillings and ninepence, to her dismay—when she felt a gentle tap on her shoulder and, swinging round, found herself staring up into the apologetic face of the hackney driver.

'Nearly left one of your parcels behind, miss,' he said ruefully. 'Found it right at the bottom of the basket when I was about to load up another fare. I oughter've checked more careful, like. Very sorry, miss.'

Eying the package as he passed it over to her, Sophie felt her heart give a little jerk, for it was none other than the atlas that Helstone had procured on her behalf and which she had rewrapped with the intention of returning it to him.

'No harm done,' she assured the jarvey, and thanked

him again for his diligence, conscious that many another
driver would simply have kept the package and sold its
contents for personal gain. 'It was very good of you to
go to the trouble of returning it.'

'No trouble, miss—I hadn't left the yard.'

And, tipping his hat at her, he backed away and disappeared into the thronging mêlée.

Sophie stared down at the parcel in dismay. Short of
paying for another left luggage ticket, which she could
ill afford, she was going to have to carry the hefty package around with her until the midday coach departed—
some six hours hence! She had originally intended to
while away the intervening hours by walking in Green
Park, and possibly visiting one or other of Piccadilly's
circulating libraries, where it was possible to sit and read
newspapers and periodicals without fear of interruption.
But having to carry so large a parcel about with her was
going to hamper her freedom quite considerably. She
frowned. The dratted book had caused her nothing but
problems from the outset! She had a good mind to—

She clapped her fingers against her lips, her eyes
lighting up with excitement. But of course! The answer
was staring her in the face. She would take the atlas back
to Broomfield's shop and persuade the bookseller to
buy it back from her! Helstone had admitted paying ten
shillings for it, so Broomfield would surely be prepared
to part with seven or eight! The walk to Maddox Alley
would help to kill time, and she could eat the breakfast
that Cook had so kindly prepared for her in Berkeley
Square gardens. The sun had come up, heralding what
looked set to turn into a fine warm day. With a determined smile, she straightened her shoulders and, tucking
the parcel firmly under her arm, set out in the direction
of Broomfield's store.

* * *

'I'd soon be out of business if I was to buy back every book I sold, young lady,' argued the bookseller, as he thrust the atlas back at her.

'But I'm not asking you to pay back the full amount,' protested Sophie, in desperation. 'Even half would do, and you would still make a handsome profit when you next sell it.'

'The way things are going, I could be out of business in a week,' returned the man morosely. 'What with constables trashing their way though all my goods yesterday, and then marching young Fisher off in irons, leaving me with a great pile of unfinished invoices to sort out, I doubt I'll ever find the time to sell another book.'

'Your clerk has been arrested?' cried Sophie, clutching wildly at a possible solution to her problems. 'I can see that that must make things very difficult for you. You are clearly in need of some help.'

'Not easy to get hold of anyone suitable round here,' sighed Broomfield, seeming almost glad to have found someone to whom he could express his grievances. 'Only took the lad on on account of being acquainted with his widowed mother, and now I'm told that both he and his brother have been mixed up in some plot to do away with some high-flown peer of the realm—wouldn't tell me which one, of course, and what it's all got to do with my bookshop, I can't begin to imagine.'

'I can see that it must be very difficult for you,' said Sophie, giving him a sympathetic nod. 'As it happens,' she then added, being careful to exhibit just the right amount of diffidence, 'I am well versed in the intricacies of double-entry book-keeping—as a qualified school-mistress...' Crossing her fingers behind her back, she drew in a deep breath and went on, 'I dare say I could probably stay and help you out for an hour or two, if that would be of any use to you?'

'You mean that you would be willing to sort out those bills for me?' asked Broomfield in amazement, jerking his head towards the huge pile of paperwork that could be seen on the desk in the rear office. 'I've been at it myself half the night, but my eyesight's not what it used to be, and what with customers interrupting—' He stopped, somewhat embarrassed, then endeavoured to hide his confusion by pulling off his spectacles and rubbing them briskly with the hem of his none too clean apron.

'I can stay until half-past eleven,' stated Sophie firmly, as she started to remove her pelisse. 'I must be at the coaching station by twelve, in order to catch the stage, and—' Pausing, she drew in a deep breath. 'You must pay me for my time, of course—I shall require ten shillings.'

'Ten shillings?' returned the bookseller at once. 'That's a great deal of money just to write out a few paltry invoices.'

Sophie raised an eyebrow. 'You would prefer to attend to them yourself?' she enquired sweetly. 'And by my estimation there are close in the region of fifty or sixty—scarcely a few.' Reaching out a hand for her discarded pelisse, she eyed him sternly. 'Ten shillings, Mr Broomfield, and in addition you may keep the atlas. Otherwise…'

'All the invoices?' he asked, his bleared eyes darting back to the pile. 'Every single one.'

'Every one—providing that I can make a start on them right away.'

'Ten shillings it is, then,' he said, backing out of the room. 'I'll leave you to get on with it, shall I?'

'Let me know when it's half-past eleven,' she called out to him, as he quietly closed the door.

Sixty-three invoices later, Sophie at last laid down her pen and, climbing down from the high stool on which she had been perched for the past four hours, pressed her hands into the small of her back to relieve the dull ache and stretched her shoulders. It had been touch and go, for there had been a good many inconsistencies in Mr Broomfield's figures and she had actually run out of ink at one point, necessitating a hurried call to the bookseller to replenish her pot. Since he had been serving a customer at the time, she had been obliged to waste several precious minutes until he could attend to her request. Now the job was done, however, and she was ten shillings to the good, making all her scrupulously checked figuring well worth her while.

'It's just on a quarter past the hour,' Broomfield pointed out, when she re-entered the shop. 'You'll find your ten shillings next to the cash box.' He eyed her enquiringly. 'You wouldn't care to take on the position full-time, I suppose?'

Sophie stared at him, considering. Might his offer be more preferable to going back home to be a burden on her mother's slim resources? she wondered. But then, realising that to accept the position would mean having to take lodgings somewhere in the nearby vicinity, she gave a reluctant shake of her head. The chances of running into Helstone in this area were far too great and a prospect to be avoided at all costs.

The previous evening's ugly confrontation, coupled with its disastrous consequences, had taught Sophie a valuable, if heartrendingly painful lesson, making it vital that she put as much distance as was possible between herself and the Viscount. She could hardly help but be aware of the fact that it was due entirely to his continual interference in her life that the whole compass of her existence had turned completely upside down. Having dissembled his way into the Crayfords' favour, with his disarming self-assurance and thoroughly irresistible smile, Helstone had then carelessly, but quite determinedly, set out to seduce her—very nearly achieving his aim with that unforgettable kiss; a kiss that had unlocked a wild and passionate facet to her nature, the like of which she had not realised lurked deep within her being. Her shock and dismay at being confronted with her own apparent inability to resist the Viscount's highly intoxicating charms had been the real reason for her sudden rage, followed by a primeval urge to unleash her fury on the root cause of her distress.

But then, as she bade the disappointed bookseller farewell and set out for her journey back to the Piccadilly change to board the stage to Dulwich, it was with doleful realisation that it came to her that, despite everything that had happened, that same unanswerable question still continued to niggle at her thoughts. What might have been the outcome had she agreed to Helstone's proposition?

Mentally admonishing herself for her wayward thoughts, she did her best to dismiss the Viscount from her mind altogether and endeavoured to concentrate her efforts on trying to conjure up some sort of acceptable explanation for her mother, since the whole unvarnished truth behind her sudden dismissal from the Crayfords was not a matter that Sophie was keen to share with her estimable parent.

In the event, Mrs Pendleton-Flint was so dismayed at learning of Sophie's constant battle to keep the son of the house at bay during her short tenure with the Crayfords that she could only express her gladness that her daughter had managed to escape the residence with her virtue still intact. Sophie, however, was honest enough to admit to herself that it was not the oleaginous Arthur Crayford who had posed the greatest threat in that particular regard, but the rakish Marcus Wolfe, with his teasing smile and that breathtakingly challenging glint in his eye, the poignant memory of which was to prove the cause of many a damp pillowcase during the long and sleepless nights that followed.

Chapter Thirteen

The reins hanging limply in his hands, Marcus peered abstractedly into the cloudy night-time gloom that surrounded the carriage. From the distressed sound of his horses' breathing, it would seem that he had run the poor beasts into the ground—an action for which he felt bitterly ashamed—in addition to which, he had not the faintest idea of where he had finally pitched up.

Having set off out of Lennox Gardens with no clear idea of where he was heading, the red mist of anger that filled his head had obscured everything but the need to remove himself from the hurtful echo of Sophie's bitter accusations. The toll-gates at Hyde Park corner and Kensington Gore figured vaguely in his memory, as did passing the gates of Chiswick House, but beyond these easily recognisable landmarks his mind was a total blank. That he had travelled some goodly distance at speed was only too apparent from the foam-flecked hides of the two wheelers who were now pawing at the ground in restive agitation.

Cursing himself for an insensitive fool, Marcus grabbed the handful of cloths that Hobbes kept tucked behind the driver's seat and, lowering himself carefully down from his perch, inched his way through the gloom to examine the leaders. Murmuring soothing words of comfort as he worked, he wiped away the excess of sweat from the animals' drenched coats, covering their shuddering backs as best he could with an assortment of rugs and other articles that he found in the box.

Raking his fingers through his hair, he peered around him. From the narrowness of the lane that they were on it was clear that he must have turned off the turn-pike at some point, but where, and—more to the point, perhaps—why?

Casting his mind back, he did have an indistinct recollection of slackening the reins and letting the leaders have their heads, but where in God's name had the beasts taken him? With only the dim and gradually diminishing light thrown out by the carriage's twin oil lamps to light his path, Marcus inched his way slowly up the lane in the hopes of coming across a gate or other such feature of the landscape that might point him in the direction of a dwelling-place of some description.

Just at that moment the scudding clouds chasing across the night sky parted momentarily, to allow the full moon to shine down on the scene in all her glory, causing Marcus to blink several times before he could believe the evidence of his eyes. But, even as he threw back his head to let out a whoop of sheer disbelief the moon disappeared to obscure his view once more. Not that the Viscount needed any such light to guide him through the gates of Bradfield, which, as had been clearly revealed in that single instance, lay scarcely twenty yards distant from the very spot on which he was now standing! The clever beasts had brought him back to his ancestral home!

Shaking his head in wonder at the extraordinary ingenuity of these four-legged marvels, he took hold of the leader's harness and set out to guide the exhausted animals up the lane towards the wrought iron gates that opened on to the Bradfield estate. A single pull of the bell brought the elderly lodge keeper, his nightshirt flapping beneath a hastily donned drab woollen overcoat, tottering out of the front door of the lodge.

'Very sorry, your lordship,' gasped the man, as he drew back the bolts and began to pull open the gates. 'Wasn't warned to expect you.'

'Sorry to get you up, Cutler,' returned Marcus, adding his weight to the older man's efforts. 'Didn't know I'd be here myself until a short while ago.' *And that's something of an understatement, if ever there was one,* he thought to himself, with an inward grimace. 'You get yourself back to your bed—I can shoot the bolts myself as soon as I've got the carriage through.'

'If you're sure, sir?'

At the Viscount's insistent nod, the lodge keeper, clutching his coat about his bony frame, hobbled back to his door, where he stood for some moments watching in total confusion as the heir to the earldom led in the clearly shattered four-horse team along with their carriage but minus both driver and groom.

Unleashing the horses from their traces singlehandedly proved to be a rather more exhausting procedure than Marcus might have imagined, but, being reluctant to rouse any of the grooms or stable lads from their hard earned slumbers, he doggedly persevered with his self-imposed undertaking until all four animals were unharnessed, rubbed down, watered and safely in their

stalls. Only then did he turn his attention to the problem
of getting himself into Bradfield Hall without waking
up the entire household—as hammering on the great
oak front door or tugging at the bell-pull would most
surely do.

The Hall, as he knew, would be well and truly
secured against intruders—thanks to the diligence of
Warren, his father's major-domo, who took a personal
pride in seeing that every one of the Hall's many entry
points was safely locked and bolted before he retired
for the night. Since it was now close to three o'clock in
the morning, Marcus doubted that anyone in the house
would still be awake.

*Looks as though it's going to have to be the well-tried
route of previous misadventures,* he thought gloomily, as
he made his way round to the rear of the building, past
the succession houses and into the neatly kept kitchen
gardens. *Thank God the clouds have blown away. At
least I'll have enough light to see by should I happen
to fall and break my neck!*

Eying the ancient walnut tree that stood in the centre
of the garden with a certain amount of trepidation, for
it was a good many years since he had been obliged
to use this method of entry into his bedchamber, he
was heartened to observe that the single upper branch
that reached as far as his windowsill still looked strong
enough to support his weight. Whether he was still
sufficiently agile to accomplish the tricky manoeuvre
remained yet to be seen. His bedroom window, he was
relieved to note, had been left in just the way he always
demanded, revealing a welcoming gap of two to three
inches in its top sash.

Unbuttoning his jacket, he flexed his shoulders and,
after taking a deep breath and casting up a prayer to

the heavens above, swung himself up onto one of the walnut's lower branches and started to climb.

Some ten or so minutes later, his hands and face having both been badly scratched in the process of achieving his goal, he found himself balanced somewhat precariously with his left knee on the windowsill of his bedroom and his right foot perched on the none too steady branch of the tree, whose ominous creaking sounds were beginning to cause him serious concern.

Reluctantly letting go of his secure hold on the branch above his head, he grappled feverishly with the window's lower sash, eventually managing to hoist it upwards sufficiently to allow him to haul the upper part of his body across the opening where, breathless from his exertions, he remained motionless for some moments, both legs still dangling limply over the outside sill.

A sudden noise from within the room had him lifting his head in alarm, whereupon, gathering up the remains of his strength, he started to heave himself over the windowsill—only to find himself being grasped by the seat of his breeches and dragged with considerable force into the room, to be dropped, face-first and none too gently, onto his bedroom carpet.

'Righto, my lad,' came Giles's unruffled voice close to his ear. 'That's quite enough of— *Good God! Marcus?*'

'Get your knee out of my back, there's a good chap,' begged the Viscount, gingerly rolling himself over and up into a sitting position as soon as his startled brother had gathered enough wits to comply with his request. 'Obviously not quite as fit as I thought I was,' he added wryly.

'A good deal more dicked in the nob though, it would seem,' retorted Giles, as he reached out a hand to help

Marcus to his feet. 'I took you for a burglar, you blithering idiot! What the devil do you think you're at, sneaking into the house in this underhand manner? What's wrong with the front door, may I ask?'

'As it happens, I was doing my best to avoid waking the entire household,' returned his brother irritably, peeling off his soiled and ripped jacket and shirt and tossing them to one side. 'So, unless you want the whole lot of them down on our heads like the proverbial ton of bricks, I suggest you try and keep your voice to a minimum.'

'Yes, but why *are* you here?' asked Giles, lowering his voice but still staring at Marcus in confusion. 'Last I heard, you were off to do the pretty at the Crayfords'. The fragrant Miss Pendleton-Flint give you your marching orders, did she?'

'You could say that, I suppose,' muttered the Viscount abstractedly, as he threw himself down onto his bed to lie glowering at the silken underside of his tester. 'Seems I lost my temper, somewhat, and made a fool of myself into the bargain!' Swinging his legs over the side of the bed, he sat up with a rueful half-laugh. 'Can't think what's got into me of late—I don't usually behave in such a crass manner—must be getting old!'

'Or just in love, perhaps?' murmured his brother, not quite *sotto voce*. 'It does tend to hit you like that, I'm told.'

'What the hell are you talking about?' returned Marcus impatiently. 'Miss Pendleton-Flint and I simply agreed to disagree and that's all there is to it.'

'Then why are you getting so riled up about it?' asked Giles, eyeing his brother steadily. 'There are plenty of other fish in the sea—as I've heard you remark often enough in the past.'

And with good cause, thought Marcus, with a wry twist of his lips. *But none of them like Sophie.* He closed his eyes in a vain attempt to conjure up the image of her face. Sadly, all he achieved was a resounding echo of the hurtful recriminations that she had thrown at him. 'I was simply trying to make the poor girl's life a little more bearable,' he grunted, clenching his fists. 'It makes me really angry to think of the way that godforsaken bunch of social misfits treat her.'

'Such righteous altruism does you real credit, bro,' observed his brother, with a dry laugh. 'And there was I, thinking that your interest in the female was purely carnal!'

A faint flush covered the Viscount's cheeks as Giles's dart hit the mark. Frowning slightly, he gave a dismissive shrug. 'I won't deny that I find myself very attracted to her—she is so utterly different from any other female I've ever come across. She is so bright and intelligent, and incredibly resourceful, yet she is constantly put upon by her employers—she even spends her own hard-earned cash on books for the schoolroom, would you believe? And yet those misbegotten savages treat her as less than nothing—it makes my blood boil just to think of it.'

Getting to his feet, he began to pace the room. 'I just wanted to get her out of that blasted house. She deserves so much better. If you could have seen her at that tavern, Giles,' he went on, his eyes softening at the memory. 'There didn't seem to be any problem that she wasn't prepared to tackle—I swear that I've never come across anyone quite like her in the whole of my life. In fact, I wouldn't mind betting that more than one of her fellow travellers could well have perished in that snowstorm had it not been for Sophie Flint's down-to-earth capability and sheer dogged determination—she even had me milking a blessed cow—did I tell you that?'

'I believe you may have mentioned it once or twice,' said his brother, turning away to hide the grin that was forming. 'Nonetheless, bro, you know the rules as well as I do—defenceless virgins are out of bounds to men of our class, and as for offering virtuous spinsters such as your little governess a *carte blanche*, I find myself questioning your sanity—apart from which, I should have thought that those two little beauties you already have in your keeping were more than enough for any reasonable man to contend with!'

Giles's pointed reference to Livvy Rayner and Cynthia Bedlington brought Marcus's pacing to a sudden halt. 'Not that it's any of your damned business,' he returned curtly, 'but it just so happens that arrangements are already in hand to discontinue both of those associations.'

Giles let out a long low whistle. 'You're paying 'em off—just like that?' he asked incredulously. 'A touch on the heartless side after all these years, don't you think?'

'Hearts have no place in business arrangements of that sort,' retorted the Viscount, striding over to the mirror to inspect the damage to his face. Grimacing at the livid scratch across his left cheek, he picked up a towel and proceeded to dab at his blood-streaked visage. 'Surely the whole point about setting up a mistress is that one is able to do away with all the emotional claptrap and enjoy a purely physical relationship without any unnecessary ties. Both Livvy and Cynthia were well aware that the association would end some day. And, in case you are wondering, I have made sure that neither one of them will be the loser. I have arranged to have the deeds of their houses made over to them both, along with suitably generous dowries commensurate with their past efforts on my behalf.' A slightly cynical smile crept across his lips. 'I take leave to doubt that it will take either lady long to find herself a new protector.'

Turning to face his brother, he offered him a slightly rueful grin. 'In fact, one could say that both of the little minxes have been shoring up their futures at my expense for quite some time now—if the recent accounts from Rundell and Bridge are anything to go by!'

Although Giles was somewhat taken aback at Marcus's relatively casual parting with his two paramours, both of whom, insofar as his brother was aware, had been under Helstone's protection for well over three years, it took the Major no time at all to realise that this sudden decision of the Viscount's was yet another indication of his growing preoccupation with the Crayfords' impoverished governess.

'So, having disposed of both Miss Rayner and Miss Bedlington to your satisfaction,' he said, eyeing his brother in some disapproval, 'I take it that you were assuming that Miss Pendleton-Flint would be falling over herself to step into the vacancy—which, I must assume from your rather crushed demeanour earlier, is the opposite of what actually occurred when you put the suggestion to her?'

As Sophie's bitter accusations assailed his memory once again, Marcus flinched. Shaking his head in weary rebuttal of his brother's uncannily accurate construal of that unpleasant scene, he said, 'I'd just as soon not discuss the matter any longer, if it's all the same to you, Giles. Suffice to say that I was deeply concerned about the lady's situation and merely harboured a desire to see her in a more fitting environment. However, since Miss

Pendleton-Flint has elected not to accept my offer of help, the subject, as far as I am concerned, is now well and truly closed.'

'Sounds rather more than just a business arrangement you were offering the unfortunate lass, if I'm any judge,' Giles retaliated, as he headed for the door. 'However, enough of your problems. I fear my bed is calling me.' Pulling open the door, he hesitated slightly, then, turning back to face his brother once more, he added, a sly grin forming on his face, 'Although, after what I've gathered from your singular obsession with her, it occurs to me that you might just as well go the whole hog and marry the girl, if you want my opinion!'

'Which I don't!' retorted Marcus, as Giles stepped hurriedly out into the corridor and closed the door behind him. *I can just picture Father's face if I walked in and announced my intention of legshackling myself to a down-and-out nobody who has been forced into earning her living as a governess,* he thought scathingly, as he wrenched off his damaged pantaloons and dived under the coverlet of his large four-poster.

Not that there was anything at all dishonourable about having to earn one's living as a governess, he then amended, somewhat shamefaced that such an idea should have even crossed his mind. *In fact,* he reflected, as the image of Sophie's sweet smile drifted into his mind, *if one were to consider it objectively, dedicating oneself to the education of young children might well be considered to be rather an honourable profession. And as for being a nobody—why, hadn't her father been a highly decorated lieutenant-colonel in one of His Majesty's top hussar regiments? One could hardly class such a fellow as a nobody. And, whilst Sophie's upbringing may have been a touch irregular by conventional standards, it was abundantly clear that her parents had made no concessions, insofar as strict discipline and correct standards of behaviour were concerned—as he, to his eternal damnation, was well able to testify!*

As the memory of those discomfiting episodes surfaced once more, Marcus let out a loud groan and, rolling over onto his stomach, buried his head in his pillow in an effort to blot out the deeply disturbing images that continued to assail his thoughts. But it was no good. The harder he tried to rid his head of all thoughts of Sophie, the more his wayward brain insisted upon seducing his mind's eye with yet another tantalising depiction of her presence: Sophie in that hideous lace cap—Sophie washing dishes—Sophie throwing snowballs—feeding ducks—swans… God! Was there nothing in the world that didn't remind him of the woman?

And then, like a clarion call, his brother's closing shot resurfaced in his mind. He shot upright, his heart pounding in rapid disorder. Dragging in a deep breath, he flung back his bedclothes, heaved his legs over the side of the bed and, for several long moments just sat there, totally impervious to the chill night air as it wafted over his naked flesh, scarcely able to comprehend the impossible thought that had succeeded in worming its way into his brain.

'Damned if I don't do just that!'

No sooner had he spoken the words out loud than everything seemed to fall neatly into place. It was really quite simple, now that he had really given the matter some thought. He had to marry some time, after all; for months now his father been pressing him to attend to his duties and responsibilities as heir to the estate and, rather than settle for one of a number of mealy-mouthed, whey-faced debutantes, fresh from the schoolroom, whose names were sure to figure on his parents' list of suitable bride fodder, he would shackle himself to Sophie Pendleton-Flint!

The more Marcus thought about it, the more appealing the whole idea seemed. As far as he was concerned there was nothing about Sophie that might prohibit her from becoming his Viscountess. She was not only lovely to look at; she was graceful, intelligent and endowed with a rare common sense to which decidedly few females of his acquaintance could lay claim. But, above all else, she was the most fascinating creature that he had come across in all his days.

And so utterly desirable, of course. It was difficult to recall his ever having wanted any woman as badly as he wanted Sophie; his whole body ached with desire just at the thought of making her his wife. He had handed both of his regular mistresses their *congées* without a single pang of regret, since neither Cynthia's pert blonde curvaceousness nor the doe-eyed Livvy's sultry Latin magnetism had the power to captivate him any longer; only the warm glow of a pair of summer blue eyes and the promise of untamed flowing chestnut tresses now had that ability.

Sliding under the covers again, he lay back and closed his eyes, ready for sleep at last, satisfied that the only hurdle that stood in the way of his future plans was his father's possible opposition. Once he'd dealt with that problem, he mused idly, as he felt himself drifting off to sleep, it merely remained to acquaint Sophie with his revised proposal…

As it turned out, both the Earl and the Countess were so relieved to see their elder son safely returned to the fold after such an extended absence that it was some little while before he was able to turn their attention to the subject that had been exercising his mind since the moment he had surfaced from the highly erotic dream-world of his slumbers.

'As a matter of fact,' he said, in answer to his mother's anxious query as to how long he intended to remain at Bradfield on this occasion, 'I do have something of an announcement to make—I trust it will meet with your approval.' Pausing, he dragged in a deep breath, conscious of the questioning stares of his listeners. 'I am pleased to inform you all that I have decided to take a wife.'

The astounded silence that followed this declaration was broken only by Giles's spluttering cough as the piece of ham he had been chewing became lodged in the back of his throat, threatening to choke him.

Getting to his feet and striding around the break-fast table to administer a hefty thump to his brother's back, thereby relieving his discomfort, Marcus took the opportunity to shoot the scarlet-faced Major a warning look, indicating that *he* would be the one to decide about which aspects of Sophie's history his parents might need to be apprised.

Resuming his seat, he turned to face his still stunned father and said, 'In case you might be wondering, sir, the lady's name is Miss Sophie Pendleton-Flint. It is my intention to bring her to meet you both sometime in the very near future. I would be glad to have your assurances that you will be prepared to receive my— fiancée—and welcome her into the family.'

A suspicious glint in his eye, the Earl regarded his son silently for some moments before saying, 'Somewhat out of character for you, isn't it, this sudden need to observe the proprieties?'

Swallowing the retaliatory retort that had instantly sprung to his lips at his father's contentious barb, Marcus curled his fingers tightly round the stem of his glass. 'Comes to all of us in the end, I dare say,' he said, striving to maintain his temper. 'I should have thought you would be glad to hear that I am finally prepared to meet your demands and relieve you of some of the burdens you carry.'

'Enough, you two. I beg of you!' interposed the Countess, reaching out to grasp hold of her son's clenched fingers. 'This is no time to re-enact past grievances! We must look to the future and I, for one, cannot wait to meet your chosen wife, Marcus. Miss— um—Pendleton-Flint, did you say? It is not a name I recognise—is the family new in Town?'

'The lady is not one of the current crop of debutantes, if that's what you're asking,' returned Marcus hurriedly, as he rose to his feet in preparation of quitting the room before either of his parents could embark upon a surfeit of awkward questions that he was not, in all conscience, fully confident that he was equipped to answer. 'Suffice to say that she is twenty-three years of age and her father was, until his death at Waterloo, a greatly admired and highly revered lieutenant-colonel in one of His Majesty's elite hussar regiments. And now, if you will please excuse me, I have a most pressing matter to attend to—I hope to be able to furnish you with further information regarding my forthcoming nuptials within the next day or so.'

Hardly had he left the room, however, before Bradfield, turning to his younger son, demanded, 'Out with it, Giles! It's quite clear that you know a good deal more about this matter than you are prepared to admit. Has that fool of a brother of yours got some young hussy in the family way and thinks to present us with his by-blow, or what?'

'Really, Edward!' protested Lady Susanna, tossing down her napkin and getting to her feet. 'You have spent the past month bemoaning the fact that Marcus refuses to come home and take up his duties, yet no sooner does he show his face than you are ready to malign him all over again. Little wonder he prefers to remain in Town with his friends. And now, when he has brought us this most thrilling piece of news—which, if I may be so bold as to remind you, is something we have been waiting to hear for some two years or more now—all you can do is reduce it to gutter level. You should be ashamed of yourself, referring to your son's betrothed in such a tawdry manner!'

'Calm yourself, my dear,' exclaimed Bradfield, as he reached for his walking stick and levered himself up out of his chair. 'I have no desire to distress you in any way, as you well know. But I surely do not need to point out that the boy seems to derive a great deal of pleasure from causing me as much aggravation as possible, and I fear that this latest ploy might well turn out to be yet another one of his—'

'I think not, sir,' put in Giles hastily, having registered his father's rapidly heightening colour and taut neck muscles—both warning signs that pointed to a swift rise in the Earl's blood pressure, a situation to be avoided at all costs, given the gentleman's weakened heart condition. Whilst Marcus's announcement had come as something of a bombshell to him, he had observed his brother's cautionary glance and had resolved to keep his counsel. Now, however, torn between a real concern for his father's health and a sense of loyalty towards his older brother, he felt that it was impossible to remain totally silent.

'I have met Miss Pendleton-Flint, sir,' he said. 'And I can assure you both that the young lady is, beyond question, entirely respectable.'

'And Marcus really means to marry the girl?'

Hesitating only briefly, the Major nodded. 'It would appear so,' he confirmed.

'Then this is truly wonderful news,' exclaimed his mother, clapping her hands in delight and turning once again to her husband. 'We must hold a ball to celebrate this great event, my dear!'

'Best wait until Marcus gives you the all-clear on that, Mother,' put in Giles hurriedly. 'You know how he is apt to dig his heels in if he thinks he's being coerced.'

'Only too well,' retorted the Earl moodily. 'A more obstinate example of manhood I have yet to come across.'

He stood for some minutes, idly tapping his finger against his lips, then, turning, exclaimed, 'I have it now! Pendleton-Flint! I had a feeling that the name rang a distant bell but I couldn't quite place it.'

Giles, who had spent some time trying to track down Sophie's father's past history without success, hastened to his father's side and, after helping him into a nearby chair, asked eagerly, 'You were acquainted with the family, sir?'

'Not as such,' replied Bradfield, his brows knitting together in concentration as he endeavoured to dredge up a vague recollection from almost half a century earlier. 'However, if my memory serves me aright, there was a chap at university—couple of years my senior, he was—name of Joseph Flint. Anyway, the *on dit* at the time was that this Flint fellow had been contracted in marriage to the daughter of his father's best friend—one Sir Jacob Pendleton by name. It appears that some sort of pact had been agreed between the two families when the youngsters were still in leading strings—something to do with the complicated entails of both estates, I believe. I wasn't really that interested at the time. I do, however, have a pretty clear recollection of the fact that young Flint was expected to add the Pendleton name to his own upon the actual marriage.' He frowned. 'The Pendleton girl's name escapes me, I'm afraid, although I do seem to remember being told that the poor lass died in childbed barely a year after the marriage had taken place.'

'And the child—did the poor mite survive?' the Countess was keen to know.

'Must have done,' Giles felt constrained to point out. 'A son too, one presumes—otherwise the conjoined name could not have carried on this far.' Then, turning back to his father, he asked, 'Any idea from which part of the country these Flints and Pendletons hailed, sir?'

Lips pursed, the Earl again racked his brain. 'Somewhere in the North Riding, I believe—Harrogate Spa, possibly—I vaguely recollect some tomfoolery regarding a proposed visit to the baths there. Flint seemed pretty well acquainted with the town, if I remember correctly.'

'And this Pendleton fellow was a baronet, you say?'

'Could have been merely a knight—can't be certain, either way—although I definitely recall Flint referring to the fellow as *Sir* Jacob. You could try looking him up in an old Debretts, if you have a mind to, Giles. I believe we still have a copy of the 1802 original somewhere in the library.'

At her husband's words, the Countess beamed. 'It would appear that Marcus's betrothed might not be without a certain standing, then,' she said, heaving a sigh of satisfaction. 'Although why he feels the need to be so very cagey about the young lady, I really cannot imagine. One would think he had something to hide!'

Chapter Fourteen

'*What are you saying, man?*'

'I have been advised to inform your lordship that Miss Flint is no longer resident at this address,' repeated Hawkins somewhat warily, the image of Helstone's violent and precipitate exit of the previous evening still vividly imprinted in his memory.

Marcus stared down at the manservant in stunned disbelief. *No longer resident? Impossible! Less than twelve hours had elapsed since he had quit the Crayford premises the evening before.* He frowned. Clearly the butler had been instructed to deny him access—a decision which, insofar as the mistress of the house was concerned, might be considered a rather daring and somewhat foolish move on her part. Although hardly surprising, perhaps, in the light of his abysmal display of temper on his last visit.

'I see,' he said, as he struggled to maintain a grip on his rage. 'Then perhaps you would be good enough to ask your mistress if she could spare me a few moments of her time?'

'I'm afraid Mrs Crayford is not at home, sir,' the butler intoned, his expression wooden. 'Perhaps your lordship would care to leave a card?'

Not at home to me, you mean, thought Marcus sourly as, with a brisk shake of his head, he turned to leave. Having had it made clear to him that he was *persona non grata* insofar as the Crayford household was concerned, the exasperated Viscount was obliged to accept that any further advances from himself were certain to be similarly rebuffed. And, as if that humiliation were not more than enough with which to cope, he was obliged to face up to the fact that Giles—the only person he might have called upon to act as his emissary—had just chosen to embark on some sort of wild goose chase up into the wilds of North Yorkshire, thereby requiring Marcus to shelve all his hastily garnered plans of matrimony until such time as his brother should choose to return.

Not that there's any real point in Giles trying to ferret out any of Sophie's long-lost relatives, he told himself, as he steered his curricle around the mass of vehicles battling to enter Hyde Park for the morning promenade. *I just hope he doesn't spend too long at it, that's all, since he's the only one who can be relied upon to gain admittance into the Crayfords' house and persuade Sophie to agree to meet up with me.*

His dark eyes gleamed with satisfaction as he conjured up her look of delight when he finally announced his altered intentions towards her—a vision that caused him to spend the remainder of the drive back to his Grosvenor Square mansion in blithe contemplation of the various ways in which Sophie might choose to reward him for providing her with so magnanimous a compromise to her earlier opposition.

* * *

Having noted her daughter's uncharacteristically withdrawn demeanour, Mrs Pendleton-Flint could only suppose that Sophie's time with the Crayfords had been rather more of an ordeal than her daughter had been prepared to divulge and she endeavoured to do what little she could to try to take the girl's mind off the experience. By sending Sophie down to the village shops daily on some pretext or other, and keeping her actively involved in as many domestic activities as was possible in such a small household, she sought to encourage her daughter to concentrate her thoughts more firmly on the here and now, rather than dwelling on the past.

Three days had now elapsed since Sophie's enforced flight from the Crayford residence and, although she did her utmost to disguise her unhappiness, the memory of the bitter words she had flung at Helstone on the evening of the ill-fated soiree still continued to haunt her, threatening to reduce her to tears at the most inconvenient times and bombarding her senses with the same unanswerable questions. *How might it have been had she accepted Marcus's proposition? For how long might such a fragile relationship have stood the test of time? Was it possible that he might, eventually, have come to love her in the way she loved him? On the other hand, and, most testing of all, could she really face a future knowing that she would never set eyes on him again?*

As if on cue, the tears would start to well up again and she would be obliged to make some hurried excuse to take herself out into the small back garden, where she would try to busy herself with the tying back of lavender, or some other mundane occupation, in an effort to prevent her mother from witnessing her anguish. And so the interminable days, coupled with the never-ending nights, drifted drearily by.

Returning to the house on the third afternoon of her enforced visit, bearing the small packet of baking powder of which her mother had insisted she was in dire need, Sophie was surprised to see a rather sumptuous-looking travelling chariot drawn up in the street outside the front doorstep. For one foolish moment her heart soared with joy as the thought that Marcus had sought out her whereabouts, having found himself unable to stay away from her, leapt into her mind. One careful look at the painted crest on the carriage's door panel, however, soon disabused her of this idea, for she had seen enough examples of the Helstone family crest on the tableware at Laurel Cottage to have committed the device of an upright lance to enduring memory.

With a disappointed sigh, she made her way into the living room, where she perceived her mother in conversation with a sweet-faced, rather plump lady of middle years, her elegant silk travelling outfit proclaiming a certain affluence. At her entrance the stranger rose immediately to her feet and hurried towards her, hands outstretched and the widest of smiles on her face.

'Oh, my dear Miss Pendleton-Flint! How pleased I am to have finally found you! Elizabeth has spoken of you with such affection—you cannot know how glad I am to be able to thank you at last!'

'Elizabeth? I'm afraid I don't…' began Sophie, only to find herself enveloped in the visitor's arms, her face pressed into the lady's very ample bosom.

'To think that without your aid my poor little Lizzie might well have died,' exclaimed the now quite tearful stranger when she finally set Sophie at arm's length, only to continue to gaze at her in the most disconcertingly soulful manner. 'And that dear little baby—oh, it really doesn't bear thinking about!'

At last Sophie began to understand. It was now obvious that the surprise visitor was none other than the recently delivered Mrs Lucan's mother—the lady to whom the Lucans had been on their way to visit when the snow blizzard had waylaid their coach on that fateful afternoon now some weeks distant.

'Do please sit down and finish your tea, Mrs—?'

Guiding the still weeping matron back to her seat, Sophie shot a questioning glance at her mother.

'Mrs Egremont,' interposed Mrs Pendleton-Flint hastily. 'It seems that the family has been searching for you ever since Mrs Lucan told her mother what a help you had been to her in her hour of need.' Since Sophie had favoured her mother with only the briefest of outlines in respect to that particular occurrence, the unexpected visitor's disclosure had come as something of a revelation to Mrs Pendleton-Flint.

'And it was not until the dear child happened to remember that you had mentioned the name of your brother's school in Dulwich that we were able to make any sort of headway,' sniffed Mrs Egremont woefully, as she dabbed at her tear-drenched cheeks with a lace-edged handkerchief. 'His lordship—Jack's father, as you are no doubt aware—even went to the trouble of engaging two Bow Street runners to seek you out, but to no avail. Although, it is true that they were told to search for a Miss Flint, of course. In the event it was not until your brother's headmaster informed me that Roger's full name was, in fact, *Pendleton*-Flint that we were finally able to ascertain your whereabouts.'

'But I still don't understand why you felt it necessary to go to such lengths to track me down,' exclaimed

Sophie, considerably puzzled. 'What I did was no more than anyone would have done under similar circumstances.' She paused as a sudden awful thought occurred to her, before adding, in a somewhat hesitant voice, 'I trust that your daughter has made a full recovery from the unfortunate experience?'

'Oh, yes, indeed, my dear,' purred Mrs Egremont, leaning forward to clasp Sophie's hand in hers. 'Both she and the babe are thoroughly blooming, thanks to your sterling efforts.'

'Perhaps it would help if I were to acquaint Sophie with a few more of the details…?' ventured Mrs Pendleton-Flint, having registered the still totally bewildered expression on her daughter's face.

'Oh, yes, please do,' replied their visitor, heaving a deep sigh of relief. 'I'm afraid I do seem to become somewhat beside myself whenever I am forced to dwell on what might well have been the outcome of that dreadful occasion, had it not been for the timely intervention of your brave girl.'

And so quite calmly, and in as straightforward a manner as was possible, given the somewhat emotional convolutions of Mrs Egremont's original outpourings, Mrs Pendleton-Flint set about furnishing her daughter with the bones of the Lucan couple's history, from which it soon became apparent that Sophie's chance involvement during that snowbound episode had achieved more than simply helping to bring about the safe delivery of the pair's firstborn child. It had, it seemed—rather more importantly from certain points of view, as it transpired—secured the ongoing line of the Lucan family, along with the not inconsiderable earldom of Whitcombe and all its attached estates.

Having been denied Mr and Mrs Egremont's

permission to marry their seventeen-year-old daughter, the current earl's younger son, the Honourable John Lucan—Jack to his friends—had, it seemed, persuaded his childhood sweetheart into a secret elopement, whereupon, following their overnight dash to the Scottish border to exchange their vows, he had taken her across the Irish Sea and set up residence in a rural retreat in Waterford, from where the pair had cut themselves off from both of their families.

Some eighteen months later, however, finding herself about to give birth to her first child, the young Elizabeth had insisted upon returning to England in order that she might avail herself of her mother's support during her coming confinement. Safely back within the family folds, following their unfortunate incarceration at the inn, however, the pair had been confronted with the tragic news that, shortly following their elopement and self-appointed exile, Jack's elder brother Charles— heir presumptive to the Whitcombe title—had met his death in a riding accident. The ancient title had thereby passed to Jack and, of course, his wife—Mrs Egremont's daughter Elizabeth—who, it seemed, now rejoiced in the lofty title of Her Ladyship the Viscountess Bingham.

'So it would seem that Master John Henry Lucan has inherited a rather more significant role in his family's history than one might have imagined at the time,' exclaimed Sophie, shaking her head in wonder at the amazing tale.

'Both families' histories,' averred Mrs Egremont firmly. 'Lizzie, being Mr Egremont's and my only child, stands to inherit all of her father's lands, which just happen to march in tandem with the Whitcombe estate, making her little boy heir to what will, in all probability, end up as being amongst the largest estates in the entire county!'

Reaching out her hand, she again gripped hold of Sophie's and as the tears began to tumble once more from her eyes went on, 'Had you not been there in that tavern, my poor, sweet Lizzie might well have perished along with her son, meaning that every last inch of Mr Egremont's property would have gone to some unknown cousin of his in the Antipodes. So you will now, perhaps, begin to appreciate the depth of our gratitude to you!'

Pausing momentarily to wipe her eyes, she then turned to Mrs Pendleton-Flint, adding, 'We—both of the families, that is—would very much like to do something to express our truly heartfelt appreciation to your daughter. Can you think of anything that might serve to show our gratitude?'

'Oh, no, really,' put in Sophie with a horrified gasp. 'That is quite unnecessary, I assure you!'

'Absolutely imperative, as far as our families are concerned, my dear child,' returned Mrs Egremont, a look of determination in her eyes. 'His lordship has instructed me to brook no refusal—apart from which, my Lizzie would never forgive me if I were to allow you to go unrewarded for your efforts on her little son's behalf. Surely there must be some way in which we can all show how grateful we all are?'

Sophie was in something of a quandary. From a purely acquisitive point of view she could not help thinking that a nice fat purse full of gold sovereigns would come in very handy, given her family's present financial situation, but, mindful of her mother's teachings, she was also perfectly well aware that any suggestion of a monetary reward would be considered decidedly vulgar.

Her thoughts a complete blank, she sat absent-mindedly chewing at her bottom lip until, in a sudden flash, it came to her.

'Well, then, what I really would like, more than anything,' she said, her eyes shining with anticipation, 'is the chance to reacquaint myself with young John Henry and his mother.'

'Oh, my dear!'

As the ready tears sprang once again into Mrs Egremont's eyes, Sophie was safe in the knowledge that nothing she might have chosen could have had the effect of pleasing their visitor more than this simple request, and, after casting a quick glance at her mother's face, she knew that she had done the right thing.

'What a splendid idea!'

Their visitor was quite beside herself with excitement.

'You shall travel home with me this very afternoon—with your mama's permission, of course?'

A questioning look in Mrs Pendleton-Flint's direction assured the now highly exuberant matron that this suggestion met with Sophie's mother's instant approval and, despite Sophie's tentative reservations regarding the woeful inadequacy of her wardrobe, her protests were immediately thrust aside and pooh-poohed as being of less than no importance.

And so it was that, scarcely half an hour later, having carefully repacked her basket with the most suitable of her belongings, Sophie found herself comfortably ensconced upon the pale blue velvet squabs of the Earl of Whitcombe's luxuriously appointed travelling chariot, about to begin the journey to the Egremont residence at Littlewick Green.

* * *

Three days having passed since he had commissioned a man to keep watch on the Crayford property, in the hopes of waylaying Sophie as soon as she emerged, her total non-appearance was more than enough to cause Marcus considerable disquiet. For it was now beginning to look as if the butler had spoken the truth when he had informed the Viscount that the governess was no longer in residence.

Whatever that might mean, thought Marcus, almost out of his mind with despair as, pacing backwards and forwards across his study floor, he raked his fingers distractedly through his hair. *But if Sophie wasn't at the Crayfords', then where the devil was she? It was beyond thought that, having finally managed to track her down following her departure from the inn, he could have been so arrogantly reckless as to allow her to slip through his fingers once again and, this time—God forbid—possibly out of his life for ever!*

Such a prospect was more than he could bear even to contemplate. As total misery washed over him, he sank wearily into a nearby armchair, dropping his head into his hands and letting out an anguished moan. *He just couldn't lose her! He loved her, damn it—he loved her!*

As the full implication of his unuttered words finally hit him, Marcus started back, his eyes widening in disbelief. *Where in God's name had that thought sprung from?* he asked himself incredulously, but then, the more he pondered the matter, the more it began to dawn upon him that his almost total preoccupation with Sophie was considerably more complicated than the simple fact of just wanting to get her into his bed—which he did, of course. That went without saying. In fact, if he were to be honest with himself, the sheer idea of making passionate love to her had ballooned into an all-encompassing desire more powerful than any he had ever experienced throughout the multi-faceted history of all his past *affaires*. But, alongside all of that, it seemed that, without his having been aware of it he had also acquired a deep, almost primitive urge to cherish and protect her and keep her safe from harm. All part and parcel of what one might reasonably expect from a man in love, he thought with a wry grimace, achingly aware that his constant cajoling of Sophie to become his mistress could hardly be regarded in a similar vein. *Small wonder that she had called him a cad.* It would be nothing short of a miracle if he ever managed to persuade her to forgive such reprehensible conduct, let alone agree to become his wife!

Filled with a sudden self-loathing, the Viscount began to take stock of the all too numerous misdemeanours of his recent history, and it gradually began to dawn on him that, at twenty-nine years of age, it was high time he put aside his juvenile resentment towards his father and started conducting himself in the manner that might be expected of one who had at least been born a gentleman—well past time, in fact, to wave an unregretted farewell to all the drunken carousing, gambling, casual assignations and other such excessive behaviour of the past six years and make a start on trying to repair the breach that had opened up between himself and the Earl.

All of a sudden it began to dawn on him that all he really needed to bring true meaning to his life was Sophie—with her at his side, who knew to what heights he might climb, what goals he might achieve? He pulled in a ragged breath, painfully conscious of the fact that,

before this highly appealing vision of an unparalleled
future with Sophie at his side was likely to come to fruition, he had first to find her. Having wasted precious
time sitting around kicking his heels, waiting for Giles to
return from his errand in the north, in the hopes that his
more diplomatically inclined brother might gain entry
into the Crayford establishment in order to ascertain
their governess's whereabouts, Marcus was no longer of
a mind to wait another second. Swearing that he would
beard the lion's den himself, and have the information
out of the Crayfords' supercilious manservant even if
he died in the attempt, he rose to his feet and started for
the door.

He had taken scarcely two steps across the room,
however, before there came a tentative tap on the door—
which then opened to reveal his butler, bearing a sealed
letter on a silver tray.

'An urgent communication from Major Wolfe, your
lordship,' intoned the man. 'One of his fellows has just
brought it round.'

*Thank God! Giles must have finally returned from his
abortive mission in the wilds of Yorkshire! Now things
can really get moving!* was Marcus's initial thought, as
he stretched out his hand to relieve Danson of his missive. Breaking open the note's seal, he hurriedly scanned
the short and decidedly cryptic message therein.

Grillons. With all poss. speed. Giles.

Having long ago given up trying to fathom the con-
voluted workings of his brother's mind, Marcus let
out a sigh. Crucial though his own mission was, the
simple brevity of Giles's message seemed to indicate
a more pressing urgency, causing the Viscount to feel

that he had little choice but to comply with the Major's summons.

'Have my curricle brought round immediately, Danson,' he ordered as, reaching to one side, he quickly retrieved his hat and gloves from the chair on which he had impatiently tossed them upon his earlier return from a fruitless consultation with his agent in Lennox Gardens.

Upon stepping into the foyer of the Albemarle Street hotel, the Viscount was greeted by Giles who, holding up his hand to silence his brother's questions, proceeded to hustle the thoroughly mystified Marcus up the stairs and through the door of one of the hotel's premier suites where, seated on an armchair by the fireside, the Viscount perceived an elderly female, elegantly clad in a most expensive looking and extremely well-cut gown of lavender coloured silk.

At her visitors' entry the lady rose gracefully to her feet and, holding out her hands, walked forward to greet the two men.

Executing a respectful bow in the lady's direction, Giles said, 'May I present my brother, Viscount Helstone, ma'am?' And to Marcus, 'Allow me to introduce you to Miss Catherine Pendleton—Sophie's great-aunt.'

Chapter Fifteen

From her vantage point at the head of the elegant curving staircase that led down into the Whitcombes' sumptuously appointed ballroom, Sophie anxiously scanned the faces of the guests thronging below, doing her best to persuade herself that there was no real likelihood of Lord Helstone being among their number. Nevertheless, having only just learned this very afternoon that her hosts, the Earl and Countess of Whitcombe, numbered his lordship's parents among their many acquaintances, along with the further information that his family seat was situated barely ten miles distant from Whitcombe Abbey, she could not help but be aware of the fact that the chances of running into the Viscount at so prestigious a function were not entirely beyond the realms of possibility.

Given that scarcely a single day had gone by since her departure from the Crayfords' without the vivid image of Helstone's angry features forcing itself into the forefront of her mind, causing her to have to relive once again the heated exchange of their final parting, it was difficult for her to suppose that he would be prepared even to exchange polite greetings with her—far more likely that he would simply cut her dead, she thought despondently. But then, with a wan smile and brief shake of her head, she was obliged to dismiss such a foolish notion as being totally unworthy of consideration, well aware that, despite his unfortunate shortcomings in certain matters, Helstone would never stoop to such unworthy behaviour. Added to which, she reminded herself, now that her circumstances had undergone such a drastic change there was always the possibility that he might even begin to regard her in an entirely different light…

'Come along now, my dear—that posse of handsome *beaux* you've acquired look to be growing impatient.'

Shaken out of her pensive reverie, Sophie turned to observe Frederick Egremont approaching. Her lips curved in welcome as he joined her, for she had made a firm friend of Elizabeth's genial father during the short time she had been with the family—so much so that it had been Mr Egremont to whom she had gone for advice after receiving the extraordinary missive from her mother telling her of the visit from her late father's aunt—a Miss Catherine Pendleton, apparently—who had come bearing the news that Sophie's brother, having inherited their great-grandfather's title, along with a not inconsiderable fortune, was now in a position to designate himself *Sir* Roger, landed baronet!

Sophie, on the verge of packing her bags and returning to her mother's side, had been dissuaded from doing so by Mr Egremont who, having perused the letter rather more thoroughly than she in her breathless excitement had done, had directed her attention to the hastily

scribbled post script on its rear, which exhorted Sophie
to remain where she was for the present, since both her
mother and brother were about to set out for Harrogate,
with their recently acquired relative, in order that they
might be on hand to deal with the various legalities that
had arisen as a result of Roger's unexpected elevation.

Although she was, naturally, thoroughly delighted
to hear of her brother's good fortune, Sophie could not
help feeling just a little piqued that Mrs Pendleton-Flint
had elected to make such a momentous journey without
her daughter's support. Even the discovery of the very
generous banker's draft attached to the letter had failed
to lift her spirits entirely, until both Elizabeth and Mrs
Egremont had taken her gently to one side to point out
to her that—since she had been unreasonably stubborn
in her refusal to accept even one of the many gifts that
both families had done their very best to press upon
her—the timely arrival of such largesse would go a long
way towards affording her the independence to deal with
her own oft bemoaned lack of suitable finery.

Sophie, who had been growing increasingly conscious
of the shabby state of the three simple muslin gowns that
she had brought with her, but had been firmly polite in
her refusal to take advantage of Elizabeth's very generous offers to supplement her meagre wardrobe, had
very soon been brought to see the wisdom of her new
friends' advice. As a result, she had very soon found
herself—following a hastily arranged visit from the local
modiste, along with the inevitable measuring and pin-
ning sessions—the thoroughly overwhelmed owner of
a whole new set of such gowns and accessories that, in
her previous existence, would have been totally beyond
anything she could ever have imagined.

No sooner had it been confirmed that Elizabeth was

well enough to receive visitors than, exactly as Mrs Egremont had predicted, the invitations had started to roll in with increasing regularity, culminating in a hectic whirl of non-stop activity, in which Sophie had found herself very much a part. Morning visits, afternoon pic-nics, routs, soirees and musical evenings, not to mention two full dress balls, had filled almost every hour of the two weeks that had passed since her arrival at Egremont Hall—all of which ought to have left her with no time to dwell upon the rift between Helstone and herself. And yet with each day that passed, and despite all outward appearances to the contrary, the ache in her heart had deepened and the painful memory of their final meet-ing had grown more and more turbulent. But she had skipped through the measures of the various dances with apparent cheerful abandon, favouring each of her newly acquired admirers with the same bright-eyed smile, and neither they nor her hosts had ever been led to suspect the true depth of her inner despair.

The welcoming smile that she now bestowed upon Elizabeth's father as she greeted him, however, was entirely genuine as, tucking her hand into his arm, she allowed him to escort her down the stairs into the Whit-combes' crowded ballroom.

'One or two of them are inclined to be a little over-powering,' she confided, referring to his earlier remark concerning the growing number of dashing young blades who constantly vied for her attention. 'Lord Bentley keeps sending me the most ridiculous poems—likening the colour of my eyes to a blue jug that stands on his mother's washstand!'

Letting out a loud guffaw of laughter, Egremont patted her hand. 'You should be grateful that the young buffoon didn't choose to use the slopbucket as an analogy!'

'Oh, I am, believe me,' she said, chuckling softly as the two of them made their way across the room to join the group presently paying court to the radiant new Viscountess Bingham. 'Especially as he also mentioned that my hair colour put him in mind of a well-polished hessian boot!'

Marcus, who in the normal way would never have even contemplated putting in an appearance at an event such as the Whitcombes' annual ball, had found himself—owing to a sudden indisposition on his father's part, coupled with the fact that his brother Giles was heavily engaged in tracking down yet another group of subversives in the capital—called upon to escort his mother to the affair.

Ever since that fateful day when Giles had ushered him into Catherine Pendleton's suite at Grillons' hotel the Viscount had been battling with a depression so entrenched that he frequently found it difficult to drag himself out of bed in the mornings. From the moment that the elderly lady had started on her tale the realisation that his cause was lost had hammered itself into his brain. His dismay at learning that his brother had actually managed to make contact with one of Sophie's relatives had been such that his mind had barely managed to register all but the barest details of the explanatory tale that Miss Pendleton had so painstakingly unfolded.

It had transpired that Sophie's father, Jonathan Pendleton-Flint—the baby son of the ill-fated Joseph Flint of Marcus's father's memory—having been raised in the bosom of his dead mother's family had, at the age of twenty-two, formed what his somewhat autocratic grandfather, Sir Jacob, had termed 'an undesirable association' with the local schoolmaster's pretty daughter,

Amelia Dwyer. Having recently inherited the not inconsiderable fortune left to him by his late father, Jonathan
had chosen to defy the old man's instructions to curtail
the friendship and had instead gone off to marry the
young woman, who was, in time, to become mother to
both Sophie and Roger. The young Pendleton-Flint, in
pursuit of a long-held ambition, had purchased himself
a commission in a dragoon regiment that had then been
garrisoned in the nearby town of York, thereby beginning a distinguished career which, by virtue of his continuously outstanding courage in the face of the enemy,
had seen him awarded various battlefield honours and
ultimately achieving the rank of Lieutenant-Colonel—
at which point his highly successful military career
had reached its untimely end during the last decisive
battle of the long drawn-out war against the Emperor
Napoleon.

Despite her father having disowned his grandson,
and forbidden his daughter Catherine to communicate
with him, it seemed that Miss Pendleton, who had been
Jonathan's primary carer throughout his childhood, had
by dint of various underhand subterfuges managed to
keep in touch with her nephew during the early part of
his career. But as the years had progressed, with the
Pendleton-Flints constantly on the move across the
continents, contact between Jonathan and his aunt had
gradually petered out, and it had been several years
since Catherine had heard anything from her nephew.

Unfortunately, Sir Jacob had not received the report
of his grandson's demise until he himself had also been
on his deathbed. In fact, it was the opinion of his elderly
daughter that it had been the unexpected shock of this
harrowing news that had finally pushed the old man
over the edge.

Having been made aware that her nephew had fathered a family, Catherine had then made every effort to trace the whereabouts of the remaining Pendleton-Flints, but it had not been until Major Wolfe had finally tracked her down that her quest was to succeed at last. Contacting Sophie's mother had then proved to be surprisingly simple, once Catherine had provided the two men with the name of Roger's school in Dulwich since—as might have been expected, had they but been aware of it—it turned out to be the selfsame one at which his father had been educated.

Forced to consider the fact that whatever reason he might once have had for finding Sophie could now be of no consequence to anyone but himself, and unable to confront the prospect of any tentative overture on his part being dismissed out of hand, Marcus had elected not to accompany the Major and Miss Pendleton on their visit to Dulwich. Subsequently, upon being advised that the Pendleton-Flints had left for the North Ridings, along with their newly acquired relative, Marcus had naturally assumed that Sophie must be travelling with her family. Having finally been forced to face up to the fact that she had gone out of his life for ever, he had shut himself up in his library and proceeded to drink himself into a life-threatening stupor in a vain attempt to expunge all thoughts of her from his mind.

The consequent hangover he had suffered as a result of this massive over-indulgence had caused him to review, yet again, the pointless emptiness of his chosen lifestyle, and no sooner had he judged himself fit enough to travel than he had called for his curricle, his thoughts agog with newly formed aspirations of making peace with his father, relieving him of the greater part of his burdensome duties and generally fulfilling all the Earl's earlier expectations of the heir to his vast estate.

These ambitions, as Marcus was soon to find out, were more easily imagined than achieved, since Bradfield was inclined to view his recalcitrant son's unexpected reformation with a good deal of suspicion—particularly after the Viscount had been forced to admit that the promised engagement of which he had spoken had hit something of a snag and would not now take place.

Nevertheless, and in spite of these unfortunate drawbacks to his somewhat high-flown intentions, the Viscount had managed to buckle down and stick to his guns, and for the past week or so the better part of his days had been filled with the perusal of account books and stock sheets, visits to tenants to discuss property repairs, renovations and so on, along with the overseeing of various planting and breeding programmes with which the estate was involved. All of which, he had been somewhat surprised to discover, had turned out to be rather more satisfying ways of spending one's days than he had formerly supposed.

Not so the nights, however, which had continued to present him with an entirely different problem, and one that persisted in proving utterly unsolvable, no matter how hard he endeavoured to resolve it. Whilst he had no reason to suppose that locating Sophie would involve him in any great difficulty, he was still left with the highly unpalatable fact that he had, on more than one occasion, attempted to persuade the former governess into becoming his mistress. How could he now seek her out and profess his undying love and devotion after having shown her so little respect in the past? Now that Sophie was protected by the wealth and security of her brother's fortune and title, any unexpected keenness on his part to renew their former acquaintanceship must only be regarded with her deepest mistrust, and would surely damn him for ever in her eyes—always supposing that Sophie even chose to receive him, which, after that last violent interchange between the two of them, Marcus was inclined to believe there was every reason to doubt.

And so, night after night, the never-ending search for some sort of answer to this vexing dilemma continued to govern the Viscount's thoughts, playing havoc with his sleep patterns until, as the first shrill cock-crow pierced the dawn of each new day, he would force himself reluctantly from his bed, do his best to banish his growing wretchedness to the back of his mind, and make every effort to occupy the whole of his attention with whatever mundane task his father had chosen to test him.

'…and you must come and say hello to John's wife—you may recall having met her at the Egremonts', when she was just a girl.'

With a sudden blink, Marcus jerked himself back to reality. *Pay attention, man!* he chided himself impatiently, hurriedly stifling the yawn that threatened, and hoping against hope that his mother was of a mind to limit her attendance at this function to the very barest minimum that civil courtesy might demand.

Bending his head over the hand that the new Viscountess was holding out to him, he murmured the accepted polite phrases, barely glancing up at her face as, thrusting out his own hand to the young man at her side, he mumbled, 'Your servant, sir.'

'I doubt that you will remember John, my lord,' came Countess Whitcombe's breathy tones at his shoulder. 'He was probably away at school when you were last…'

'*By all that's holy! It's our Mr Wolfe!*'

Viscount Bingham's startled ejaculation at once shook Marcus out of his semi-torpid state as, with a perplexed frown, he forced himself to focus his attention on the young man whose hand was still grasping his own. Then, his brain suddenly clearing, realisation hit him in a blinding flash. There in front of him stood the young father-to-be from that godforsaken inn from which all his present problems had sprung! Viscount Bingham and Jack Lucan were one and the same man! *But Lucan? It was hardly possible—his family had known the Lucans for most of his life! How in God's name could he have failed to make so obvious a connection?*

His mind in a state of utter confusion, he found himself being hustled in the direction of a group of guests that had congregated nearby as the young Viscount's voice rang out excitedly, 'Do look, Sophie. You'll never guess who I've got here!'

Sophie?

Marcus's heart stuttered to a standstill as one of the splendidly attired young women turned a questioning face in his direction. 'Sophie!' he stammered in disbelief, as he reached out towards her.

Chapter Sixteen

'My lord.'

Ignoring Helstone's outstretched hand, Sophie lowered her eyes and dipped him a respectful curtsey. Her shock at seeing Marcus descending the stairs some minutes earlier had almost brought her to her knees, with only Egremont's quick thinking preventing her from actually sinking to the ground. And, although her hurriedly concocted tale of having caught her heel in the train of her evening gown had seemed to satisfy her concerned escort, it had very soon come to her that it was simply a matter of time before she would be required to confront the Viscount face-to-face.

As the minutes dragged by, with her every nerve attuned to the looming threat of his approach, she had struggled to keep the rising panic at bay. Eventually, by using every tool at her disposal, she had managed to steel herself to turn and greet him in a relatively calm and dignified manner.

'Your lordship is well, I trust?'

Utterly transfixed by the heart-wrenchingly lovely vision that stood before him, Marcus found himself lost for words. Gone were the prim hairstyle and dowdy grey dress of the one-time governess's previous lifestyle, and in their stead a riotous tumble of shining chestnut curls and a stunning gown of oyster-coloured satin, whose clinging folds seemed to accentuate every single one of its wearer's only too memorable curves, and whose fetchingly low-cut neckline served merely to emphasise the entrancing creamy swell of her shapely bosom.

Conscious of several pairs of eyes upon him, Marcus finally managed to marshal his stunned senses into reciprocating Sophie's curtsey with a polite bow and the standard exchange of courtesies, before forcing himself to stand aside and allow her to return to her friends—whereupon he found himself having to drag in a hefty breath in order to quell his aching awareness of her all too captivating presence barely three feet away from him. Try as he might, he found it difficult to concentrate his attention on the conversation that was going on around him.

'…knowing him as Mr Wolfe, and never having met his lordship before, it simply never occurred to me,' Bingham was explaining to the group. 'Besides which, of course,' he added, shooting his prettily blushing wife an affectionate grin, 'I was more immediately concerned with Elizabeth's problems at the time! Thanks to our dear friend Sophie—or Miss Pendleton-Flint, as I should more properly refer to her—everything turned out just splendidly!'

Amidst the general murmur of laughter and approval that followed these remarks, Lady Susanna turned to her son in some confusion.

'Did he say Pendleton-Flint?' she asked, a bewildered frown furrowing her brow. 'But surely that is the—'

'Not now, Mother, if you please!' muttered Marcus urgently, catching hold of her arm and manoeuvring her firmly out of Sophie's earshot. 'I would prefer that you didn't mention that particular matter just at the moment, if you would be so good.'

'Ah, yes, I remember now,' returned his mother with a perceptive nod. 'You did tell us that your plans in that direction had gone somewhat awry, as I recall.' Her eyes travelled shrewdly towards Sophie who, having returned herself to the safety of her former companions, gave the impression of being fully engrossed in whatever the earnest-looking young man at her side was telling her. 'Such a pity. The girl is rather lovely—as indeed are those diamonds around her neck. The family is quite well-to-do, I imagine?'

'So I believe,' grunted Marcus, eyeing Sophie's eager attendant with some disfavour. His attention having been distracted by rather more emotive issues at the time, any jewellery that Sophie might have been wearing had totally escaped his notice.

'I presume that there is no reason why you may not ask the young woman to dance?' Lady Susanna then enquired of him. 'Even supposing that the two of you have had some sort of a fall-out, I cannot imagine that Miss Pendleton-Flint would be so ill-mannered as to refuse such a request.'

'If you don't mind, I had just as soon...' began her son, but then, after a slight pause, during which his mother seemed to discern some sort of inward tussle taking place, Marcus twisted his lips in a somewhat wry smile. 'Why not, indeed?' he said finally.

Thrusting his way into the circle that had again

surrounded her, Marcus manoeuvred his way to Sophie's side and sketched a brief bow. 'May I crave the pleasure of this next dance, Miss Pendleton-Flint?' he asked, his fingers mentally crossing as he awaited her reply.

'Oh, dear—I'm not certain that—I believe another gentleman…'

Having finally managed to bolster herself sufficiently to perform the customary exchange of courtesies, it had not escaped Sophie's attention that Helstone had lost little time in distancing himself from her. She had done her best to hide the pain this obvious lack of interest on his part had caused her by endeavouring to focus her attention on the words of her nearest companion. But to suddenly discover the Viscount standing there in front of her had the effect of catching her badly off guard and barely able to muster her thoughts.

'For old times' sake, perhaps?' murmured Marcus softly, willing her to meet his gaze as he held out his hand.

Unable to prevent herself, Sophie raised her eyes to his, only to catch her breath as she read the patent appeal therein. Oblivious to the muttered protests that were emanating from several of her followers, and as if in a dream, she found herself laying her hand in Helstone's and allowing him to lead her out on to the dance floor where, as she was soon to discover, a waltz was already in progress, with several other couples energetically engaged in showing off their capabilities.

'I appear to have cramped the style of one of your admirers,' observed Marcus as, executing a nimble side step in order to avoid collision with an over-enthusiastic pair who were about to barge into them, he dextrously swung her into the fast moving mêlée of dancers.

'Lord Murcheson.' Sophie sighed, casting a distracted

look over her shoulder to register the look of simmering fury on the face of the young man from whose side Helstone had just removed her. 'Although I feel obliged to point out that he does have the right to look somewhat disgruntled—this was to be his dance and you have stolen it.'

'Murcheson? His Viscountcy is barely sixty years old,' retorted Marcus with a careless shrug. 'Mine, on the other hand, is well over two hundred—I shall claim seniority of rank.'

Since her nervous system had not entirely recovered from the shock of Helstone's impetuous action, Sophie found herself unable to conjure up an adequately disapproving reply to this somewhat high-handed remark, added to which she could not help reflecting that, despite the apparently imperious manner that he was exhibiting, the Viscount did not seem entirely at ease with himself.

Registering her silence, Marcus, cursing himself for a fool, tried again.

'You certainly look to be enjoying this new life of yours,' he ventured. 'You must be delighted to have been reunited with your father's family.'

'Oh, yes, I am—of course,' she replied, in a somewhat offhand tone of voice. 'Although I must confess that I have not, as yet, had the pleasure of meeting my great-aunt.'

'Oh, you will like her, I am sure,' said Marcus, guiding her adroitly across the floor as he spoke. 'My brother was good enough to introduce the two of us when Miss Pendleton first arrived in the capital—I thought her a most charming lady.'

Feeling duty bound to thank him for the Major's efforts on her family's behalf, Sophie did so, wondering all the while how she might turn the subject to one that was of far more concern to her.

'I was wondering—' she began nervously, as soon as a suitable bout of silence offered itself.

'You must—' blurted out Marcus simultaneously.

Pausing, they both laughed. Then, 'Please go on,' he said.

'No, you first,' she insisted.

Hesitating only briefly, Marcus took a deep breath. 'I dare say you may have been wondering why I have not approached you to beg your pardon for my appalling conduct at our last meeting,' he said.

Sophie's eyes widened in dismay. Having spent a good many sleepless nights castigating herself for her own unseemly behaviour on that unforgettable occasion, she could not allow Helstone to shoulder the entire blame for the event.

'Oh, no, my lord,' she exclaimed in protest. 'Surely it is I who should apologise to you for having vilified you so dreadfully?'

A pensive frown on his face, the Viscount shook his head but, finding himself obliged to direct his attention to the avoidance of yet another maladroit couple in his pathway, it was some few moments before he was able to consider his reply.

'I have little doubt that I deserved every condemnation you threw at me,' he grunted. 'I had every intention of offering you my apologies first thing the following morning—only to discover that you had left the Crayfords.' He paused briefly, before adding, 'I take it that you were asked to leave?'

Sophie gave a perfunctory nod. Mrs Crayford's harsh condemnation of her on that evening was still fresh in her mind. 'I thought it best that I went,' she said diffidently. 'It would have been difficult to remain, given the circumstances.'

Correctly reading the expression on her face, Marcus, heaping mental curses upon her erstwhile employer, tentatively tightened his hold before saying, 'Unfortunately, I was then unable to establish your whereabouts—although my brother did gave me the impression that you had travelled to Harrogate with your family.'

'Oh, no, it was decided that I would do better to remain with the Egremonts for the time being,' replied Sophie, her breath catching as she felt the increased pressure of the Viscount's hand at her waist. 'The family has been extremely kind and generous towards me.'

'No doubt they feel they owe you a debt of gratitude,' acknowledged Marcus, his mouth curving in a mischievous smile. 'It would seem that your intervention at that godforsaken tavern helped to ensure the Whitcombe succession—which must be a matter of great moment, after all!'

An unbidden chuckle escaped Sophie's lips.

'I have the feeling that Mother Nature would have managed very nicely without my assistance,' she replied, her clear blue eyes filling with laughter as she smiled up at him.

His heart seeming to swell within him, Marcus pulled her more closely still. Perhaps all was not lost, after all, he told himself, as he swept her across the floor. If he could just persuade Sophie to overlook his past misdemeanours, he reasoned, perhaps he could set about wooing her in the time-honoured fashion. Given time, and a little help from Lady Luck, it might yet be possible to regain some of the ground that he'd lost.

Her former concerns now fully satisfied, Sophie allowed herself to relax in the Viscount's hold, more than content just to have him shepherd her around the room, their steps perfectly matched to the hypnotic rhythm of the lilting music. Any further conversation was, as far as she was concerned, entirely superfluous; simply to find herself once more in Helstone's arms—for however fleeting an interlude—was, to her, far more than she could ever have hoped or dreamed of. Her whole being deliciously alive to the realisation that Helstone was holding her rather more closely than was generally considered proper, she closed her eyes, tipped back her head, and surrendered herself to the supreme rapture of the moment.

Inevitably, and all too soon, the captivating rhythm drew to its close and, with a sweeping flourish, the final chord rang out across the room, bringing the exhilarated dancers to a laughing, breathless standstill. Marcus, gazing down at the still rapt expression on Sophie's beloved face, found himself wishing that he could just lift her up and spirit her away to some secret hideout, where the pair of them could cloister themselves away from prying eyes and where he would have all the time in the world to demonstrate the true extent of his feelings towards her. The horde of fawning admirers who battled so eagerly for her attention not having escaped his notice, it had very quickly come to him that there was a very real danger of one or other of those toadying dissemblers securing Sophie's hand before he himself was able to conjure up a suitable opportunity to convince her of his sincerity. The sudden ripple of fury that coursed through his veins at the thought of Sophie being pledged in matrimony to any man other than himself was swiftly overtaken by a feeling of sick dread as he was forced to remind himself that his cause was not yet won.

Consequently, and only because there were no other options open to him at that point, it was a very reluctant Marcus who finally returned Sophie to the bosom of her waiting court. His half-hearted attempts to soothe the still somewhat aggrieved Lord Murcheson's ruffled feathers having been grudgingly accepted, it was with a gnawing disappointment that he then discovered that Sophie's dance card was already filled. Her satisfyingly eager suggestion that the Viscount might care to escort her into supper, however, went some way to bolstering Marcus's spirits, but, rather than suffer the indignity of having to stand to one side while a succession of would-be suitors made increasingly outrageous attempts to capture his beloved's attention, he quickly excused himself and went in search of what had become a much-needed drink.

Having procured himself a glass of champagne, Marcus then quit the ballroom and wandered out into the corridor in search of the card room, in the hopes of having his mind distracted from its present preoccupation by means of a few highly concentrated hands of either faro or vingt-et-un.

Even his fervent belief that most of the apparently ardent young bloods who made up Sophie's court were rather more likely to be interested in whatever fortune she might bring with her than they were in her personal charms brought him little solace, since he was sufficiently versed in the ways of the *Ton* to realise that any similar overtures on his part would be regarded in very much the same light. Not that he had ever been particularly concerned as to what the *beau monde* thought of him, as he hastened to remind himself. Sophie's good opinion of him, however, was an entirely different matter, and had suddenly become utterly paramount to his well-being.

On peering into the room designated for card-playing, he was irritated to observe that all the tables were fully occupied, with several other gentlemen already standing by in expectation of taking up any relinquished places. Preferring not to add his name to that number, the Viscount then decided to venture further along the corridor, with a view to ensconcing himself in the library, the quiet comfort of which he had fond memories of having enjoyed back in his youth.

Upon entering the room which, apart from the two wall-sconces at its entrance, was illuminated only by the gently flickering flames that issued from the logs burning in the fireplace, he was pleased to find that, not only did he have the place to himself, little seemed to have changed during his prolonged absence: the high-backed soft leather chairs were still dotted around the room in abundance; the huge map table still graced the wall between the two sets of French windows that opened out on to the terrace, and the faint but unmistakable aroma of musty books coupled with stale cigar smoke still hung in the air.

With an appreciative sniff, Marcus made at once for the carved wooden box that had always stood on the mantelpiece where, to his immense satisfaction, he was to discover that Whitcombe's well-remembered habit of keeping the box replenished with prime Havana cigars had not altered in the intervening years.

Having helped himself to a cigar, he then selected a taper from the nearby receptacle, and was just about to thrust it into the fire when his attention was caught by a soft snuffling noise that seemed to be coming from the far side of the room.

His curiosity aroused, Marcus, setting both cigar and taper down on a side-table, moved quietly across the library floor towards the source of the noise which, he was fairly certain, gave every indication of being the sound of a female in some distress. Not that he had any particular desire to intrude upon the unknown lady's apparent grief, he told himself, but, having inadvertently been made party to it, it was more than he could do to simply stand by and ignore the plaintive whimpering.

Having judged that the sounds were emanating from one of the high-backed armchairs that nestled in a dimly lit corner of the room, he crept towards it and peered over the back of the chair, where he was confronted with the sight of the most piteous looking creature—hardly more than a girl, he concluded—who was doing her utmost to stifle her anguished sobs in the absurdly inadequate handkerchief that she had pressed against her lips.

Finding himself at something of a loss in the face of such overwhelming distress, Marcus was momentarily stopped in his tracks. But then, as commonsense prevailed, he reached down and extracted his own, rather more serviceable handkerchief from his pocket, before stepping round in front of the weeping female and attempting to thrust it into her hand—only to have the panic-stricken girl recoil in fright as she suddenly became aware of his presence.

Struggling to her feet, her tear-drenched eyes wide with apprehension, she raised both hands, as if in self-defence, and backed hurriedly away from him. Sadly, in her frantic haste to flee from the unwelcome intrusion into her wretchedness, she misjudged her step, catching the heel of her slipper in the lace-edged flounce of her gown, and, had not Marcus's reactions been as prompt as they were, would most certainly have tumbled to the ground.

'Do please calm yourself, ma'am,' he begged her, as he steadied the struggling female against his chest. 'I won't harm you, I swear—I am merely trying to be of service. Has someone hurt you? Can you not tell me what has caused you such distress?'

At his soothing words, a fresh bout of tears overcame the girl, sending shivers of apprehension coursing through Marcus's veins.

'Come, please tell me what ails you,' he urged her as, with some difficulty, he managed to pry her violently trembling form away from his own and lower her back into the chair. 'Are you ill? Is there someone I could fetch for you? Will you not allow me to help you in some way?'

More sobs ensued as the girl gave a despairing shake of her head. 'P-please go away, s-sir, I b-beg you!' she choked. 'I am b-beyond help. Beyond both help and h-hope! Oh, how I wish I were d-dead!'

'Oh, come now,' protested Marcus, his original sympathy beginning to evaporate somewhat at the girl's somewhat histrionic outburst. 'I cannot believe that whatever it is that has upset you can be so dreadful as to warrant so desperate an inclination!'

Making a valiant effort to control her sobs, the girl buried her face in Marcus's handkerchief and, after heaving in a shuddering breath, dipped her fingers into her beaded reticule and drew out an expensive-looking pearl choker. 'I have d-damaged the c-clasp.' She gulped nervously. 'It belonged to m-my husband's first wife— when he discovers what I have d-done, I c-cannot begin to imagine w-what he will d-do to me!'

Staring down at the necklace in bewildered astonishment, Marcus found himself unsure whether to burst out laughing or to deliver a sharp lecture to the young woman for having allowed herself to get into such a state over a mere trinket. He rose to his feet, his irritation increasing by the minute. 'Nonsense,' he chided her. 'You are exaggerating, I'm sure. I find it extremely unlikely that any sane man would stoop to punishing his wife over so paltry a matter as a broken necklace.'

'Then it's clear that you do not n-number my h-husband amongst your acquaintances.' The girl sighed, as she dabbed dispiritedly at her damp flushed cheeks.

'Possibly not,' retorted Marcus, who was beginning to regret his impulsive attempt at chivalry and was wishing that he had never involved himself in the foolish creature's absurd problems. 'My name is Marcus Wolfe— Helstone, if you prefer. May I be permitted to know who you are?'

'I am Christabel Sa—I mean Dawlish,' she amended hastily. 'Christabel Dawlish—wife of Sir Randolph.'

Marcus stilled, a frisson of unease trickling through him. Good God, he thought, staring down at the girl's bleak expression in appalled silence. *Randolph Dawlish!* The man was old enough to be the girl's father! Having come up against the elderly baronet on more than one occasion during his own rather too frequent expeditions into the seamier side of London's night-life, he had become sufficiently well acquainted with Dawlish's singularly unpleasant nature to now realise that his young wife's fears in regard to her self-confessed clumsiness might not be entirely without foundation.

'Randolph Dawlish?' he repeated slowly. 'I am slightly acquainted with him, as it happens, but I must confess that I was unaware that he had remarried.' *And his first wife barely cold in her grave,* he thought contemptuously. *Yet how typical of the sadistic swine to*

*find himself another pathetic victim to vent his spite
on so soon!*

Unsuppressed tears gathered in the new Lady Dawlish's eyes. 'Just a l-little over three w-weeks ago,' she
choked, as she hurriedly turned her face away in a futile
attempt to hide her rising distress. 'You have been very
k-kind, sir, but I would be greatly obliged if you would
leave me n-now.'

'No, ma'am, I fear I shall do no such thing,' returned
Marcus, with a determined shake of his head. 'It is clear
that you are in no state to be left here on your own. You
must allow me to escort you as far as the ladies' retiring
room, or to call for assistance at the very least.'

'Oh, no! P-please go, sir, I b-beg of you,' cried
Christabel, her mounting anguish clear to see as she
twisted his soaking wet handkerchief between her fingers. 'I really do not wish to be s-seen by anyone just
at p-present!'

Instinct telling him that it was imperative that he get
the weeping female such help as was humanly possible,
Marcus tried again.

'I really must insist that you come with me now,' he
adjured her, holding out his hand. 'I cannot simply walk
away and leave you here on your own, and you must see
that it would not do for us to be found in here together.'
With more than enough problems of his own to deal
with, he could hardly help being aware that the very last
thing he needed at this juncture was to be discovered
in a dimly lit room in the company of another man's
wife.

Thankfully, the implied threat behind his warning
was enough to bring the clearly petrified Christabel
to her senses. With a frightened gasp she leapt to her
feet and, placing her hand in his still outstretched one,

allowed Marcus to lead her across the room. Upon reaching the doorway, however, she halted and, letting go of his hand, hung back timorously, twisting her fingers together in apprehension before clutching at his arm and whimpering, 'Not past the card room, sir, I beg of you—*please*!'

Biting back a withering retort, Marcus found himself at somewhat of a standstill. Having only just recently observed her husband in the gaming room, he could appreciate the girl's concern, realising that there was every chance the pair of them might well be spotted as they passed by the doorway. Unfortunately, he was also aware that the only way they could possibly reach the relative safety of the ladies' room was by means of the corridor outside.

He stood for a moment, totally nonplussed, as he racked his brains for a solution to the dilemma. And then, in a sudden inspiration, it came to him that if there was anyone who would know exactly what to do in such a situation, it was Sophie! His brow cleared as a simple way out of his predicament at once became obvious. All he had to do was deposit the now softly weeping Christabel back into her chair and go in search of Sophie. Having witnessed the one-time governess's infallibility in the face of the numerous problems with which the marooned group had been beset during that freak snowstorm, he had little doubt that she would be able to come up with some sort of solution to this particular problem. In fact, it would hardly surprise him to learn that Sophie also had at her disposal some fiendishly clever means by which the damaged necklace might be fixed, thus saving the poor misguided Christabel from Dawlish's malicious spite.

Fully convinced that the answer to his current

difficulty was now well within his grasp, Marcus finally
persuaded Christabel back into her chair and headed
once more towards the door—only to open it and discover that the passageway was now swarming with all
manner of people. The absence of music clearly signalled that the supper hour had begun. Within moments
hordes of laughing, chattering guests were making their
way out of the ballroom into the corridors, out onto the
brightly lit terrace and into the gardens, intent upon
making the most of the balmy evening air before returning to the supper room to indulge themselves in the
sumptuous repast that the Whitcombe cooks had worked
so diligently to provide.

Muttering a string of curses, Marcus retraced his
steps, grabbed the now violently resisting Christabel's
hand and hauled her to her feet, having realised that their
only hope of salvation now lay in exiting the library by
way of its terrace doors. With luck, they might be able
to lose themselves among the thronging crowds.

Just as they were about to step out onto the terrace,
however, the library door was suddenly thrust open to
reveal none other than Sir Randolph Dawlish himself
standing at the threshold! With a terrified yelp, Christabel hurled herself at Marcus and buried her face into
his shirtfront, whimpering, 'Save me—oh, I beg of you,
don't let him hurt me, sir!'

Sir Randolph, a tall, spare man with thinning grey
hair, whose pale and deeply lined face bore testimony
to his chosen life of reckless dissipation, stood rigidly
in the doorway for some moments, his thin lips twisting
in a contemptuous smile as he surveyed the unfortunate
scene. Then, striding across the floor with an angry
snarl, he reached forward and attempted to wrench his
wife away from Marcus who, despite his dismay at the

baronet's unexpected appearance, had automatically raised his arms to cocoon the ashen-faced Christabel against his chest.

'So, madam wife!' sneered Dawlish. 'You think to creep off with your lover the minute my back is turned, do you?'

'You are mistaken, sir,' retorted the Viscount, raising his eyebrow in haughty disdain. 'Lady Dawlish appeared to be in some distress when I came upon her. I was just on my way to seek assistance—'

'A likely tale, sir!' Dawlish interrupted, his lip curling in disbelief. '"Tis common knowledge the sort of "assistance" Hellcat Helstone usually has in mind as far as the female of the species is concerned, but this time, my lord, I fear you have met your match, for I refuse to play cuckold to your scheming Lothario! I must insist that you release my wife at once, sir, and do me the courtesy of naming your seconds!'

'Don't talk rot, man!' returned Marcus shortly, while doing his level best to unclasp the disobliging Christabel's hands from the back of his neck. He shot a hurried glance at the growing crowd of curious onlookers who were eagerly converging upon the scene, in the futile hope that one or other of her friends might be among them and come to her rescue. 'I have no intention of meeting you. I assure you that neither your wife nor I have behaved in any way that would require me to do so.'

'Your assurances are worthless, sir!' ground out the now thoroughly enraged baronet, drawing himself up to his full height. 'I doubt that there is a single person here present who is unaware of your dubious history.' He paused, sneering. 'Do I take it that you are refusing to accept my challenge?'

Having finally freed himself from Lady Dawlish's clinging embrace, Marcus now found himself on the horns of a dilemma. Whilst there was no question in his mind that his unlooked-for sojourn with the baronet's young wife had been of an entirely innocent nature, it was not difficult for him to see how such a situation might appear to the average bystander—especially given the highly embellished reputation he had gained over the past few years. Up until about twenty or so minutes ago he would have had no difficulty in accepting Dawlish's challenge, and taken considerable pleasure in wiping the supercilious smirk off the slimy toad's evil visage, but now, having only just succeeded in getting himself back in Sophie's good books, Marcus was not at all happy to find himself embroiled in a scandal that was not of his making. He could only hope and pray that word of this unpleasant event had escaped her ears.

Casting a wary glance over the assembled onlookers, he very soon realised that such optimism was doomed to failure—for there, on the very fringe of the crowd, stood Sophie, her wide blue eyes luminous with unshed tears. The Viscount was beset by a wave of despair, and only just managed to stop himself from howling out his innocence to her. *This is none of my doing, believe me!* his eyes strained to tell her. *This is not what it seems, I swear!*

Having waited for Helstone to return to the ballroom and accompany her into supper, as previously arranged, the somewhat puzzled Sophie had finally made her way out onto the terrace in search of her errant escort. Curious as to the noisy throng of guests surging outside the library doors, she had drifted towards the scene, only to find herself confronted with the appalling sight of Marcus locked in the arms of another man's wife.

Scarcely able to believe her senses, she had stood, almost paralysed with shock, while she listened to Dawlish issue his challenge. It was beyond her understanding that Marcus, who less than half an hour previously had been practically begging her to look favourably on his suit, should have chosen to while away the intervening minutes in a clandestine liaison with some other unsuspecting female—and a married one, at that! Righteous anger began to bubble up inside her chest, and she was just about to turn away from the distasteful scene in shuddering revulsion when she caught sight of the anguished appeal in Helstone's eyes. She froze, as wild seeds of doubt began to plant themselves in her mind, and, unable to prevent herself, took a hesitant step forward—only to find herself being held back by Lord Bingham who, having been notified of the commotion by a diligent manservant, had recently arrived at her side.

'What's going on, Sophie?' he asked, a concerned frown furrowing his brow as he attempted to make sense of the scene unfolding at the library's threshold.

'I'm not absolutely certain, Jack,' she answered him shakily. 'It seems that Sir Randolph discovered Lord Helstone in some sort of compromising situation with Lady Dawlish and has challenged his lordship to a duel!'

'Good Lord!' exclaimed Bingham, casting a nervous look over his shoulder. 'Let's hope my father doesn't get wind of it—a thing like this is enough to put the dampers on the whole proceedings. Ought I to step in and put a stop to it, do you suppose? Wouldn't do to upset the ladies, now, would it?'

Since it was clear that a good many of the gaping bystanders were of the female gender, Sophie could only suppose that the Viscount was attempting to lighten the atmosphere by uttering such a frivolous jest. She herself was unable to find any humour in a situation that might easily lead to Marcus being hurt or, God forbid, *killed*! No matter what he might have done to deserve it, the thought of him losing his life was more than she could bear to contemplate.

'I was under the impression that duelling had been made illegal,' she said worriedly.

'Yes, it has,' returned Bingham distractedly, his eyes still intent upon the interaction between Helstone and Dawlish. 'Still goes on, of course—the participants just have to be careful not to get caught by the authorities. Certain imprisonment, I believe.'

'I insist that you name your seconds, sir!' barked Dawlish, his cheeks purpling with rage as the scowling Viscount continued to refuse to accept his repeated challenge. Then, with a derisive sniff, he turned to face the several other men who had accompanied him into the library, smirking. 'It would appear that the great nonesuch has finally lost his bottle, gentlemen!'

Closing his eyes briefly, as a ripple of frustrated rage ran through his veins, Marcus was finally forced to concede that Dawlish had left him with no choice. Not that he was particularly bothered about having to face up to the man but, having registered Sophie's look of total revulsion, it had become painfully clear to him that any hopes he might once have harboured in that direction were now doomed to failure. Alongside that depressing thought, the possibility of severe injury suddenly seemed of little importance.

But as to the matter of seconds? Marcus was not at all sure that any of his one-time associates would be interested in supporting him, given that he had made a point of shunning all such delinquent company since his recent renaissance. He had no doubt that his brother Giles—after treating him to a severe dressing down for landing himself in such hot water—would have been willing to oblige him, but unfortunately Giles was up to his neck in Home Office affairs and not immediately available.

A pensive frown sifted across his forehead. It was hard to believe that he, with so many friends and acquaintances, should be finding it a problem to drum up a single name.

'Well?' demanded Dawlish belligerently, thrusting his face mere inches from the Viscount's own. 'Are you going to admit you are at fault and apologise immediately or name your seconds—the choice is yours!'

Sophie was beside herself with wretchedness. 'Do something, Jack,' she beseeched Bingham, clutching frantically at his arm. 'I don't think I can bear another minute of this.'

'I'm not altogether sure that there's anything I *can* do now,' returned Bingham, looking somewhat abashed. 'Looks as if Sir Randolph might have a point, after all— messing about with another fellow's wife, you know...' His voice trailed away awkwardly.

But Sophie, having taken a good look at the quietly weeping Christabel, would have none of it. She was finding it impossible to believe that such a little mouse-like creature as the curled-up female on the chair seemed to be would appeal to the Viscount in any way whatsoever. It was becoming increasingly obvious to her that not only was Marcus's supposed transgression distinctly out of character, it would seem that there was a good deal more behind his clear reluctance to accept the baronet's challenge than appearances might suggest. And then, as her mind dwelt upon the decidedly anguished look that had crossed his face when he had spotted her in the crowd, she became immediately convinced that, for some obscure reason or other, he had allowed himself to become a scapegoat.

'You *must* do something about it,' she said stoutly. 'I'm sure that there has been some dreadful mistake. Helstone is not at fault—I would stake my life on it!'

Incensed at Marcus's stubborn refusal to countenance either of his demands, Dawlish suddenly lashed out at the Viscount with both fists. 'Name your seconds, damn you!' he spluttered, becoming almost apoplectic with rage as Marcus, his highly tuned reflexes leaping instantly into action, moved himself well out of the baronet's range.

All at once a ripple of excitement, followed by an expectant hush, ran through the by now utterly spellbound spectators as the young Viscount Bingham shouldered his way through their midst and stepped into the room.

'If you're in want of a second, my lord,' he said, favouring Marcus with a brief smile. 'I would be more than happy to offer my services!'

Chapter Seventeen

'I still don't understand why you just didn't give the fellow my name and have done with it?' exclaimed the exasperated Giles who, when the rapidly spreading rumours concerning Marcus's unfortunate clash with Dawlish had reached his ears, had immediately downed tools and hastened back to Bradfield Hall. 'Surely you must have known that I would support you?'

'I wasn't too sure how to get hold of you,' returned his brother, emitting a weary sigh. 'Quite apart from the fact that I really had no intention of taking up Dawlish's challenge. None of it would have happened had the foul-minded swine been prepared to listen to reason but, no! It was clear from the very start that he was determined to make full capital out of the matter.'

'You think the chap has some sort of a grudge against you, then?'

'Well, it's true that I've managed to relieve him of several thousand pounds over the last year or so,' replied Marcus with a careless shrug. 'And I did catch him trying to cheat in a poker game a couple of months ago—not that I mentioned it at the time, but I've always had the feeling that he knew I'd spotted his careless gaffe. But to involve that pathetic little scrap of a wife of his in the way that he did, simply to get back at me, must surely be the action of the lowest cur on earth! For that reason alone it would give me the greatest pleasure to put a bullet through one or other part of his slimy form!'

Giving a disapproving shake of his head, Giles felt constrained to point out that Sir Randolph was known to be a pretty fair shot himself, adding, 'Don't you think it might be better if we were to try and reach some sort of compromise? That, after all, is what a good second is supposed to do in circumstances such as these.'

'Well, I refuse to give him some sort of grovelling apology, if that's what you're about to suggest,' growled Marcus, heaving himself up out of his chair and striding across to the sideboard to replenish his empty glass. 'I've had more than enough of that particular topic from the mater.'

'Good Lord, man!' exclaimed Giles, a concerned frown crossing his face. 'You're not telling me that the parents have got wind of the affair?'

'Just Ma,' Marcus took pains to assure his brother. 'Luckily, the vast majority of Whitcombe's guests only learned of it long after it was all over, but naturally, Ma being Ma, she had to know everything, down to the last detail. And, since she spent the entire ride home last evening badgering me, I was finally goaded into confessing, on the strictest understanding that she kept it from the old man.'

'Well, thank heaven for small mercies,' breathed the Major, much relieved.

'I'll have you know that I'm not quite as dicked in the nob as you seem to be implying,' muttered his brother, somewhat affronted. 'I'm well aware that a shock of this sort is enough to bring on another attack—which was yet one more reason why I wasn't too keen to drag you into this affair. I'm perfectly capable of dealing with the matter on my own—it's not as though I haven't had plenty of practice!' he finished dryly.

'Don't be a fool!' retorted Giles, glowering. 'If you're determined to go through with it, then I'm happy to support you all the way—as you well know!' Then, after taking a pensive sip from his glass, he leaned forward again. 'You didn't tell me how Dawlish reacted to Bingham's offer,' he observed. 'I imagine the fellow wasn't best pleased at the thought of Whitcombe's son taking your side?'

'Well, there was quite a bit of teeth gnashing going on, as I recall,' replied Marcus, a faint smile creasing his face. 'Then Dawlish just grabbed hold of his wife's arm, yanked her out of her chair and was about to drag her out of the room when young Lady Bingham intervened and insisted on taking Christabel to the ladies' room to recover from her ordeal—Bingham must have sent his wife some sort of sign, I suppose. Anyway, the long and the short of it is that Dawlish stormed straight out of the building, leaving his wife to God and good neighbours, as it were!'

'Let's hope the poor lass has the sense to remain there until this miserable business is over and done with.' His brother sighed, as he reached for his glass once more. 'Not that I would care to be in her shoes when she finally does put in an appearance.'

Marcus grimaced, his lips twisting slightly, as he replied, 'Oh, I dare say Miss Pendleton-Flint will drum up some sort of solution to that particular problem—as soon as young Christabel recovers sufficiently to unburden herself of her troubles, that is.'

'Miss Pendleton-Flint?' repeated the Major, suddenly alert. 'You didn't mention that she was present at this event.'

'Did I not?' returned Marcus, with a self-deprecating shrug. 'As it happens, our one-time governess was very much present, and had little difficulty in making her feelings on the matter pretty clear, as I recall.'

A curious expression on his face, Giles regarded his brother in silence for some minutes before asking, in a slightly offhand manner, 'Do I take it that you are still carrying a torch for that young lady?'

'Something of the sort,' grunted Marcus, shifting restlessly in his seat. 'Bit pointless, really, since it would seem that this latest escapade of mine has put the final damper on whatever chance I might once have had in that direction. The only husbandry that is likely to affect me in the near future is that which involves crop rotation and milk yields!'

Less than ten miles away, at Whitcombe Abbey, the subject of Helstone's morose introspection was seated at Christabel Dawlish's bedside, endeavouring to piece together that young woman's tearfully stilted version of the previous evening's melodrama.

Although Sophie had no doubt in her mind that the Viscount was innocent of any of the charges that Sir Randolph had flung at him, she had to admit to being distinctly curious as to how the whole distasteful affair had actually come into being. Unfortunately, trying to extract the bones of the matter between the various sniffles, gulps and self-condemnatory tears of the still badly affected Christabel was proving to be no mean task.

Eventually, however, her confidence bolstered by the many sympathetic nods and expressions of commiseration from both Elizabeth and Sophie—not to mention the numerous cups of hot chocolate and soft buttered rolls with which she had been plied throughout the night—Christabel managed to satisfy her listeners that their joint decision to whisk her away from her husband had been well and truly justified.

Having arrived at the scene just in time to witness Bingham offering his services to Helstone, his young wife had demanded to be told what was going on. After hearing Sophie's brief but pithy explanation, Elizabeth had taken one long, lingering look at the wretched-looking creature still cowering in her armchair and had then, after a hurried consultation with her friend, taken it upon herself to waylay Sir Randolph on his exit from the library. Although, to begin with, it had been their intention merely to afford the baronet's wife some sort of temporary respite from the ugly scene that was being played out in front of a score or more of voracious onlookers, neither Sophie nor Elizabeth could find it in themselves to feel a great deal of sorrow upon learning that Dawlish had taken off without Christabel.

A hasty discussion involving both Mrs Egremont and Countess Whitcombe had resulted in Christabel being tucked up in one of the abbey's many guest bedrooms, but, since it had become clear that the girl had suffered too great a shock to allow her to fall asleep, Sophie and Elizabeth had taken turns at keeping her company throughout the night.

'And now,' hiccoughed the girl wretchedly, at the end of her long drawn-out recital, 'the p-poor man is about to get himself k-killed—and all because he tried to h-help me!'

Since Sophie had spent the past several hours endeavouring to rid her mind of such a devastating thought, Christabel's unpleasant reminder was more than enough to send a shudder of dread running through her. Biting her lip, she took a steadying breath and forced herself to concentrate on ridding Christabel of the feelings of remorse that so clearly burdened the grief-stricken girl.

'Come now,' she said soothingly, as she patted Christabel's hand. 'I refuse to believe that it will come to that—Lord Bingham has assured his wife that he intends to take whatever steps are necessary to bring about some sort of conciliation.'

'Sir Randolph is not the sort of man who can be easily appeased.' Christabel sniffed and gave a mournful shake of her head. 'He is so utterly self-centred that the only point of view that has any meaning for him is his own.'

Their eyes meeting across the bed, Elizabeth and Sophie shared a brief moment of compassion for the girl. That there was little love lost between Dawlish and his young wife was very plain to see.

'Forgive my vulgar curiosity, my dear,' ventured the Viscountess tentatively. 'But how came you to marry such an unpleasant man?'

'He had advanced my father a large sum of money for some business venture or other,' Christabel sighed. 'Unfortunately, when the time came to repay the loan, Papa had insufficient means at his disposal and was obliged to ask Sir Randolph for a postponement. Having already learned that the quite substantial amount of money that I was due to inherit from my grandmother on my twenty-first birthday would be paid if I were to marry in advance of that date, Sir Randolph agreed to forego the debt on condition that I married him—otherwise he threatened to haul my father into the debtors' court.' At the memory, her already red-rimmed eyes filled once more with tears as she hid her face in her hands with a choked, 'I couldn't allow that to happen, so I simply went along with it!'

'Dear God!' whispered Sophie, in the certain knowledge that her own father would rather have sold his own soul to the devil than sacrifice his daughter in such a way. Having observed clear signs of bruising on Christabel's arms and back while helping the girl to undress, she could not forbear from adding, 'And, not content with helping himself to your inheritance, it would appear that the horrid fiend beats you, too!'

'It's not the beatings I mind so much,' faltered Christabel, dropping her eyes as her colour mounted. 'It's the—the other ways in which he chooses to punish me that I fear most of all.'

Even though the unspoken meaning behind the young Lady Dawlish's hesitant disclosure was only too clear to her stunned and horrified listeners, both Sophie and Elizabeth were uncomfortably aware that there was little that they could do in regard to that particular aspect of the girl's pitiable existence, other than try to keep her here at the abbey for as long as was humanly possible.

'We'll just have to tell Dawlish that his wife has suffered some sort of mental breakdown and cannot possibly be moved,' whispered Sophie as, with a brief flutter of her eyelids, accompanied by a shuddering sigh, their exhausted patient finally allowed herself to succumb to the sleep that had eluded her.

'Which is hardly a lie, in the circumstances,' returned

Elizabeth fiercely. 'If I were a man, I'd gladly put a bullet into the vile creature myself!'

Her heart seeming to jump into her throat as she was confronted with yet another reminder of the looming threat to Helstone's life, Sophie, clutching at her friend's hand, drew her across the room towards the window, well out of hearing of the now soundly sleeping Christabel.

'Has Jack managed to put a stop to this fiasco yet, do you know?' she asked, her eyes full of concern.

'He was very reluctant to tell me anything at all!' sniffed the Viscountess in disgust, still somewhat piqued that her husband had refused to take her into his confidence. 'However, I did manage to worm out of him that he had spent the better part of the night in consultation with Sir Reginald's seconds—he wouldn't give me their names, of course, but he does seem pretty certain that Dawlish has no intention of pulling out.'

'He didn't say when it would take place, then?'

Elizabeth shook her head. 'Not as such—apart from letting slip that he hoped the Cromptons' ball this evening wasn't going to last all night. So my guess is that the meeting is set for first thing tomorrow morning.'

On hearing Sophie's sudden intake of breath, she paused, regarding her friend with a certain amount of curiosity. 'You seem unduly concerned about Viscount Helstone's safety—I was under the impression that the two of you barely knew one another.'

Unable to prevent the rosy blush that was beginning to flood her cheeks, Sophie turned hurriedly away, simulating a keen interest in a somewhat bland-looking watercolour that hung on the wall nearby. 'We don't,' she replied, with a feigned nonchalance. 'It just doesn't seem fair to me that the poor man should feel obliged to put his life at risk just to satisfy the lunatic ravings of a devil like Dawlish—we both know that his lordship is not at fault, after all!'

Elizabeth, continuing to study the back of Sophie's head, was struck by a sudden thought. 'I was watching the pair of you dancing together last evening,' she said slowly. 'I remember thinking that I had never seen you look so happy—so alive!' Her eyes widening, she took hold of Sophie's arm, spinning her round in order that she might see her friend's face as, in almost breathless fascination, she challenged, 'You love him, don't you?'

Unable to bring herself to deny the charge, Sophie gave a brief nod, her lips quivering with barely suppressed anguish as she blurted out, 'I know it's stupid of me, and I've tried so very hard not to, but I just can't seem to help myself!'

With that, she buried her face in her hands and burst into tears. Elizabeth, thoroughly caught up in her friend's misery, flung her arms around her and, hugging her tightly, murmured, 'Oh, you poor, poor thing—it must be devastating for you not to know what's happening—I swear I'll make Jack tell me if it's the last thing I do!'

Chapter Eighteen

The early-morning mist was still wreathing its diaphanous plumes over the heath's scrubland as Marcus's carriage drew to a halt beside the clump of trees that had been designated for the meeting place. Leaping lightly from the vehicle, his lordship was surprised to note that two other carriages were already in attendance at the scene, despite the fact that the time was still more than fifteen minutes short of the appointed hour.

'Colder than I expected,' remarked Bingham, as he cast a somewhat nervous glance in the direction of Dawlish's waiting group.

Never having been involved in anything of this sort before, he was slightly unsure what to expect. He had heard a good many tales, of course, and had taken pains to acquaint himself with the proper procedure. Since he had already made a thoroughly conscientious attempt at mediation—a second's primary duty, according to his sources—he was reasonably satisfied that he had fulfilled all his requisite obligations. All that remained now, as he understood it, was for one or other of the parties to deal his opponent a relatively harmless injury—a slight nick on the upper arm usually served, it seemed—and justice would be seen to have been done, with neither party having lost face. He had also managed—after some considerable difficulty and the promise of a hefty fee—to persuade his family doctor's junior partner into attending what was, when all was said and done, the sort of activity now punishable by law. But, having observed that Dr Felsham, whose maroon landau Bingham had recognised, had chosen to remain well out of sight at this juncture, the young Viscount could only hope that his father never got to hear of his own part in the illicit proceedings!

Giles, meanwhile, was busily engaged in examining the weapons, which on this occasion had been supplied by Dawlish, whose skill as a crack marksman was common knowledge—not that the Major had any doubts as to his brother's own expertise in the sport, having seen him shoot out a pip at a distance of twenty yards or more.

Having checked the silver-handled duelling pistols to his satisfaction, the Major stood back and watched as one of Sir Randolph's seconds, Captain Dempsey by name, tossed a coin to decide which of the participants should be given first choice of weapon. Dawlish's harsh 'heads' allotted the choice to Marcus, when the coin landed tailside uppermost.

Extracting a battered chronometer from his pocket as the muffled chimes of a distant church clock struck the hour, Dempsey flipped open its case to declare that the time had arrived for Helstone and Dawlish to take their places.

Pistols in hand, the two stood back to back, awaiting the count.

'Time for last prayers, you despicable swine,' grated Dawlish through clenched teeth, his mocking words inaudible to all but the Viscount.

'*One…two…three…*'

His lip curled in derision, Marcus stepped forward. *So the cur actually means to kill me, does he?* he mused, almost unconcernedly. Having spent the better part of the past twenty-four hours putting his affairs in order, including willing all his worldly possessions to his younger brother, he had very little interest in the outcome of this morning's meeting. In fact, once he had registered the look of sheer contempt on Sophie's face after his attempts to signal his plea of innocence to her, the Viscount had discovered that he really had very little interest in anything at all.

'*Four…five…six…*'

His initial anger at Dawlish's accusation had dissipated some hours ago, especially since he had been obliged to face up to the irrefutable fact that, having gone out of his way to acquire the unsavoury reputation with which the name Helstone had become synonymous over the past six years, such a charge had become almost inevitable, given the decidedly incriminating circumstances in which he had been discovered. In fact, it had become depressingly clear to Marcus that it was going to take a darned sight more than a couple of weeks of fixing tenants' roofs and calculating milk yields to cancel out his now deeply regretted history of loose living and self-indulgent profligacy. Unfortunately, as he had also come to realise, without Sophie by his side to help him overcome the stumbling blocks that inevitably lay ahead of him, he was not at all sure that he would be able to summon up either the inclination or the enthusiasm to deal with so momentous a task. In losing Sophie, Marcus was starting to realise that he had lost everything that was truly worth living for.

'*Seven...eight...nine...*'

His brain automatically cutting to the matter in hand, the Viscount tensed, his finger poised to squeeze the trigger on the turn. Just as he was about to take the final step forward, however, he was astounded to find himself staggering to remain upright as the force of Dawlish's bullet ripped through his left coat-sleeve, biting into the tender flesh of his underarm. His shock and anger was so great in that moment that any pain he might have been feeling was thrust immediately from his mind. The treacherous bastard had pre-empted Dempsey's count! Whirling round to confront his assailant, he slowly raised his pistol.

Scarcely able to comprehend that his carefully aimed shot could have missed its intended target, the by now thoroughly shaken Dawlish stood utterly transfixed, his brain refusing to function. Not only had he committed the indefensible offence of discharging his pistol in advance of the call, but he had also failed in his attempt to put a period to his hated enemy's life! But then, as the awful realisation that Helstone was aiming his as yet still loaded weapon in his direction finally captured the horrified baronet's attention, his heart seemed to stop in its tracks and he let out a whimper of despair.

His eyes fixed unwaveringly on Dawlish's panic-stricken face, the Viscount took aim.

'Hold hard, Marcus!' howled Giles, as he leapt across the space that separated him from his brother. 'Lower your weapon, man!'

Temporarily sidetracked by the Major's frantic shout,

Marcus was momentarily diverted from his intention. Seizing his opportunity, Dawlish swung round and, taking to his heels, tore frantically across the grass in an effort to reach the safety of his carriage.

His lips curling in contempt as he watched the baronet haul himself into his waiting carriage, Marcus, lowering his pistol, turned to face his irate brother. 'I wasn't about to kill him, if that's what you were afraid of,' he grunted, somewhat aggrieved at Giles's apparent lack of faith. 'I merely intended to part the swine's hair!'

'You're a damned fool,' retorted the Major, looking suitably shamefaced. 'I can only thank God that the lily-livered cur wasn't as good a shot as he thought he was!'

'Not half bad, though,' muttered Marcus as, suddenly aware of the burning pain in his underarm, he stared down in fascination at the rivulet of blood now dripping from the cuff of his jacket. 'Another inch or so to the right and—'

A wave of blackness swept over him and then… *nothing*.

'What exactly do you mean by "slightly injured",' asked Sophie, eyeing Bingham suspiciously.

'He took a bit of a nick in his arm, that's all,' replied the Viscount with a nervous laugh. 'The doctor didn't seem too worried about it—just a flesh wound, he said.'

Having seen more than enough 'flesh wounds' in her time, Sophie was still not nearly satisfied with Bingham's very sketchy description of Helstone's injury. Having set upon him the moment he had arrived back at the abbey, both she and Elizabeth had proceeded to badger the Viscount until, with the utmost reluctance, he had eventually been browbeaten into divulging the very barest details of that morning's happenings.

'Was his lordship losing a great deal of blood?' she demanded to know.

'Oh, I think we might be spared that sort of detail,' interposed Elizabeth hurriedly, her face paling. 'If Dr Felsham was of the opinion that Helstone's wound wasn't serious, then surely we ought to accept his verdict.'

'Simple flesh wounds have been known to turn very nasty,' Sophie countered in reply but then, having taken note of her friend's rather sickly-looking expression, she swiftly changed the subject to demand of Bingham, 'So, where exactly is his lordship now?'

'Major Wolfe had Felsham accompany them both back to Grosvenor Square,' the Viscount was at pains to assure her. 'Where you can be sure that he will receive the very best of treatment. Anyway, if you ask me, Dawlish is the one we should all be feeling sorry for at this moment!'

'That cur!' retorted Sophie with an angry glare, while Elizabeth merely gave a derisive snort. 'Why on earth you think that anyone would feel a moment's pity for that odious creature is beyond my understanding. After the way he's treated that poor defenceless wife of his, the evil swine deserves everything he gets—not that his punishment for behaving in so outrageous a manner is likely to amount to much more than being blackballed from one or two of his clubs for a couple of weeks,' she added scathingly. 'The brunt of which will be borne by Lady Dawlish, if I'm any judge!'

'And I fear that you would be quite wrong in that assumption,' said Bingham, giving a decisive shake of his head. 'Seems the poor devil suffered some sort of apoplectic seizure not long after climbing into his carriage. Captain Dempsey—one of his seconds—sent a note round to the major indicating that it's highly unlikely that Dawlish will last the night!'

There followed a somewhat awkward silence as Sophie and Elizabeth tried their level best to avoid catching one another's eyes, the guilty remorse on both girls' faces bearing testament to their vociferous and far-reaching condemnation of the baronet earlier.

'I suppose one of us ought to go and break the news to Christabel,' ventured Sophie at last. Not that she was looking forward to imparting such gruesome tidings to Dawlish's young wife, particularly after having spent the best part of the night castigating the man. Added to which, since she was fairly sure that Christabel would immediately assume the mantle of guilt for the whole wretched affair, she had the distinct feeling that the girl's previous display of grief would be as nothing when compared to the one which would erupt upon being informed of her husband's imminent demise.

Having already spent a good many hours at the highly distressed girl's bedside, Sophie was now thoroughly exhausted and would have liked nothing better than to bury her own head in a pillow and devote her thoughts to trying to figure out what might be going on in Grosvenor Square at that moment. As her many years of experience had taught her, even the simplest of flesh wounds had a nasty habit of festering and turning putrid. Tiny threads of fabric could get caught under the skin, setting up an infection. Instruments were often contaminated, and bandages weren't always as clean as they might be—not to mention the very real danger of lead poisoning—all of which might easily lead to amputation and—a violent shudder ran through her as she did her best to suppress the thought that followed—even *death*!

Biting her lip to stop the tears that threatened, Sophie knew that there was no way that she could be satisfied that Helstone's injury was really as trivial as Jack had attempted to imply. She was just going to have to go up to London and discover for herself the actual extent of the damage to his lordship's arm! But first, as she was reluctantly forced to remind herself, there still remained the rather depressing task of dealing with the soon to be widowed Christabel Dawlish. Murmuring a short prayer of absolution, Sophie could not forbear from keeping her fingers tightly crossed as she entered the sleeping girl's room.

'Absolutely not!' Marcus gave a mutinous shake of his head. 'I've already told you! I have no intention of putting in an appearance at Bradfield until this damned arm of mine is on the mend!'

'But if Ma should get to hear of your injury, she'll be pretty offended at you not wanting her at your bedside,' protested his brother. 'You can't have forgotten what she was like when we both went down with scarlet fever that time!'

'There's no reason why she should get to hear of it,' riposted Marcus with a weary sigh, while privately thinking that the only person he really wanted—*needed*—by his bedside at this particular moment was the chestnut-haired, blue-eyed goddess who had so clearly rejected him two nights ago. 'Neither of Dawlish's cohorts is going to want word of their chum's gutless behaviour to get out—especially as the poor sod seems about to cash in his chips, if Dempsey's note is anything to go by. Young Bingham has been doing his damnedest to keep the affair from his father's ears and I certainly don't see Felsham blabbing about it.'

'Well, I'm not entirely happy about leaving you here on your own,' remonstrated Giles. 'You lost a fair amount of blood—you were out for almost half an hour, I'll have you know!'

'So you keep telling me,' retorted his brother dryly. 'However, in case you have failed to notice the fact, I can hardly claim to be on my own, being surrounded by an entire household of highly trained staff whose only desire in life is to pander to my every need. The noble Ferris is on hand to deal with my more personal requirements, and our reluctant medic has promised to drop in at regular intervals to change my dressings. Satisfied?'

'I suppose so.' The Major stood undecided for a moment, before adding, 'But you really do need to rest, if you want that wound to heal properly, so positively *no* visitors allowed—I shall inform Danson on my way out.'

Having spent the better part of the morning suffering the ministrations of the none too happy Dr Felsham, Marcus was feeling decidedly wrung out and only too pleased to comply with his brother's instruction. Particularly in view of the fact that it had been entirely due to the Major's quick response that he had been prevented from falling to the ground when he had collapsed—an achievement that had doubtless saved him from even further injury. Not that the Viscount could recall a great deal of what had followed, other than finding himself back in his own bed being poked and prodded with what he had felt at the time was undue savagery but what he now supposed was quite normal procedure, given the unusual circumstances. Incredibly, and although it had taken off a slice of his skin in the process, the ball from Dawlish's firearm had ripped straight through Marcus's coat sleeve, finally ending its journey at some point on the grass in front of him. And, despite the fact that the surface wound had bled rather profusely at the time, Marcus had been gratified to learn that there had been no damage to the underlying muscle. Felsham had assured the Viscount that a few days' rest and recuperation were all that were needed to return him to full health.

Gradually allowing his eyelids to droop to a close, Marcus was still unable to banish the truly gut-wrenching image of Sophie's horrified face from the forefront of his mind. Would she even care that he had been hurt, should she ever come to hear of it, he wondered, as sleep began to wash over him. Very probably not, was his last distinct thought.

Several hours later, having eventually persuaded Jack to allow her use of a carriage, Sophie, accompanied by one of the abbey's footman, arrived at the front door of Marcus's Grosvenor Square mansion only to find that both bell-pull and knocker had been removed from their housings—the latter a generally accepted signal that the dwelling's occupants were not in residence. Since there were clear sounds of activity issuing from the basement below, with sinking heart Sophie could only assume that Helstone's injuries had been far worse than Jack had been prepared to admit, and that the Viscount must be, at this very moment, lying at death's door!

Ignoring the footman's muttered disapproval, she raised her hand and rapped briskly on one of the door's panels. To her surprise the door, swinging open almost immediately, revealed the odd sight of a rather stately looking individual—the butler, Sophie assumed—who was regarding her with a severe frown on his face while one of his fingers was pressed firmly against his lips.

'If you please, miss,' the man whispered, casting a nervous look towards the highly impressive-looking stairway that stretched away to his right, 'we have illness in the house. I'm afraid I must ask you to state your business and be on your way.'

'But his lordship—' began Sophie, her voice tremulous with apprehension, 'Is he—? That is—I really need to know that he is all right!'

'I'm afraid his lordship is not receiving visitors at the moment, miss,' came the butler's haughty reply. 'If you would care to leave your card?'

Since Sophie had not yet availed herself of the Egremonts' offer to order her a set of visiting cards, she was at something of a loss. A sudden sob rising in her throat, she gave a reluctant shake of her head. 'Just tell your master that Miss Pendleton-Flint called,' she choked and, turning swiftly on her heel, she hurried down the steps, desperate to gain the sanctuary of her borrowed carriage before finally dissolving into the tears that she had succeeded in holding back for the past two days. *If only I had had the courage to accept Helstone's offer,* she found herself thinking, *none of this would ever have happened. Please, God, don't let him die—even if I can't have him, please keep him safe!*

In spite of Danson's determined efforts to achieve absolute silence throughout the building, it was actually the sound of Whitcombe's somewhat aggrieved footman slamming the carriage door rather too vigorously that roused Marcus from his sleep. Feeling much refreshed, he hauled himself up into a sitting position and reached out his hand for the pitcher of water that sat on his bedside table.

'Allow me, your lordship.'

Ferris was there before him, already pouring water into the waiting glass.

'What the devil was that infernal noise outside?' demanded Marcus, as he quaffed back the much needed liquid. 'Sounded like an explosion of some sort.'

'Just a carriage door, sir,' soothed his valet who, having had little else to occupy his time while his master slept, had been standing at the bedroom window aimlessly contemplating the passing traffic. 'The Earl of Whitcombe's, by the look of the door crest.'

'Viscount Bingham, I suppose,' murmured Marcus lazily, allowing his eyes to close once more as he leaned back against his pillows. 'Dare say he'll call again tomorrow.' Having been unable to express his thanks to the young Viscount for his part in that morning's events, Helstone was determined to make sure that Jack was fully aware of how grateful he was for his support.

'No, sir,' returned Ferris, stretching across Marcus to straighten his covers. 'The visitor was a young lady.'

His eyes flying open, Marcus shot up. 'A young lady?' he croaked in disbelief as he flung back the bedclothes and staggered across to the window. Sophie! It just had to be Sophie! Who else but Sophie would be calling on him in one of Whitcombe's carriages?

'Sir, I beg you!' cried Ferris, his face a picture of distress. 'I must insist that you return to your bed immediately.'

Having discovered that Whitcombe's carriage had disappeared from view, Marcus turned on his valet in disgust. 'Rubbish!' he retorted, already engaged in the rather intricate task of trying to remove his nightshirt with only one good hand. 'Stop wittering, man, and get me out of this damned thing.'

'But, sir!' protested his hapless valet. 'Major Wolfe gave specific instructions—'

'No doubt he did,' grated Helstone, doing his utmost to fight off the disturbing sense of weakness that was threatening to overcome his efforts. 'However, unless I am much mistaken, I am still master in this house! So, do as I say and sort me out something to wear—and while you're at it ring for Kimble and tell him that if my curricle isn't round at the front door in ten minutes flat, he can start looking for another position!'

Muttering fierce imprecations under his breath, Ferris felt he had no option but to carry out his master's orders, although he managed to retain sufficient forethought to send down for the brandy decanter while Marcus was engaged in dowsing his head in the basin of cold water that stood on the room's marble-topped washstand.

'Good man!' exclaimed the Viscount when, having dried off his face, his gaze fell on the drinks tray. 'That ought to do the trick!'

Exactly seven minutes and a couple of hefty swigs of brandy later, he was up on the driving seat of his curricle, an anxious Kimble at his side, intent upon chasing after Whitcombe's carriage in the hopes of making some sort of peace with Sophie.

But even as he unhooked the whip from its mounting it became clear to him that, with only one good arm at his disposal, such a task was going to prove well-nigh impossible. A resigned sigh left his lips as, reluctantly passing the reins to his groom, he urged, 'Spring 'em, Kim!'

Having finally cried herself out, Sophie dried her eyes, straightened her bonnet and cast an indifferent look out of the window, simply to ascertain how much further she had to go. As far as she could make out, the carriage was just passing through Chelsea village. As the sudden memory of that magical afternoon flashed into her thoughts, her lips curved in an unbidden smile. Leaning forward, with no clear understanding of what she was doing, she gave a sharp rap on the front window.

'Take the next left, Clifford,' she instructed the coachman. 'I have another call to make.'

Just one little peek, she told herself, as the carriage drew up outside the driveway leading to Marcus's secret hideaway. *I won't even go up to the house. I'll just creep round to the lake and take a quick peek at the view, just to see if it's really as perfect as I remember it!*

Two breathless minutes later and there it all was, exactly as her mind had pictured it…the rose arbour…. the white-painted pavilion…the ducks at the waterside. In a sudden rush, the closely guarded memories of that truly wondrous afternoon came flooding back to her. The scent of the honeysuckle…the warmth of the sun on her face…the succulent taste of the strawberries…the touch of Marcus's hand as he draped the soft woollen shawl over her shoulders…the captivating smell of his cologne…

Countless minutes drifted past as the poignancy of all she had lost threatened to overcome her. She stood silently on the pavilion steps, doing her utmost to ignore the relentless ache in her heart and heaving in deep breaths of the softly scented air, until at last her senses were once more beguiled by the peaceful beauty of her surroundings.

She still had not moved when Marcus rounded the corner of the house. The sight that met his eyes stopped him in his tracks. Whilst he had always considered this vista to be the most attractive of his secret hideaways it seemed to him that, at this moment, Nature had surpassed herself. The exquisite loveliness of the scene now took on a new and more compelling meaning, the fundamental essence of which was Sophie, the captivatingly winsome beauty who had stolen not only his heart but his very soul. How could he ever have imagined that taking her as his mistress would ever satisfy the deep hunger he felt for her? He knew now that, should he live to be a hundred, it would never be possible to have his fill of her.

But what if he was too late? His heart executing a painful somersault at the thought of such a possibility, the Viscount squared his shoulders, took a deep breath and, with no little trepidation, strode purposefully towards her.

Her reverie shattered by the sound of booted footsteps on the gravel path, Sophie, her eyes widening in shock, spun round to face him, a bizarre combination of intense joy coupled with faint apprehension coursing through her body.

'W-what are you doing here?' she gasped, her eyes anxiously raking his body for outward signs of injury.

'I might ask you the same question,' replied Marcus, stepping up into the pavilion and positioning himself directly in front of her, the breadth of his shoulders completely blocking her view of the lake.

Even though his expression was unreadable, Sophie could not prevent her heart from giving a little skip at seeing him standing there before her. 'I just wanted to take one last look—shouldn't you be in bed?'

'Very probably, but that's beside the point at this particular moment. I believe you came to see me. May I ask why?'

'I just wanted—needed—to see how you were,' she said, finding herself incapable of tearing her gaze away from the penetrating look in his eyes.

'Needed?' Marcus's pulse quickened. 'I rather got the impression that you had washed your hands of me.'

A puzzled frown crept over Sophie's brow. 'No such thing. If you really must know, I—'

She stopped, her colour rising rapidly as she struggled to find the words.

'Yes?' he prompted her. 'I really think I must know, as it happens.'

'I came to tell you that I had changed my mind,' she said in a low voice.

Marcus held his breath. 'Changed your mind about—me?' he asked softly.

Sophie shook her head, the words tumbling out almost without thought. 'About accepting your offer—if you still want me!'

Want her! Scarcely able to believe what he was hearing, Marcus stared down at her, his mind in a whirl. *She couldn't be referring to the* carte blanche *he had offered her, surely? He had long since dismissed that idea as being quite out of the question!* Needing to make sense of what Sophie seemed to be saying, Marcus, passing his hand across his forehead and uttering a faint groan of dismay, turned on his heel and made for the water's edge, his eyes fixed unseeingly on the placid scene before him.

Having come to realise that she could no longer envisage a future without him, Sophie had already made the momentous decision that the only way she could have Helstone in her life was to accept the proposition he had offered her. But now, as she studied the rigid stance of his body, her heart seemed to shrivel within her. She could only assume that the Viscount was regretting his former offer and no longer desired her. Bitter chagrin swept over her as she watched him turn and retrace his steps to stand, once more, directly in front of her.

Unsure how to begin, Marcus cleared his throat. 'I'm afraid that I am obliged to decline your very generous offer,' he said eventually. 'The truth is that I no longer find myself in the market for a mistress.'

Dropping her eyes, as every vestige of colour drained from her cheeks, Sophie was too shaken to formulate any sort of reply. Her lips trembling, she made to turn away from him—only to have him reach out his hand to catch hold of hers.

'I do have another suggestion that might be of interest to you, however,' he ventured, with just the hint of a smile on his lips. 'But first I have to know what caused you to change your mind.'

Another suggestion! thought Sophie bleakly. *A quick and tawdry dalliance in some out-of-the-way hotel or other,* she could only suppose. But then, she found herself reasoning, if that was all that he was prepared to offer her, could she really find the strength to turn him down, only to live out the rest of her life dreaming of what might have been? Having already thrown the last vestiges of her pride at his mercy, she resigned herself to the realisation that she really had nothing to lose by acquainting him with the true reason for her unexpected *volte face.* Stiffening her shoulders, she raised her chin defiantly and looked him directly in the eye.

'I love you,' she said simply.

Marcus, closing his eyes briefly, felt a surge of exhilaration flooding through his body, temporarily nullifying the throbbing pain in his injured arm. 'Oh, God, Sophie,' he gasped, as he pulled her towards him with his one good hand and buried his face in her hair. 'My dearest, darling girl! You can have no idea how I've yearned to hear you say those words!'

Almost convinced that she must be dreaming, Sophie pulled back and stared up at him, her face full of confusion. 'Are you trying to tell me that—?'

'—that I love you, too,' Marcus interrupted her, as he tightened his hold. 'Utterly and to distraction.'

'You love me?' faltered Sophie in disbelief.

'Now, always and for ever, sweetheart,' Marcus assured her. 'With every fibre of my being and with every breath I take.'

Even as a wild torrent of joy coursed through her veins, Sophie was unable to contain her mystification. 'Then what was the suggestion you were about to make to me?' she challenged him.

The Viscount gave a self-deprecating shrug, a rueful expression crossing his face as he replied. 'I was going to suggest that you might care to take pity on me and do me the honour of marrying me instead. I find that my life seems to make very little sense when you are not part of it.' His eyes darkened as he held her rapt gaze. 'The truth is that I simply didn't recognise that what I felt for you was a good deal more than just unadulterated lust.'

He paused, shooting her one of his lopsided grins. 'Although I am bound to admit that I cannot, in all honesty, claim to have noticed any lessening in that particular area, I've come to realise that I would truly far rather have you as my wife than as my mistress.'

A mischievous smile played about the corners of Sophie's lips. 'I dare say it would be possible to fulfil both duties, if I were to really put my mind to it,' she replied demurely.

Although he was not entirely sure that he had understood her aright, Marcus's eyes lit up as hope flared wildly within him.

'You mean you're prepared to accept my proposal?' he asked, in breathless amazement.

'I accept both of your proposals, my darling!' breathed Sophie, tears of joy filling her summer blue eyes as she flung herself into his waiting arms. But then, as she felt Marcus sag against her, a flicker of alarm ran through her. 'But first, I really do think I ought to get you into bed.'

Pressing his lips against her forehead, Hellcat Helstone—devil to the last—let out a roguish little chuckle. 'Whatever you say, my beloved angel,' he whispered into her ear. 'What man in his right senses could resist so enchanting a suggestion?'

* * * * *